AFTER THE COMING

THE GREAT
DESPAIR

book one–2014

GREG ELLIOT

ECHO BOOKS

First published in 2014 by Barrallier Books Pty Ltd,
trading as Echo Books

Registered Office: 35-37 Gordon Avenue, West Geelong, Victoria 3220,
Australia.

www.echobooks.com.au

Copyright © Elliot, Greg A.

National Library of Australia Cataloguing-in-Publication entry: (paperback)

Author: Elliot, Greg A., author.

Title: After the coming - the great despair / Greg A. Elliot

ISBN: 9780992588052 (pbk.)

Subjects: Science Fiction, Romance, Drama, War

Dewey Number: A823.4

Book and cover design by Peter Gamble, Ink Pot Graphic Design, Canberra.

Set in Garamond Premier Pro 12/17 and Nyala Regular.

www.echobooks.com.au

Contents

Terran Earth
Continental Territorial Divisions
2081

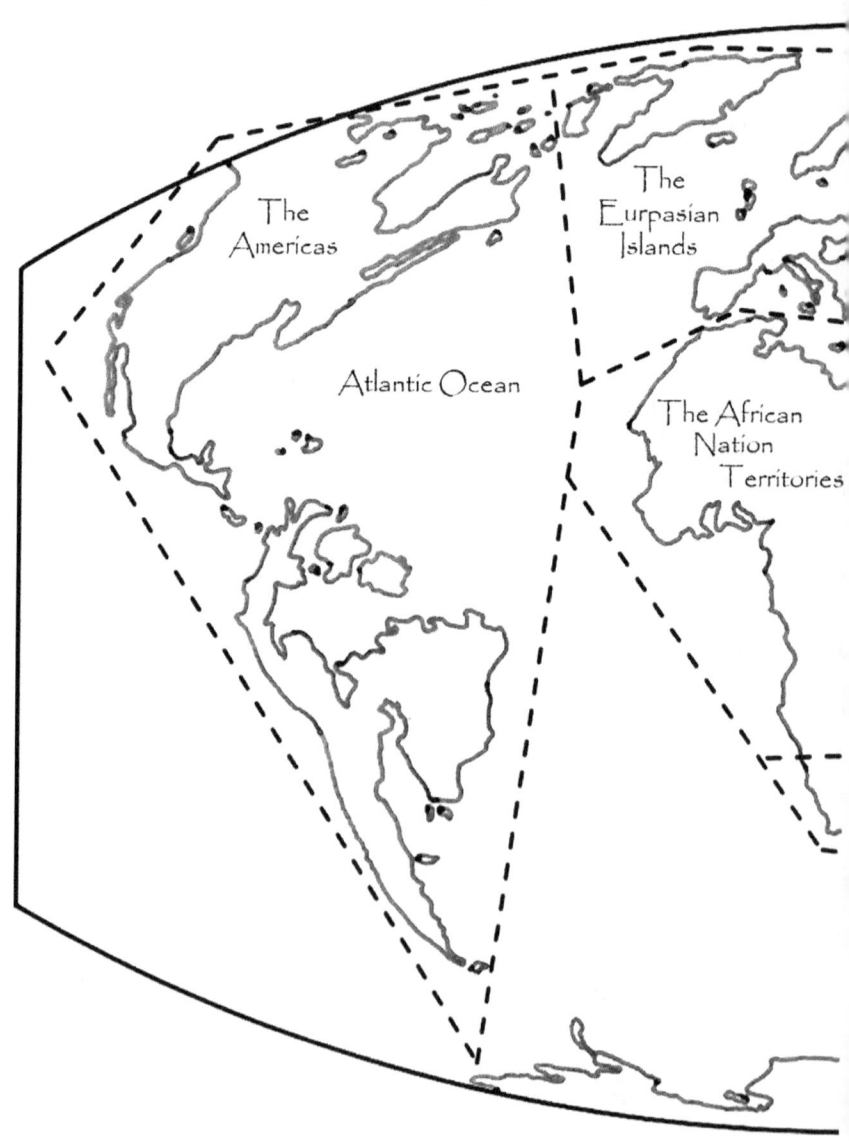

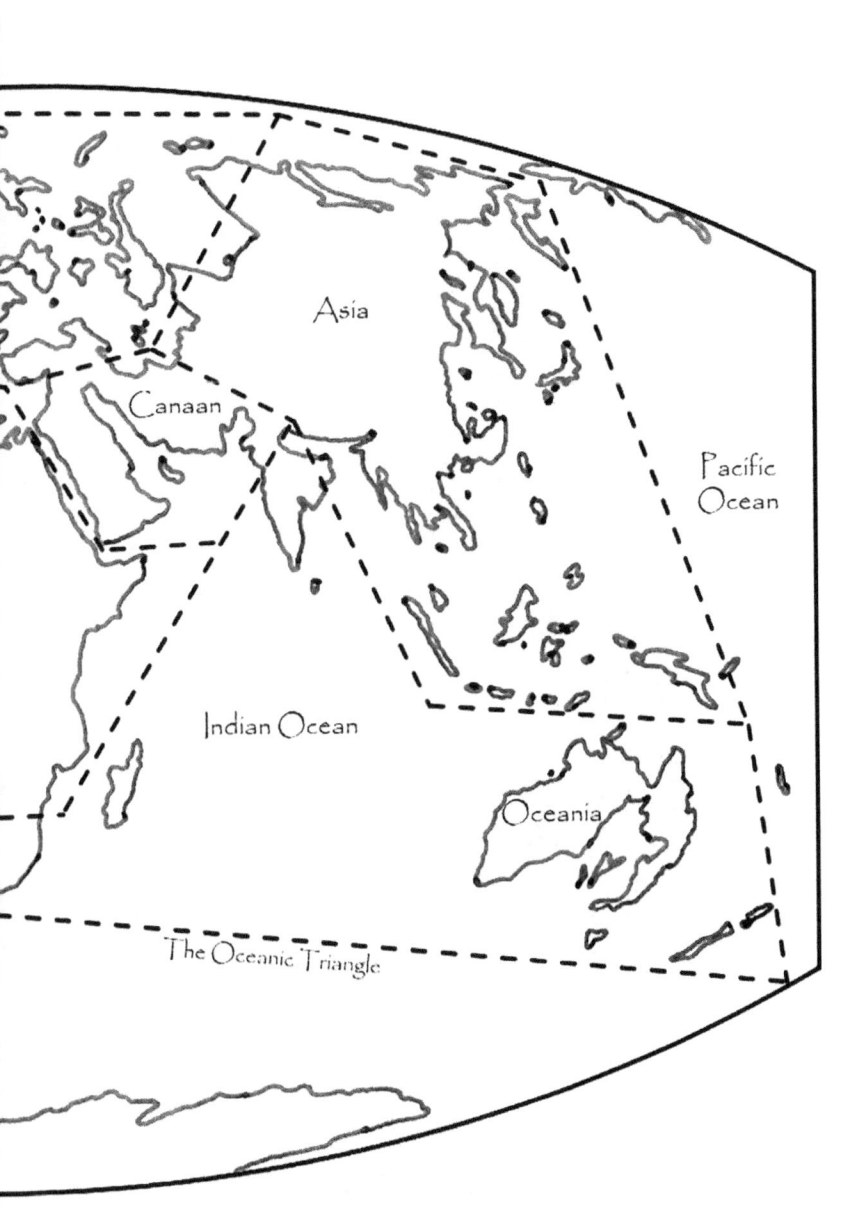

Asia

Canaan

Pacific
Ocean

Indian Ocean

Oceania

The Oceanic Triangle

Prologue

Continents had been changed by the melting of the polar icecaps. Long dormant underwater volcanos had since erupted and in doing so had wiped out vast coast lines. In some cases, complete countries now lay deep under the ocean's waterline. What they were taught from the old text now ceased to exist. Where there was land, there was now ocean, where there was life, only the remains of a civilisation past.

Most people born into this reality just go about their daily business. They live life as they have always done, for they had never known any different. To them, this was life as they knew it for they had not lived in the time before now; that is the time before the Coming. Today, people refer to the Coming as the Great Despair, a term which represented the feelings and emotions in the hearts and minds of those who lived through this period.

This was also the name given to the conflict that created the Coming, this was the War of the Great Despair. This was when the sleeping darkness arose and took hold of them all. Stories their elder carers told them as children, of a time when the sun shone through clear skies. A time of beaches that presented an image of pristine white sands and crystal blue oceans. It all just didn't seem real to them now, like it had never existed.

To those born into this time, it sounded fake to them. That was a time when the air was not filled with the deadly toxins that rapidly changed one's genetic being, or rain that did not sting one's skin when touched. It was all a distant dream from a time and place that seemed to have never been of this land.

There aren't that many poor souls still left around that can remember the time before. Most have now grown old or have become part of the terran ground they once walked on. When once they have cometh from the earth; so shalleth they be returned. For those that are in the here and now, live in a time governed by the Consortium of Trust under a United Federation of Terran Nations known as the UFTN. Its legions of Peace Makers always vigilant and at the ready to preserve their utopian dream.

Since the Coming of the Darkness, transcontinental borders and allegiances have developed into the five main Divisions of the UFTN. The Americas, both north and south continents; the Eurpasian Islands once known individually as Europa and Eurasia and now with many of its former countries laying deep under sea level; Asia; and residing in the centre is Canaan which is still very much considered sacred as the birth place of Christ. Finally, the last member of the UFTN are the wide sweeping plains and tropical forests of Oceania.

Oceania had been somewhat saved from the devastating effects of the Great Despair and was now considered a safe haven. It is also the lands guild where the capital of Terran Earth resides, a place called Destiny. Only the African Nation Territories still remain separate from the UFTN. These untamed territories are now considered as the wild lands or frontiers, unstable and dangerous, but hope still remains. The AN Territories is a continent that the Consortium of Trust desperately wish to bring into the UFTN as the sixth Territorial Continental Division.

After many years of hardship and uncertainty, the peoples of the new world rebuild societies founded on peace, trust, and understanding, however; fear still exists. All could come undone by the growing unrest in the wild frontiers of the AN Territories. This is known as the AN Uprising. The UFTN had tried on many occasions to welcome the AN Territories into this new world, but time and time again they refused citing differences of equality. UFTN Peace Makers had on more than one occasion been called upon to settle the unrest in the frontiers. But these had been rather small skirmishes and nothing really to be concerned about. They would hope to bring the AN Territories into the fold as the sixth Territorial Continental Division.

Now mostly unified, the people of Terran Earth would collectively serve to protect and uphold peace from all threats. Their terran home, earth, one planet based on five Territorial Continental Divisions, controlled and administered by a Council of Elders known as the Consortium of Trust. For those born into this time accept their fate and place in this new society. All have purpose and all serve Destiny for the salvation and longevity of all life. From destiny springs new hope that once again as a race of people can they rise and prosper together as one in their never ending search of knowledge and wisdom.

Soon Destiny will mark a special day in the new calendar year. Time had seemed to stand still for a period following the end of the War of the Great Despair. Records had been lost, days and months melded into one as birthdays and other special occasions remained left unknown. It appeared no-one would celebrate anything ever again. To start life again with a new beginning, the clock would have to be reset. It would represent the hope that the lessons of the past would never be repeated and symbolised a civilisation's rebirth.

After these twenty-three years of ungoverned lawlessness, the Consortium of Trust, upon creating the UFTN, started again at year one. However they would still maintain the Christian year even though, unfortunately, the precise date was left unknown to them. Being lost in time, historical scholars calculated the Christian year based on the research of evidence they could gather. Now as the year draws to a close, the peoples of the UFTN will celebrate the 35th coming of the Christmas Union since the Consortium of Trust united Terran Earth.

For thirty five years this had been the tradition. Resurrected and kept alive by the stories their forefathers, the elder-parents, had told their young. But for the inhabitants of Oceania, particularly Destiny, this would be an extra special sacred event. For it was here in Destiny that the bricks and mortar were laid for their rebirth. Not only was this day remembered because it marked the day Christ was born, but it would also now be remembered as the day the UFTN was born. This was the day that destiny returned to the people. This 25th day of December in the year of our UFTN founding, 2081.

Chapter One

The sun as usual struggled to peer its brightness through the dark grey clouds that were a constant reminder of what this land had become. The seasons were much different than what they had once been. The winter months in this part of the world bought welcomed relief with clear blue skies and water that fell from the heavens requiring very little in the way of purification.

It could be said that life was pretty good for the Untouched Citizens South of the Equator, commonly referred to as the Ucusee. But for these citizens, this was summer and as predicted, it would be another harsh one. Though this place was fortunate, as most parts of the world received almost little to no relief from the now changed landscape all year round regardless of season.

The oncoming Christmas Union would be a day in which would change the lives of many, but for one family in particular, this would see a chain of unspeakable events unfold. The patriarch of this family was about to head out for the day with his family to do some Christmas Union shopping. His schedule would be long and hectic as he knew this particular day and the ones that followed would be. He would hope to be finished this days outing quickly and return home just after midday due to the stinging rains of the Darkness that would surely come.

All would have the same idea. This way of life was nothing new to those who lived in this part of Terran Earth. They had been born into this world and had never known any different. For as long as any of them could remember, the rains came at this time of day and every day during these summer months of the year. Indoors were the only safest places of refuge from the stinging sub-tropical rains.

Their destination, the City of Queenstown was filled with electronic billboards and advertising of all sorts that blinded the city urban landscape with images of business and trade. Although it was some distance from Destiny, Queenstown was a large northern thriving metropolis. Busy as ever and with an ever growing population proving that once again that the human race could overcome any obstacle placed in front of it.

The remains of the old city that once stood here are now just a distant memory, except for those on the outer fringe further inland and along the old Brisbane River. New buildings and homes cramped the new city centre and the streets were organised in a circular pattern, culminating with the district head of government at its centre.

He would know what awaited them when once they had arrived at their destination at the Queenstown Centre Shopping Village. After parking the family APAM in the underground vehicle lot, he would usher his family quickly inside. The APAM was an All Purpose AutoMobile suited to this type of country terrain. It was large enough to comfortably fit a family of five and it provided protection from the harsh elements that surrounded them.

The drive from Glassenville in the outer mountainside fringes had been far and people were already starting to amass in eager anticipation for the stores to open. After which, consumers would rush in, going in search of various products and goods from the traders and merchants willing to take their terra marcs. As he stepped from the vehicle with his family, the humidity had already reached eighty-five percent and was still climbing. They would all much prefer the comforted surroundings of the environmentally controlled conditions of the Village.

His decision to be there with his family this day had been driven by his desire to avoid the large crowds that would increase by the number as Christmas Union day drew nearer. He had come to dread large crowds due to his time spent in the Terran Wars against the Republic of Free Nations and more recently in the African Nation Uprising. He knew that if he could, he would try to minimise his exposure amongst the masses as much as possible.

Christmas Union day was still some time off, but it had made no difference. During his prolonged stay overseas, the population of Queenstown seemed to have doubled. There was also a notable increase in the amount of new Ugbee and Trap citizens to this part of the world. He assumed that they were obviously abandoning the harsh conditions of the north, in favour of the relative safer environment that the south had to offer. More importantly though, this day's outing gave him precious time with his family, and that would outweigh any selfish thought he may have had. His family had always come first and today would be no different.

For this UTFN Peace Maker of the Oceania Terran Division; it had been a year since he had spent some quality time with his wife and children. The Peace Maker high command had deployed the OTD to the AN Territories to quell the uprising in the Northern provinces, in particular, the Sudan. The world had changed a great deal over the years, but the Sudan was still essentially, the Sudan. Sand dunes remained a prominent feature, however; lush vegetation now covered many more previously isolated pockets of the country. It had been and still is, one of the harshest environments to live in, let alone to put down an uprising. Blistering hot sub-tropical winds and rains were a year round event.

He knew that he only had twelve months at home with his family before he would be called back to the OTD to re-join the 46th Pioneer Striker Division. This had been a special division developed from the Federal Continental Ranger Corps during the last years of the Terran Wars. Its purpose was to strike hard and to strike fast as the spear head carving their way through enemy lines. The FCR commanded all brigades of the Pioneer Corps and for this Ranger, he had been the first to volunteer upon its raising. Just as his grand elder had done during the War of the Great Despair when he commanded one of the very first Continental Ranger Battalions before federation.

Now he was home, the place of his birth and united with his family. He loved them a great deal and would savour every moment he had with them. He had seen some terrible events so far from his recent action, but where he was headed next would be far worse. The 46th Pioneer Striker Division would be headed into the Congo where the heart of the AN Uprising was believed to have its Headquarters. The mid-land frontiers of the AN Territories was not known for its compassion. This was a brutal and barbarous environment. One was not simply captured and held prisoner, no! This would be far worse than that.

His wife knew the life her husband led and accepted the fact that one day he may never return from war. Realising it was one thing, but it didn't mean that she had to like it. She too would cherish their short one year reunion and dream of better days beyond this life and this land when all of Terran Earth was truly one. But for now, this OTD Ranger, her husband, was home and they would settle on that, at least for now. He would choose to spend as much time with his family as possible, even if it did mean going shopping in Queenstown's biggest shopping mecca.

Once the initial surge at the front doors had passed, they proceeded to make their way inside. This would only be one of two trips he or his wife would have to make into Queenstown. The first was for the window shopping, and the next would be for the purchase of the Christmas Union presents that he or his wife would return to buy without their children's knowledge. He would enjoy today as he knew that soon his children's eyes would grow wide with excitement when they saw all the wonderful toys inside. They would no doubt plead with their parents to buy them then and there. But that was the joy of it, seeing the happiness within his children, especially on Christmas Union day when Saint Nicolas had delivered all their presents.

They had been there since nine that morning and it was time to take a break. It was also coming close to lunch in which his children were starting to make him painfully aware of. Their stomachs were like clockwork and as with children from all walks of life, they were getting hungry as it neared midday. So they all decided to venture into the food court for a bite to eat before continuing with their window shopping. He was also starting to tire; he may have been a Federal Continental Ranger, but running after children fixated on toys and gifts for three hours was another matter entirely. His children were starting to wear both their parents out. None the less, they would sit down, have their lunch and then decide whether or not to continue. He was also very much aware of the time regarding the coming of that afternoon's Darkness rains.

Typically, they had chosen a table that was positioned by a wall. Siobhan knew this was her husband's preference. He didn't like having people, strangers that is, being at his back without knowing what they were doing. His time in combat and the seemingly unknown outcome of many missions behind enemy lines he had experienced, had more than likely fed his paranoia. But more times than not, his paranoia had saved him and that of his comrades on more than one occasion. He was just cautious, that's all.

As they all sat down, Siobhan decided that she would take the children to the food stalls to see what they would like to have for lunch. Once he was alone at the table and as he gathered up his thoughts, he began to feel a presence, one which he had felt and sensed earlier that morning. Was this his paranoia? Or was there someone actually watching him from afar?

But those feelings he had sensed earlier that morning had quickly evaporated due to his attention being drawn to his youngest son's antics. At the time, Marcus Angelus had spotted the toy he wanted most and in doing so, dragged his father by the hand to have a closer look. Now however, the feeling had returned and he began to scan the area for anything out of place.

As a Ranger, he had been trained as a scout and was often sent out on missions alone or in small groups of two or four. These missions had taught him to trust his sixth sense. By now, the feelings he was having intensified. He couldn't just put this down to unfounded paranoia. The sense that someone was watching him was too strong for him to ignore, as his stomach started to twist in knots. He looked over to where his wife and children were. It seemed that lunch would have to wait a little longer as he watched Siobhan being pulled in all directions by their children in an effort to decide on a food outlet.

Poor old Siobhan he thought. She had been solid as a rock over all these past years, especially when he was sent away overseas in the performance of his duty. He knew that she had always kept a thought in the back of her mind the fear that one day he may never return. But she learned to live with this thought, pushing it deep into the recesses of her mind. She would continue to be the best wife and mother she could to her husband and children. She would always support her husband, and provide for and nurture their children.

—⚋— ✝ —⚋—

The seven years he was away fighting in the Terran Wars had been especially hard on Siobhan. The two of them would be inseparable during his periods of granted leave and as a result Siobhan fell pregnant twice more. During that time she had already been caring for their eldest, Alexander, who was just a one year old at the outbreak of the war. Now she had given birth to a daughter, Elyssa-Jayne and another son, Marcus, and without her husband by her side. Luckily she was from a large family and had plenty of support.

To make matters worse, Alexander was diagnosed with TerraOxygenen Syndrome; a skin disease common in certain areas of the world bought on by the earth's atmosphere. At that time, his military career had seen him relocated on an accompanied posting to Brazil for three years. It was during this posting that in 2067, Alexander had been born. Scientists and doctors speculated that the disease was a result of the coming of the Darkness after the time of the Great Despair. However, this disease is only found in a third of the earth's children which brings into doubt their theory.

The symptoms causes large flakes of skin to randomly peel away from the body's surface, and although very easily treatable, it is not curable. Adults with this disease are able to live quite comfortable and productive lives as long as they adhere to a strict daily regime of self-administered medical injections. But this is a very different story for children as these injections are often very painful for the young to receive. All of which Siobhan has had to administer ever since Alexander was born.

In fear of giving birth to another child with this disease, Siobhan decided to relocate back to Australia, to Melbourne where she and her husband called home. The Terran Wars had started by this stage and it made sense to be back in safer surrounds. She couldn't take care of a two year old and be almost nine months pregnant with their daughter on her own. Not while her husband went off to fight the RFN Rebels.

In addition, Siobhan has also had to watch over Marcus who was born with Retina Light Focal Aperture Sensitivity. Doctors refer to this as RLFAS or more commonly known in recent times as, RFN Eyes in recognition of the RFN Rebels who were the cause of this condition. For those afflicted, symptoms are poor eyesight, red dry skin around the outer eye and a sclera that turns an algae green colour which glows in the dark. They are so bright, that even with eyes closed can they be seen.

It has been proven that with age, the condition will completely heal of its own accord. Cases have been documented that people as young as nineteen years of age have fully recovered from this condition with no signs remaining that it ever existed. This all depends on what age the person first contracts the condition. In the case of Marcus, who is already ten years old, it is hopeful he will be free from RFN Eyes in the next five to ten years.

In the meantime, the effects of this condition have already made a large impact on his quality of life. It has been the center of a great deal of stress and discomfort for Marcus since his birth. Although his condition has markedly improved over time, it has affected his ability to study and learn and presently, he is academically below the required standard. But what Marcus lacks in one aspect of his life, he makes up for in others. His intuitive nature has seen him succeed in areas whereas others would have failed. The lack of vision suffered by Marcus has also been counter acted by the enhancement to his hearing and sixth sense. In many ways Marcus possesses the same sixth sense ability and gift of his father.

Confirmed links to this disorder have been traced back to a terrorist style attack during the Terran Wars when a group of RFN Rebels set and detonated a series of Improvised Explosive Devices. These IEDs were each laced with chemical agents and set off during the Destiny Christmas Union celebrations of 2071, marking 25 years since the founding of the UFTN.

As fate would have it, Siobhan had decided to visit her younger twin sisters that year for the celebrations. Ciara and Coailainn were just twenty years old at the time and living in the UFTN Capital of Destiny. She was also pregnant with Marcus and although she had managed to stave off the chemicals from the IEDs herself, the same could not be said for her unborn child. Siobhan has had to deal with many things in her life, still through all these challenges, she continued to strive ever forward.

—m— ✝ —m—

They had met at secondary college when Siobhan first appeared out of no-where. She was the girl next door type, sweet and innocent looking, but she had a devilish side of her, a streak that ran a mile long and she knew it too. She would play on this characteristic trait of hers throughout their initial courtship period, but he saw right through her and to the astonishment of all around, they would eventually become known as the perfect couple.

Their initial meeting had taken place in the Christian earth year of 2062 at Melbourne's Senior Institute of Technology and Science. It had been the first day of a new school year and they had all been seated in the large auditorium where the Headmaster Elder would give his opening address to his charges.

From the very first moment he laid eyes on her, he knew he loved her. But what was love? For they were only teenagers at the time. They couldn't possibly know its meaning, or could they? He was, after all, just a young sixteen year old boy with endless opportunity while she, was a seventeen year old girl and just new to the school. She had yet to make any real friends and yet to be known by all. How would she be received?

The students hadn't quite yet all assembled and the Headmaster Elder could be seen up on the stage flicking through his notes in preparation.

It would no doubt be another awe inspiring speech that would be sure to raise the roof and rally the students to great new heights. Well judging by last year's speech, the students assumed that it would be that which he would be aiming for. And just like last year's speech all the students would once again, and as usual, turn a deaf ear to it. They had all heard his speeches before throughout the years and this one would be no different.

The students were mindful however, to pay respect to their Headmaster Elder and they would remain very silent throughout the oncoming speech. It had occurred at times that the Headmaster Elder would sometimes experience a flash back or two, back to his time in the War of the Great Despair. Suddenly, out of nowhere, there would be an outburst of military orders given along with panic and confusion, as slowly he would realise where he was. He would come to know that these weren't his soldiers at all, but in fact just children under his care and tutelage.

He had entered and fought in the War of the Great Despair when just eighteen years of age during its last couple of years. The students respected and admired him paying tribute to his courage for the freedom they enjoy today. They just didn't enjoy the endless speeches that seemed to never end.

But this day it wouldn't be the Headmaster Elder's speech that would try and grab this young sixteen year old boy's attention. As a matter of fact, there would be nothing at all that morning he would pay heed to, regardless of what it was. Nothing that is, except for one thing. That moment came like a dream when all around him seemed to come to a standstill in one pure innocence in time. He didn't know that his gaze would soon be fixed upon the young girl that was about to enter the building and forever change his life. As he turned to say something to his friend that was sitting next to him, he caught site of her.

She was now the only thing on his mind and that which occupied his thoughts. The sight of this alluring young girl had stolen his now racing heart, which missed a beat with every step she took. He watched as she walked through the ancient archway and into the building. Two other girls she had only just met that morning before school had started, walked in with her, the three of them in unison.

The way she moved her hips as each step followed the next, her long jet black hair swaying from side to side and her slender athletic legs that seemed to go on forever. It was almost too much for this poor boy who felt his heart quicken, as she came steadily closer. A bead of perspiration formed and trickled down the back of his neck. Suddenly he remembered to breathe and so took a deep breath.

He had always been cool, calm and collected when it came to girls and was one of the more popular students of the school, but this was different, why was he so nervous? She got closer and closer as she finally came to rest sitting in the seat directly in front of him. You could see that she was brimming full of confidence. As she sat down, she turned around to him and said,

'Hey sexy boy.'

She then quickly turned around again to face the front giggling along with her two new girlfriends.

She was playing him right from the start and had chosen to sit down in the seat in front of him because she too had been taken, taken that is for the love she felt for him. When the assembly concluded and the Headmaster Elder had finished his speech, neither of them had heard a word that was spoken. He just continued to stare at her as she would, every couple of minutes, turn her head to sneak a glance at him. As she did this and he caught her looking at him, she would quickly turn back again pretending to ignore him. But as she got up to leave, she spoke words of her introduction.

'See-ya round fella and by the way, I'm Siobhan. Siobhan Kelly.'

He was about to introduce himself as well, but was interrupted when she gave him a little punch to his arm winking as she did and walked away. This girl was very cheeky and appealing at the same time. He had thought what a little devil she was for her confident persona, but he could not resist her, not for one second. As the rest of the assembly got up to leave, he was stilled fixed on her trance as the friend who had been sitting next to him tried to bring him back from his awaking coma.

'Ash, hey man it's over we can go. Ashleigh, snap out of it will ya.'

As the two grew and got to know one another, no-one, not even their closest friends ever thought they would end up together. All they were to each other was a couple of mates hanging out together. They hardly ever liked the same things and argued on occasion over differences of opinion. And when they argued, wow, they really argued, but they would seldom leave each other's side when they were together. They loved one another immensely but their lives were worlds apart when it came to their families. Siobhan had been raised in a strict Irish family, her parents being devout Catholics from the old ways. As a child, she had been made to go to Sunday school and attend church sittings with her parents.

Both her parents were born to refugees of the War of the Great Despair. Siobhan's grand elders, as with many of the population of Ireland and the UK fearing the worst, fled their homelands for safer ground. It had been a wise decision as Ireland and most of England are now at least a hundred meters under the Atlantic Ocean. Her grand elders on both parents' sides decided to immigrate to Australia where her father, Reilly Kelly and her mother, Lucienne Murphy, were both born. In fact they had been born the very year the war ended.

Times were tough then when all around seemed lost, however; the southern continents seem to fair well. Life had to be worked at though and the only way they could survive was to cling to their faith and to the old text. When after nearly twenty years of uncertainty, hope was once again on the horizon. Reilly and Lucienne, desperate to have children, decided that now would be a good time to start. Siobhan was subsequently the first of six children to be born into the house of Kelly, just two years before the creation of the UFTN. Born and raised in what is now called Sydneyton.

She had only moved to Melbourne because of her father's work, for he had to relocate his family or be found without employment and income. As with many citizens, they weren't that financial and they had to also care for Siobhan's three younger brothers and two younger sisters. Life continued to be a struggle for this family and she had been caught right in the middle of it.

Being from such a strict upbringing and as she was the eldest, she would have to quite often conduct work beyond her years. This had been due to both her parents' working day jobs with long hours. She would have to prepare supper, make her siblings lunches for school and do the clothes washing amongst other chores. Most nights she would even read her younger brothers and sisters bed time stories, even though she herself was falling asleep as she read. She also had her own school work to get done, but she never complained about her life, not once. She was proud of her family and loved them all. So it could be said that Siobhan's devil streak was born out of a sub-conscious rebellion and where she could, she would let her hair down and be free of all responsibility, even if this just was during the school hours.

Ashleigh on the other hand had come from a middle class protestant family, his lineage going back nine generations of Australian born Maynard of English descent. The old text of his family's scriptures state that the house of Maynard had immigrated to Australia from England during the gold rush days in Victoria, and from there, had carved out a little piece of Australia to call their own. He was also only one of two brothers and the youngest. Both had been raised by their grand elders due to a terrorist attack by a group of Trap left wing extremists. Ash was just five years old at the time and really could not remember what his parents were like.

Because of this, he wasn't burdened with the same pressures of life that Siobhan had been borne to. He and his brother still had to do chores around the farm, but their grand elders would also allow them to be children as well. They would enjoy and learn about the life around them and be guided by the wisdom and knowledge of both their care givers. But Siobhan and Ashleigh did have one thing in common, they were both born before the rise of the UFTN. In fact Ashleigh was born just one month before.

Their parents would never allow such a union between the two from very different backgrounds. But neither of them cared about that, they would be together regardless of what anybody thought, and if they were forbidden, they would defy it, if they were separated by distance, they would find a way to be together, and it she was locked up for all eternity, he would break down the walls of injustice and embrace his love. They would never be torn apart.

Years later, the two became one under a sacred union, he converting to Catholicism to appease Siobhan's father, for he considered family very important. He would not see family torn apart if it could be averted and he embraced his newly acquired faith. Coming from a great and honourable house, his family name remembered throughout history for great deeds committed, he would take his pledge of Catholicism very seriously.

He would respect and honour thy father and mother of one for which he was now joined with. In respect of her father's wishes, he had agreed to a handfast marriage, an old Celtic tradition kept alive by the elders. This tradition, cast upon two with intentions of marriage under sacred vows, tested their resolve. It would be by which one would prove themselves in each other's eyes before committing to union under God and Jesus Christ. Normally the two undertaking the handfasting would remain together for twelve months and one day. If the couple had found themselves incompatible come the end of that twelve months and had borne no children, the following day they could then go their separate ways thus legally dissolving their union and ending their marriage.

Siobhan's father, Reilly, being the master of the house came to realise that he could never keep these two apart, no matter how much he would try or had wanted. He saw that these two were deeply in love and he would seek to please his daughter and see her happy. He knew that throughout her life, she had been asked of many things, and it was now time she enjoyed the greater things that life had to offer. He knew that by this union, his precious daughter would be loved and cared for, for the rest of her life.

Chapter Two

I t was now coming up to the 35th Christmas Union and they were window shopping for presents for their children. He began to have a sickly feeling in the pit of his stomach. He hadn't felt this way since the time he lost two of his soldiers in a green on blue attack in England during the Terran Wars. That particular morning had started like any other morning in England. The Republic of Free Nations had seized control of the new capital in York and Peace Maker Federal troops were moving down from Edinburgh to engage.

By this stage of the war, RFN regiments had started defecting to the UFTN after learning the truth that their rebellion had been based on a lie. These defecting soldiers had now pledged their allegiance to the UFTN and would now fight side by side with the Peace Maker Federal troops.

And just like that day in England, this day here in Queenstown had also started without incident but would soon take a turn for the seemingly worse. This day had started like any other day over the last couple of weeks. He was enjoying his time back home from the AN Uprising and his family were well. Marcus had even started to see a lot clearer. However, like this day, that day in England would see his life turned upside down as his, and that of his mate's and fellow Ranger's hearts would be ripped out.

The Federal Continental Ranger Corps of the OTD had harboured up for the night on their march to York. He had decided to take the lull in activity the next morning to call his wife. As he entered the number code into the Visual Image Display Communications device, otherwise known as the VIDCom, a screen message appeared informing him that all UFTN public communications services had been blocked. That could only mean one thing, a White Out had been enacted.

White Outs usually meant that there had been another incident involving Oceanic or other Peace Maker Federal soldiers in engagement with RFN rebels, either by a direct fire attack or IED blast. He could only hope that it wasn't his guys, but the pit in his stomach told him something different. Rangers had been killed in the line of duty before, but something felt off this time, this time it was different.

As he opened the door to his mobile command centre, he was informed that there had been an insider attack at one of the advanced forward OTD Ranger Company's within his Regiment. One of the rebel soldiers from the defected RFN militia had turned his weapon on Peace Maker Federal troops. At that stage, the information coming in was fairly sketchy. All that could be heard on the TacComRad (Tactical Communications Radio) was that three OTD soldiers were shot, followed by the news of two Eurpasian soldiers and an RFN interpreter also being shot.

There were choppers coming and going as these men were evacuated to the various medical facilities around the old Northumbria Province. The pit in his stomach tightened. He had men out there, and he knew that they would have most certainly been amongst the action, but were they wounded? Or worse, had they been killed?

Only weeks before had he been witness to, and involved in an In Direct Fire attack on a base, IDF. The attack maimed two English soldiers of the Eurpasian Terran Division, decapitating the leg of one. The base alarm warning system that was there to alert soldiers and every one of incoming rockets, known as the Air Projectile Alarm Warning System or APAWS for short, had gone off just as people were moving into the dining facility about to have their lunch.

These rockets had sometimes been sporadic where they landed due to the shoot and scoot techniques employed by the RFN, but this one rocket had found its mark. It was only a second or two after the APAWS had gone off when it hit the ground, as he too was also going to have lunch, sending him backwards from the concussion caused by the blast.

This was a very busy and dangerous period in the Terran Wars against the RFN, as tensions between the UFTN Peace Makers, the RFN soldiers that were defecting, and the rebels that were still sided with the RFN were at an all-time high as political relations worsened. The pit in his stomach confirmed his worst fears. From the three OTD soldiers shot, two had been confirmed as killed in action, two that had been Federal Continental Rangers and which had been under his direct command. One of the English soldiers was also confirmed as killed in action.

Although this wasn't the first time he had lost Rangers under his charge, it was the first time he had lost them killed by a supposed ally. Unfortunately there would be many more days like this to come, but as that day in England changed his life forever, so too would this day. But this particular day would have far reaching affects and consequences as the oncoming drama would be played out and made clear.

He continued to scan the crowd in the shopping centre but nothing seemed out of place. Siobhan was still trying to get the children settled on lunch. But the pit in his stomach remained. He did not know it at the time, but this would be his coming of being, a culmination point which decisions he had made along the way have bought him to. His decisions and that of future decisions would affect our way of life, perhaps that of the UFTN itself. But it would be a much more personal and darker path for that of his family, just how much so was yet to be determined. He wouldn't know the extent of which this change would impact on all their lives.

As he continued looking around him, the unlikeliest of events would unfold. Here he was looking for the mischievous, looking for the sly, looking for the things that should not be when all of a sudden he heard a voice come from over his left shoulder. The owner of the voice must have been timing his looks, as he moved his head from left to right, with perfection. For when the voice spoke, it seemed to have been right on top of him.

'Are you Ashleigh?'

The question coming from a whispered voice in a somewhat nervous and unsteady tone. Startled, he quickly turned back around to see where the voice had come from. He had been looking for the misgivings from an adult with sinister intensions. What he heard however, had come from what sounded like a very young and shy girl. He then fixed his gaze on the voice's owner, it was that of a young slender figure belonging to a teenage girl.

'Ashleigh?'

The voice once again spoke, but this time in more of a quizzical tone, its pitch rising as it rounded out the question. For a moment, he could not speak, he was somewhat taken aback by the girl, for she had seemed to remind him of someone. Someone he knew or had once known, he just didn't know who or from where.

She was about to walk away as he had not yet given his answer. The young girl must have thought he was ignoring her and she was clearly very, very nervous. He just sat there and stared at her for what seemed like a lifetime. In reality it was only a couple of seconds, but taken by the moment, seconds can often feel like an eternity, especially when meeting someone for the very first time. Nerves and anxiety can be powerful monsters if unleashed. After all, he was thirty-five years old and she, well she must have been about fifteen or sixteen. Still the silence remained and as she slowly began to turn away, he quietly answered her.

'Yes, yes I am Ashleigh, but who are you? And how do you know me?'

The girl stopped, turned around again and asked Ashleigh if he had once known a girl by the name of Evonne, Evonne Taylor. All of a sudden he had then realised why the girl had looked so familiar to him and why he had thought he recognised her. This must have been Evonne's daughter he thought to himself. But why now? It must have been at least twelve or so years since he last saw Evonne, and if this was indeed her daughter, what did she want with him?

Ashleigh replied in answer that yes he had once known a girl by that name. He explained to her that she was considered to be a very good friend of his once, but that was a long time ago. This was very strange he thought, why was this girl here asking him these questions and who was she to Evonne? He pressed her for the answer to that question but instead of a reply, he only received silence as a tear could be seen trickling down the girls face, down her cheek.

She was clearly upset, but by what? Had something happened to Evonne he thought? Was she or this girl in some sort of danger? There was still something that didn't quite gel. The pit in his stomach which he had thought would have started to relax a little by now, instead tightened even further. There was something definitely not right here and he sensed that she may have been hiding something or that she herself was in some kind of trouble.

Ashleigh again asked the girl why she had come seeking him out and how she knew Evonne. He would also ask her what her name was, but still the girl said nothing; she just lowered her head further as her shoulders slumped increasingly downwards. A shiver began to take hold of the girl's body as she started to form the words with her mouth in answer but was abruptly stopped in her tracks.

'Who's this?'

Alexander had come up from behind him. The girl, her gaze firmly fixed on Ashleigh, jumped in startled fright. She had not noticed Alexander had come walking up to them. It wasn't that she wouldn't have recognised him; quite the contrary, it was just that she never noticed. In fact, she had knowledge of all the children. She had known where they went to school and had known where they lived. She had been watching this family for about a week now trying to confirm if this was the man she was indeed looking for. She had also been trying to build up the courage to approach this man and strike up conversation, but she had wanted to do this away from his family. The only problem was, he had never been left alone without them either being with him or being very close by.

Ashleigh had given so much of his life to the UFTN Peace Makers that now every time he is home, he would spend as much time with his family as he could. But she had now seen an opportunity now that his wife and children had gone off to get lunch. She decided to seize on the moment. She couldn't walk away could she? Not now, not after everything she had been through to find him. She would not let the interruption by Alexander stop her from what she had come here to say.

For a brief time, she paused from speaking the words that were desperate to escape her lips. Instead she quickly covered the left side of her face with her long reddish auburn coloured hair, turning slightly as she did. Ashleigh told his son that he didn't know who the young girl was, but he was going to find out.

By now, Siobhan had returned to the table carrying their lunch. As she placed the tray of food down on the table, she too asked the question of Ashleigh about who this strange girl was. The girl now surrounded by Ashleigh's family, began to fidget as she nervously glanced left and right. She was completely out of her comfort zone and would do anything if she could only find a hole and crawl into it to escape and hide from all these prying eyes.

As those eyes intensified with their piercing glare, she felt like shouting out and running, but she didn't, she kept her cool and remained calm. She had found the man called Ashleigh, she had found the man that had known Evonne, and she had many more questions that she would ask of him, but the moment had been lost, or so she had thought.

She slowly turned as if to walk away. Ashleigh quickly asked her to stop and sit down with them. He even offered to buy her lunch, she looked like she hadn't eaten in months and would surely appreciate a good meal. But she just shook her head and continued walking without saying a word.

'Wait!'

Ashleigh had wanted her to stay.

'You don't need to leave, we can sit and talk and you can tell me why you wanted to find me.'

But again the girl said nothing; she only quickened her pace as she walked away. Ashleigh instructed his family to remain where they were and to finish eating their lunch. This girl was obviously seeking to speak to him alone and the presence of his family had strayed her from her course. He would see her return to it.

'I'll be right back, stay here for a moment'

He walked up to the girl who had now hidden herself from sight.

She had not wanted to be seen by Siobhan and the children. What was all this secrecy about? Ashleigh had thought to himself. He needed to get to the bottom of this. As he reached the young girl he stretched out his hand in an attempt to grab her so she would stop and talk. But as he did this, and as his fingers gradually grazed the skin of the young girls arm, she stopped and turned to him, and began yelling in a loud voice.

'Don't touch me! Don't you dare! No-one will ever touch me again!'

The people standing around in the shopping centre all stopped from what they were doing to see what all the commotion was about. One bystander even came up to the girl and offered his assistance, but she didn't require his assistance. She never asked for it and she didn't want it, instead she just told him to get lost, calling him a jerk as she said it.

Ashleigh was amazed by her response to his touch, she must have had some trouble in her past. Was it abuse, and if so by who? The worried look of concern and puzzlement now embraced the contours and lines on his face. This place here in this shopping centre was clearly not the spot to be having this conversation. Conversation he thought, so far it had been one way and he was no closer to discovering the answers to the questions which now occupied his thoughts.

He would have to make a decision, one which could result badly as he feared another outburst like the one just witnessed. He decided that a firm voice was required.

'Ok, the time for games are over, you really need to tell me who you are, and why you felt the need to interrupt me and my family during lunch'

'Can't you see it? I'm Evonne's daughter and my name is Josephine, and you don't care!' she yelled.

'If you did care, you would have never left me!'

What was she talking about? Would never have left? He needed to know more. He told her that whatever she had thought he had done, he was sure that he didn't know it, and he would certainly have never wanted to hurt her by it. He pleaded with her to believe him and explained that he had no idea what she was talking about.

He quickly realised that if this was Evonne's daughter, then where was she? Was she here in the shopping centre somewhere? She couldn't be, she would never allow an encounter like this to take place without her being present. So why was this girl here and did Evonne know where she was? Ashleigh had thought to himself that on one hand, he wanted to have her here with them so she could clear this whole thing up, but on the other hand he was glad she was not, for it would be an uncomfortable encounter if she were. The last time they had met didn't exactly go that well.

—⊶— ☦ —⊷—

Ashleigh had held feelings for Evonne a long time ago when they were just a couple of young Federal Continental Rangers just starting out. He as a Tactical Communications Specialist and she venturing into the Intelligence, Surveillance and Reconnaissance field as an ISR specialist. His military training with the FCR Corps had meant that he had to live a great distance from Siobhan for a number of years until his training was complete.

While he was in training, he was forbidden to live with, or have members of the female persuasion in his accommodation on the barracks. On occasion, he would travel to Melbourne to visit his sweet girl, the two staying ever loyal to one another. Their love never wavering not even for a second. Although he had thought Evonne attractive, he would never act on anything he felt for her.

At that stage, the two of them, Evonne and he, were just close friends. They enjoyed each other's company and from time to time it was good for Ashleigh to get away from all the male bravado and testosterone of his male counterparts. He enjoyed being able to go out and have a good time and share a dance with an attractive girl. It was almost as if he was her big brother and he now had someone else to watch over, which he welcomed.

But their feelings for one another slowly began to change as the two spent more and more time together. It could almost be considered a natural evolution that over a time spent, sharing the same challenges and hardships that their Ranger training had thrown at them over the last three years that a romantic relationship would spark up between them. And it did, towards the very end of their training and just as he was about to leave to return to Melbourne.

He would never have the same feelings for her as he did for Siobhan. This relationship was born more out of lust and circumstance, and time and place than anything else. Ashleigh was confused about his future, Siobhan was the woman he loved more than life itself, so why was he putting himself through so much turmoil?

He had already asked Siobhan for her hand in marriage which she happily gave. The two of them had agreed that they would choose the traditional path of being engaged while they were separated due to his initial training. It would be on his return to Melbourne that the two would be joined together in a handfast ceremony that her father had directed them to do.

But now he was at a place that provided very little emotional comfort and during this turmoil, and against he's better judgement and the undeniable love he felt for Siobhan, he gave into his lust and found comfort in another. He found comfort in Evonne. He knew that what he had done was a crime of sin, as did he know that his actions could have grave consequences one day. Was it this day? He considered it a personal character flaw of his that he was able to give his heart so willingly to others who would have it.

After that fateful night and a time spent in self-imposed solitude reflecting on his bad decisions, he knew and came to the conclusion that the only correct thing to do was to say his goodbyes to Evonne and return to Melbourne. He would return to his true love; he would return to be with Siobhan. He had pledged that he would never leave her, ever; and he knew that when once he again fixed his eyes upon her, just like that first day he laid eyes on her, everything else would become a distant memory.

Ashleigh had met up with Evonne some years later after that sinful evening back in '65' to have coffee. He had been granted a reprieve from the Terran Wars and while home, had received a message that Evonne had wanted to catch up. After all that had taken place between the two of them, he still considered her a good friend. He would have coffee with her and talk of days past remembering the happy and joyous moments they spent together. Moments when all was innocent and his true path clearly lit. They would meet up in old Lygon Street, still one of Melbourne's most revered restaurant and café strips in the city.

Siobhan had knowledge of the feelings her husband once held for Evonne, and given the chance would deny such a meeting, for she did not hold much credence in her. The lord says to forgive is divineness. Siobhan would hold true to this and stay the course. She would respect her Catholic beliefs, but it didn't mean that she had to forget or like it.

She would see to it that she was present when the two of them met. This was not to be taken as mistrust for she loved Ashleigh more now than ever before. They were starting to carve out a life for themselves and the future looked bright. The conflict with the RFN Rebels had been going the UFTN's way and looked like it would soon be over. But that devil streak Siobhan possessed meant that she would present herself as a strong authoritarian and commanding figure, thus letting it be known that Ashleigh was hers, and hers alone.

When they all met, things seemed to be going smoothly. Conversation was struck up quickly and times of past were reminisced about, however;

just as fast as the talk began did it quickly end, as the topics soon became a scarcity. At one stage it appeared that Evonne had wanted to tell him something, but her look of wanting quickly dissipated. Next a deafening silence befell the trio and that of uncomfortable glances toward one another ensued. For the next fifteen minutes they each sat silently, finished their Lattes and Cappuccinos; got up from the table and left, going their separate ways. It was not the best of meetings and since then he has never again had contact with her.

Chapter Three

He would belay his concerns about seeing Evonne again and ask Josephine if her mother was here with her now. Josephine explained that she was not and that she was still in Melbourne. The more this story revealed itself, the more Ashleigh became increasingly concerned. Josephine, in her mid-teens was looking gaunt and sickly. She was also very emotionally upset. The current state of her mind would mean she could be at risk and vulnerable to those that would seek to take advantage of her. And what did she mean when she said that if he had cared he would never have left?

His thoughts were racing a million miles an hour. He had to make some sense of it all and tried to put the pieces in place. His main concern was that of the young girl now standing affront of him.

'You mean to tell me, you are here on your own? Does Evee at least know where you are?'

There was no reply from her as he again asked if her mother knew where she was. All Josephine could do was collapse onto a nearby seat as she started to whimper.

At this stage, he still did not know what he had done to make her so angry with him. Suddenly she looked up at Ashleigh and gazed deeply into his eyes, her own now glazed over and filled with tears, and asked him if he really did not know why she was there and why she had come looking for him. Didn't he know who she really was? He had yet to figure this out for himself as he struggled to comprehend the information coming his way.

She continued explaining that she had spent six long months searching for him and that she came seeking help. Evonne had once spoken to Josephine of a man she knew a long time ago. A man that was kind, a man of compassion, and a man that protected and looked after her when she was younger. This was a man that could be relied upon. So was this all she wanted out of him, a man that Evonne had once loved and that could now provide assistance? But assistance with what?

Evee, as he called her, would never have sent her daughter out all alone to find him he thought. Besides, if she had wanted to contact him, there would be far easier and safer ways of doing so. He was still with the OTD FCR Corps as was she at one time. There would be people they would both still know; a network of friends each joined to the next. It would only take a phone call from one person to the next and then to the next before eventually he would be found. So why would it have taken six months for Josephine to find him? Unless she had run away from home and didn't know where to start looking.

'Are you hurt? Do you need terra marcs?' he asked.

He took a seat and was now sitting down beside her still in the middle of the Queenstown Centre Shopping Village and it was getting late. It had already passed one in the afternoon and soon the rains of the Darkness would fall. If they didn't all leave soon, it could be another five hours until it was safe to again venture outside without the aid of protective clothing.

As he sat down, she continued looking down towards her feet and remained silent. Her hand moved and reached down inside the front pocket of her denim jeans and with it she pulled out a folded up photograph with a worn image on it. She handed the photograph to Ashleigh, it was a picture of her family, Evonne, her, a man which must have been her father and two small infant boys that must have been twins.

She told Ashleigh that the man in the picture was her stepfather and the two boys were her twin step brothers. She continued on to say that this fact had only just revealed itself to her and she was now looking for her real father. She had wanted to know why he had left her and why he had never come looking for her. She explained that her full name was Josephine Van den Berg, but she much preferred to go by her mother's maiden name of Taylor.

Ashleigh concluded that she had run away from home in search of this man she called her real father and figured that she had thought him to be that man. That's why she was so angry, that's why she said if he had cared he would have never left. But this couldn't be so, it simply couldn't be true. But if she was angry about her real father leaving her at childbirth, then why would she come looking for him and why would she request his help?

'Are you going to have lunch dad?'

A small voice appeared out of nowhere.

'Hey, she looks like me.'

Elyssa-Jayne, or EJ as her friends called her, had come to collect her father for lunch. EJ was only twelve years old and very innocent. She did not know that the girl in front of her could be her half-sister. At last he had put some of the pieces together. He now knew who she was. She had not only looked like her mother; she had also looked like EJ. Was it true? Did they really share the same father and which was the reason why they both looked similar? Back at the table when she hid her face from view with her long hair, did she feel she might have been recognised? For anyone to look at the pair side by side, they could easily have been mistaken for sisters.

Josephine was very nervous and was trying to also be very cautious. She had wanted to approach this with a level of maturity and sensibility, but she was a teenage runaway girl who was obviously having troubles at home. The emotion of the occasion would of course have taken its toll on her as she was gradually overcome by it and as it would have done anyone else. She was only a child after all. The puzzle was now coming together easier than before as if the pieces themselves were lining up and waiting their turn to be laid into place. The family photograph she had shown clearly displayed the image of a teenage girl much older than her brothers, and if she was fifteen or sixteen, this would clearly fit the timeline.

Evonne must have become pregnant that last summer they had spent together, that summer in Destiny just before he had to leave her and travel to Melbourne. Was this girl that was now sitting next to him really the result of their illicit affair? This would be too much if this were to be true. Would this be the karma that came back to haunt him as he had once thought? The karma to perhaps drive a wedge between him and Siobhan and their marriage?

He stood up from the seat and started pacing back and forwards. EJ meanwhile was still looking at this older girl in amazement by how much she looked like her. While he was pacing and trying to figure all this out, Josephine in a tender caring voice quietly instructed EJ to go back to her mother, and told her that her daddy would be along shortly. Ashleigh had forgotten about everything around him, he had forgotten that EJ had walked away, he had forgotten that Josephine had asked for his help and was obviously in some kind of trouble, and he had forgotten that he was standing in the middle of a shopping centre surrounded by people.

For the first time since recently returning home from the uprising in the AN Territories, he didn't feel nervous or paranoid about people behind him. In fact, he didn't even know they were there at all. All he could think of is, would Siobhan leave him over this? It would shatter his world if she did, but he then took stock of himself, pulling his emotions and fears back into check. He suddenly stopped pacing and realised there were more important issues at hand here. He again remembered his surroundings. He would not put himself first; he would not be that selfish. Whatever was to come next, he would handle it with dignity and honour as he had tried to do his entire life.

As he stopped pacing, he turned, stood, and stared at Josephine in stunned silence. Then came the words that he feared with uncertainty the most.

'That's right.' she said.

Tears now streaming down her face.

'I am your daughter.'

The words sent an icy shiver right down the center of his back, right down his spine and into the pit of his soul. Again he thought this couldn't be, he was careful wasn't he? They did use protection didn't they? It was so long ago that he all but put it behind him. How could he be sure though? In defiance and bewilderment he told Josephine that he couldn't be her father. He explained that her mother and he would never have been so careless and they wouldn't have made such a huge mistake like this. So much for dignity and honour, he cursed the very words that came from his mouth wanting to stop them as they did, but they just seemed to keep on going.

'A huge mistake!' she yelled.

'Is that what you think I am, a damn huge mistake?'

The face that was previously overcome with tears was now becoming an angry scowl which continued hurling abuse at him. A crowd was now gathering as the sound of Josephine's yelling and shouting soon grabbed Siobhan's attention. She told Alexander to stay at the table and look after

EJ and Marcus for her while she rushed over to see what was happening. As she reached the point of all the commotion, she heard all of what Josephine was saying to her husband.

'I am a living person!'

She clenched raised fists and continued.

'Blood courses through my body, through these veins! I have feelings just like anyone else, but you wouldn't know it, would you DAD? It's obvious you don't care after all!'

Dad? Siobhan thought. What was she talking about? She didn't know it at the time, but she was going to find out.

Josephine didn't want this anymore and turned away from Ashleigh just as Siobhan reached his side, close enough to hear Josephine say to him that she knew it was a mistake trying to find her real father.

'What does she mean real father?'

Siobhan had a stern and yet puzzled expression on her face as she asked this question.

'What is going on here husband?'

Ashleigh told his wife he would explain it all in good time, but that would have to be later. Right now he just needed her to trust him and give him some time and space. He felt like he was being ripped apart from both sides. The action he had seen during the Terran Wars was nothing compared to this he thought. On one side he had his wife wanting answers from him and on the other, what now appeared to be his daughter and thought must be true, was walking away from him. He couldn't let her leave.

'Wait!' he yelled.

'Pheeny, STOP!'

Suddenly Josephine came to an abrupt halt and turned around. No-one had ever called her Pheeny, no-one that is, except for her mother. She asked him how he knew that was the pet name her mother had given her. It just seemed to be right, he explained to her. He again pleaded for Siobhan to give them some space, reluctantly, she agreed.

As the pair calmed down, they decided to take a stroll through the shopping centre and to move away from the large crowd that had now formed around them. He had apologised to Josephine for the cruel and insensitive words he had belted out earlier. He was just stunned by the revelation; that was all. He would not turn from this girl or say such hurtful things ever again to her. She had come seeking his help and he would see to it that it was given.

Now that he had accepted the truth of it, he once again asked Josephine if her mother knew where she was, and how it was that she came to find out the truth about who her biological father really was. She revealed to him that she had run away without her parent's knowledge in search of him, in search of the man named Ashleigh. She told him that she had overheard her mum call out his name one night when she was having an argument with, what was now revealed to be, her stepfather.

She overheard Evonne say to her stepfather that she wished Ashleigh had never left her and her daughter and that she had always wanted to be with him. She continued to say that she wished she had never married the man she was with now. Josephine at the time couldn't believe what she was hearing, but it had all made sense now. She had often felt the sting in her stepfather's words when he spoke to her and the sting of his belt when he lashed out at her.

He had never laid a hand on the boys though, the twins seemed to be his favourite and now she knew why. Besides all this, she was born on the 23 of September in 2066, and as it turns out, nine months after Evonne and Ashleigh had shared that moment together. He at least now knew her age, fifteen years old and a runaway. But this was only one answer of many more to come, for there was becoming an ever increasing sum of questions that seemed to exponentially double with each passing revelation. He would have the answers to these questions that lay in wait for her.

Every now and again however, disbelief would re-enter his thoughts as he would again listen to the doubts of uncertainty in his head. Was there a chance that maybe, just maybe, she wasn't his daughter? It was really a null question; he was clearly the girl's father. Any person with half a brain could see that, but reason would vacate itself at times with all abandonment.

Had she worked all this out prior to their meeting? Maybe it was some cruel hoax. Did she want currency? Did she want something else from him? What? But as quickly as those thoughts entered his mind, they were as quickly dispelled as he would again look into her eyes and know, undoubtingly, that she was his offspring. The more he looked at her, the more he could see the resemblance and no it to be true.

More importantly however, even if this child was not his daughter and regardless of any motive she may have had, she was far from home and had come looking for help. Here stood a fragile and vulnerable teenage girl. Where was she staying? Who was she living with and how was she living? Did she have no-one at all to care for her? He couldn't just walk away from this even if he had wanted to. It wasn't the Ranger way and thanks to the teachings of his grand elders, it wasn't his way.

Ashleigh needed to take control of the situation. This was no place to be having this conversation, and what of his family? They would surely be getting worried by now. Siobhan would want answers, and they had better be good. But there was no way he could sugar coat this. He had loved Evonne at one time and had betrayed his love for Siobhan for here was the evidence. He would have to try and convince her that it was such a long time ago and that there were more important things to worry about and take care of now.

He turned to Josephine and told her he wanted to take her back to his house with his family so they could continue with this conversation. He wanted to take her to somewhere safe and where they could really sit down and talk in private. But Josephine was hesitant of this, the leers of those piercing eyes she felt earlier still lingered. She surely would not be welcomed in the home of his wife. This time he pleaded for her to go with him until reluctantly she agreed, but not before pulling out her phone and showing him another picture. This would be the reason she came looking for him in the first place.

Those stories that she was told of a man that was generous, kind and loving. The stories she had heard so many times as a young girl. That of a man she believed to be a knight in shining armour that would one day come bursting through the door to take both her and her mother away, away from her tyrant stepfather, had kept her going strong through all the times she had felt like giving up.

However, as she got older and more cynical with age and with the life around her, thoughts of her knight in shining armour quickly evaporated. Such stories were only for stupid naive little girls she told herself. She had thought that her mother had made these stories up, only reciting them to her to provide comfort for a daughter that was clearly in need of it. These stories, she thought, were fiction in an effort to take her mind off things by placing her into a fantasy world of make believe. She believed they were designed to put her in a place much gentler and kinder than the one she was currently in, at least in her thoughts anyway.

Gradually, she believed the story to be a lie and that no such person existed. How could a person like that exist she told herself? Men just aren't that way inclined. They aren't built to be loving and caring. This is what she knew to be true, this is how she saw the world around her and the men that filled her life. But since that night when her mother yelled out those words to her stepfather, did she start to believe again.

Chapter Four

O n the night of her most startling revelation, she now knew the truth that she was not the daughter of Dirk Van den Berg, but she also now had questions, uncertain questions. She thought to herself, what of this man her mother had been telling her stories about for so many years? Did he really exist? Was there hope after all? Later that night after learning the truth about her stepfather and after Dirk had once again collapsed drunk on the sofa, did her mum come into her bedroom to give her a tender caring hug telling her that she loved her with all her heart.

She told Josephine that she was sorry for this life she had given her and not to sorrow too much in despair for her destiny had yet been set. She told her daughter that greater things awaited her. Josephine gave her mother a little smile and asked if she could tell her those stories again. Evonne had known her daughter had overheard the row earlier that evening, so instead of telling her another story as she had done when she was younger, and to which she now admitted to embellishing from time to time, Evonne chose to tell her daughter the truth. She would tell her everything about her real father and why he wasn't with them now.

Unfortunately some of the truth became skewered and twisted in Josephine's mind and she misunderstood some of its content. Was it because she was overwhelmed with emotion? No-one can be sure, but what did hold true is that Evonne had told her daughter the whole truth. Josephine, however; in hearing that her real father had left them to go back to his fiancé, never heard the part about Ashleigh never being told about a child being born. Evonne confessed to her daughter that she had tried to tell him once before when they had met up again years later, but couldn't bring herself to do it.

Evonne had chosen at the time of her daughter's birth to keep that to herself. As she saw it, she didn't want to ruin Ashleigh's life by revealing she was pregnant with child, his child. Despite Josephine's omission of this fact due to selective hearing, she still loved this man. A man she had never known except for an image she had painted for herself in her head. Mum still held love for this man she thought, and if mum still loved and trusted him, so would she. She would therefore try and find him to help them.

Josephine still holding her phone while Ashleigh viewed the image, revealed what was an atrocity. The picture displayed on the phone showed an image of Evonne. But it was an image that shocked and angered him. Evonne had a bruised lower lip with the left side of it stitched together; dry blood could be seen around the edges. Her left eye was swollen and bruised. A deep blue could be seen with tinges of red and brown around Evonne's eye as she struggled to see out of it.

She had been beaten with malice and he would not stand for this. The bastard was going to suffer no matter what it took. His whole body tensed up as he clenched his fists in rage. The Ranger corps may have been family to him, but this was his real family, this was his blood. Josephine started to panic, maybe she had done the wrong thing in finding her real father. Maybe it wasn't a good idea after all.

Since she was born, Josephine had been around the angry tempers of men. She was now seeing another man, a man she believed was good and kind show this same temper. Had she placed misgivings in him? She had recognised the rage that now filled his eyes and started to become very frighten and scared of him. She started to back away from Ashleigh with an uncertainty, after all she did not know him at all, other than from the stories her mother had told her when she was little. But those were stories of a man her mother had known years ago. What was he like now? What had he been through?

Josephine had never known of the horrors of his military service as a Ranger and what it had given him. She didn't know what he had been through during the Terran Wars, how could she have? She hadn't known that he had killed before in the line of duty, and that upon returning home from such wars did he wake in cold sweats night after night with the nightmares that lingered in his memories. It was only through the love and support of Siobhan that he was able to assimilate back into civilian life.

She did not know that he took the sacrament of family very seriously for the affair with her mother had proven to her otherwise, but still, that was a long time ago and many things have changed since then. Family was sacred and honoured and he would now consider Evonne and Josephine a part of his. He would see it defended.

Slowly the colour of his face began to turn a deep red as he walked with purpose.

'Daddy?'

Josephine quietly spoke with a hint of fear in her voice. Ashleigh suddenly stopped. He hadn't heard someone call him daddy since EJ was little and now she only said it on rare occasion. He turned to look at his new found daughter, tears again filled her eyes which by now were red roar from all the crying she had been doing. A tear trickled down her face followed by another, and then another.

What was he doing to this poor girl he thought. Josephine repeated her previous word, but this time she took a pace forward reaching out her hand.

The muscles in his body began to relax as he too reached out with his. They had come to new ground which was openly embraced by the both of them, and as their hands touched, right at that moment; that very second in time, Josephine knew that here was a man that would love and protect her for the rest of her life. Ashleigh knew that she in turn would reciprocate that love in him.

Right now, the best course of action would be to not place himself in harm's way, but rather make it a matter for the State Division Police and the UFTN law to handle. He would not take matters into his own hands as this was one of the acts of humankind he and his fellow Rangers fought to stamp out. The SDP was created to uphold law and order at the forming of the UFTN, he would let them handle it. But that being said he would ensure that he would be the catalyst of change for Evonne and Josephine. He would ensure that he would have a part to play in the coming days that would soon be upon them.

They had returned to the seats and the table where Siobhan and their children were still waiting. He had known his wife would still be there. It would take a lot to separate these two, especially after all they have been through to be together in the first place, and have gone through since. That fact didn't remove the look of anger on Siobhan's face however. Ashleigh explained that he had a lot to tell her and asked Josephine to show Siobhan the photo of her mother he had seen only moments before.

Siobhan was stunned to silence, her look of anger turning to sorrow and pity for Evonne, and for this poor girl that has been living in such an awful environment. No matter how she felt about Evonne, past events would take a back seat as these seemed insignificant to what was happening now.

It was true, Ashleigh had an affair, but at least is was out of love. But this was something different altogether, this was domestic violence and wife bashing. She knew the matter had to be resolved and she knew her husband of sixteen years would not, could not, walk away from this. She knew he would be the one to see it resolved. He was an honourable man and would see justice served.

Ashleigh had convinced Josephine to come home with he and his family to talk some more. They would continue to discuss this matter and get to the bottom of this and many more issues in the privacy of his own home and away from prying eyes. But first he would collect Josephine's belongings from where she was staying. It had been just as well that he had chosen to park the All Purpose AutoMobile in the underground vehicle lot. The rain was now beating down upon the empty streets below as all had ventured inside to escape its dangerous effects.

But being a Federal Continental Ranger of the OTD had meant that he was always prepared for any eventuality. In the rear of the APAM he always carried PARTNAR Suits, one for each member of his family. These were the Personal Anti-Rain Toxin & Nerve-Agent Repellent Suits designed for a person to live in through any environmental condition. From the extreme cold, to the scorching heat and everything in between, including the stinging rain. A person experienced enough with these suits could survive months, even in the most extreme conditions. With a little adjustment, he could fix one that would fit Josephine and keep her safe.

The PARTNAR Suits were skin tight and had many utility pouches down the legs and arms. A breathing apparatus was fitted over the nose and mouth and special vision goggles, known as VEPEW goggles, protected the eyes from any ingress from harmful toxins. These were electronically controlled Vision Enhancement and Protective Eye Wear goggles that could be adjusted to enhance the sight of the wearer. The ensemble was completed by an outer covering resembling a full length trench coat with hood. The trench coat also doubled as a shelter that one could use to protect themselves during prolonged storms if caught unawares.

When they reached the APAM, Josephine still had reservations about collecting her things. She had wanted her belongings but did not want to reveal to her real father where she had been living. This was of no consequence to Ashleigh, he would just want her safe and under his care and protection. He knew that Evonne did not know where her daughter was, he also knew that she had run away from home and could easily tell that she had not been eating that well. She would either have no funds left or if she did? Well, it would be very little. For all he knew she could have been living off the street. No daughter of his was going to be living in squaller if he had anything to do with it.

Still Josephine resisted and refused to tell her father where she was staying. Maybe she was ashamed or maybe she would be embarrassed by it, but he would convince her otherwise and that it would be the right thing to do. She had come looking for her real father to help her mother, but she obviously needed help herself. He would not let her or Evonne down by neglecting to offer his care and provide a safe haven for her to rest.

Josephine finally agreed it was for the best and gave directions to where she was staying. Much to his surprise, her directions were starting to take them to an older part of the metro city of Queenstown, the fringe limits, and he started to wonder just where she was taking them. As they turned each corner weaving their way through the city streets, his vision through the dark and heavy rain had deteriorated to a point where it was becoming impossible to see. With the push of a button he adjusted his VEPEW goggles and instantly his field of view became a lot clearer.

The rain pelted down onto the city streets and the cloud cover had increased to almost darkness as the city high-rises added to the effect. The further they drove, the more his understanding of where they were going became painfully apparent as he slowly began to recognise where she might have been staying. He couldn't know exactly which house or what building, but he had guessed the suburb which made him fear for her safety, and that of his family as well as his own for that matter. He would not know what would await them when they arrived.

When they reached their destination, his thoughts had been correct and they pulled up outside a little refuge where the less fortunate had made their home. It had been a little hostel in Sinton, a place referred to in the old text as Fortitude Valley, or Sin Town as people used to call it during the years of unrest that immediately followed the War of the Great Despair. The years before the Consortium of Trust and before the peoples of earth were united under the UFTN. The old text had referred to this suburb as the seedy underbelly of a city that once thrived along the river that ran through it.

Over the years and somehow, Sinton had survived and remained the same to what it was back then, only now it was far worse and had become a thorn in the side of the new city of Queenstown. It was cheap, it was dirty, and it was nasty. Not to mention that it was also a very dangerous place to be especially if you were a fifteen year old girl. This was a place where drug deals were made and illegal prostitution ran rampant. It was said that a person could disappear in this place never to be found again. Sinton had everything, if you wanted it, it would be there no holds barred and with no questions asked.

The criminal element in this part of the city took care of themselves and strangers were considered unwelcomed. Not even a Ranger could be safe here, especially one with his family. But he had modified the APAM and it was fitted with a tough exoskeleton that would be hard to penetrate.

Siobhan and his children were also no slouch when it came to self-preservation. Just as with his own upbringing, Alexander and EJ had been taught the life lessons of Terra Earth. He knew they would remain safe while he and Josephine would venture into the building. But every minute they stayed there, lessoned their chances and shifted the odds in favour of the criminal underworld. He would have to act fast and not bring attention to the fact that he was a Ranger.

What a God almighty dangerous place his daughter had found herself in. Was she even aware of the gravity and the seriousness of this place? As he thought about all the possibilities and dangers his daughter could have been exposed to, a sickly thought entered his mind. What if Josephine had turned to prostitution as a way to earn terra marcs? He shuddered at the thought but the reality was he didn't know this girl at all. For all he knew, she could've been capable of anything. The local Sin Skin Bosses were always on the lookout for new talent, especially the young and untouched. Josephine certainly fit the bill and would provide an easy target for the less scrupulous to prey upon.

He quickly put those thoughts from his mind however, he needed to stay focussed on the task. If she had succumbed to the unthinkable, he would find out and deal with that later. Now wasn't the time to be asking her those type of questions. She was still very emotional and vulnerable at the moment. She had tried to walk away from him once already and he didn't want to give her another excuse to do it again. The most important thing right now was her safety and he would stay the course and remove her from this place post haste.

As they pulled up outside the hostel, he told Siobhan to stay in the APAM with the children while he escorted Josephine up stairs to grab her things. He then proceeded to unlock a secret compartment inside the APAM and handed his wife a small projectile weapon. Use this if you have too he told her, they were only words really as he knew he could have left the vehicle without giving his wife any instructions at all. Siobhan knew exactly what to do in the case of an emergency. She told him they would be fine, but also told him not to take his time. Again, this needn't had been said, but it was their way to reassure each other that everything was going to be fine. If trouble broke out, he would know the sounds of this particular weapon he handed her and would come back down to assist immediately.

The building was run down and he could only assume was filled with the disease of vermin; both of the rat infested and insect kind, to the human occupants that called this place home. He and Josephine put on their PARTNAR Suits and stepped from the APAM. He led the way entering the building with Josephine close by his side as they both commenced the climb up the stair well. As they did, they passed a woman sitting on the landing, completely zoned out of this world. Visible traces of herorain abuse could be seen up her arm by the puncher marks she had and her appearance was very gaunt, especially around the midriff and facial cheekbones.

Herorain had now been the drug of choice for the poor. Ever since the coming of the Darkness and the rains that came with it, Heroin poppies now grow in abundance. But because these grow abnormally fast with the aid from the stinging rain, the poppies mutated becoming more lethal, hence the term herorain. Very easily addictive, very cheap and very lethal. The expected life of a user from inception to death would only be about ten years. Considering that most were teenagers orphaned as young children by their parents, most users never saw past their thirtieth birthday. It was a sad indictment on this seemingly utopian world the Consortium of Trust had created, but one in which measures were introduced to stamp out. Unfortunately there would always remain persons harbouring the most sinister of intentions.

The next part of the stairwell on the third floor presented a man leaning against a wall and as Ashleigh and Josephine passed him by, he muttered out some words.

'Hey man, looks like you got a good one there, nice and young the way they should be.'

It was all he could do to refrain himself from knocking this guy on his arse, but he had to keep his temper, he had to stay the course. He was there for his daughter and the sooner he had removed her from this environment, the better.

Chapter Five

Finally they reached the room where she had been sleeping. As he opened the door, a sleeping bag could be seen all rolled up and with what looked like a bundle inside of it. Josephine had said that this was hers and as she removed the hood of her trench coat and facial equipment of her PARTNAR Suit, she quickly rushed over to get the backpack that she had rolled up inside it. In her naivety, this was the only thing she saw that she could do for security.

Ashleigh later asked her why she had left the bag there in the first place instead of taking it with her. She answered that she had trusted the other people she shared the room with. Her mother had been a Ranger, did she teach her daughter nothing of the world around her?

She was so young and innocent. Her untrained ways of the world presented a real fear in him. Her reaction back at the Centre Shopping Village when he first reached out to grab her indicated that she had been physically hurt in some way. He had put it down to Dirk mistreating her and his obvious dominance over Evonne, but as he walked around the apartment and had seen where she had been living, he asked himself, had something else happened to her here? He only hoped that she would come away from this not that emotionally scarred, now he feared about her physical being. He knew that when the dust had finally settled on all this, there would be some serious hearts and souls to mend.

Josephine unrolled her sleeping bag only to find a heap of newspaper scrunched up inside made to look like her backpack. Her trust in her room mates it had seemed, had been mislaid. Suddenly a noise could be heard coming from another room that led off just to the rear of the kitchen. On the bench were the remains of used needles and dried blood stains just underneath where a bowl of cereal was resting.

A lone cat that was unnoticed upon entry now made a hissing noise at the two of them, rearing back with its back arched as they approached the kitchen to investigate the sounds. It had seemed that they had interrupted the feline in its afternoon snack as it went back to licking the blood stained milk that was in the cereal bowl. Ashleigh had dealt with feral and wild animals before during his time in the Burmese Jungles in the first years of the Terran Wars, so he quickly disposed of the creature and continued walking towards the door at the rear of the kitchen.

The sound, Josephine had thought, was being made by the others that she had been sharing the apartment with, and she rushed over to investigate. Had they taken her backpack? Ashleigh quickly stopped her and placed her behind him for protection. He would see what was going on from behind this closed door for himself first. It could be anyone doing anything. They could be high on herorain or worse, have a weapon and panic, and injure someone in the process.

There is nothing worse or more dangerous than a drugged up dope addict with a firearm, they were unpredictable. At least those he fought in the Terran Wars had a purpose, albeit one he strongly disagreed with and which later came to light as being a lie, but these people, potentially kids themselves only had one desire in mind and that was when and where they were getting their next score. Everything else was irrelevant and inconsequential to them.

As he open the door, he saw two young boys. One of the young boys had been holding a plastic bottle which he had been using for modern day chroming. As a cheap thrill, those desperate enough would risk safety to themselves and go out into the rain unprotected to collect the dangerous water falling from the sky. This water when added to simple aspirin would be shaken vigorously until a toxic vapour would emerge. After that, one would simply remove the bottle cap and inhale its treacherous fumes.

The other young boy, however; was seen holding his daughters backpack. This had been what they had come for. The pair must have been around eighteen or nineteen years of age and they started hurling abuse at Ashleigh as he entered the room. It wasn't until he removed the hood of his trench coat and breathing apparatus that had concealed his face, along with the sight of his 9mm Mk4.0 Berretta that he had holstered to his thigh that the pair began to show signs of panic. Even the most dim-witted of people couldn't mistake this man for anything other than a Ranger, as they were the only ones allowed to carry such a weapon.

The fear in their eyes intensified as he took a step forward and the realisation of their situation slowly began to become a whole lot clearer. It would be the most futile of attempts to stand against a member of the FCR and as they gazed upon the sight of this tall solid figure standing over the top of them, they quickly backed down. They were clearly stoned and although this pair had the sense of mind for self-preservation, they were barely capable of any other coherent thought or speech.

'Hey give that back!' Josephine yelled.

But the boy holding her back pack just clenched it tighter.

'u,u,u,you given it to Maarrrty after he, he, laid wit ya last nigh.' One of the boys said.

'eh,eh,eh,enyways, you diden't care about of it, you was, em? sleepen'

What! Ashleigh thought to himself.

'Who's Marty and where is he?' he ordered.

They told him in their almost incomprehensible speech that he had left and wasn't coming back. They also hadn't known his full name. It was quite often like this in these run down cheap and dirty hostels, particularly here in Sinton. Half the time, there would be no guarantee that the other person would introduce themselves by their real name in the first place. These people that sort refuge in such places were either dead poor or had wanted to hide from something or someone. If they didn't want to be found, then they wouldn't be.

It would be certain that this Marty had most likely left as the boys had said and was now long gone from this place. He concluded that the boys would be most likely telling him the truth. They were both now cowering in a corner of the room and were obviously afraid of what was going to happen to them next. Ashleigh's rage was intensifying more and more as he stepped closer to the two boys.

Josephine's look was one of regret and shame, she had made a huge mistake and had gotten herself into what now seemed liked serious trouble. And now from this young boy's mouth, she had heard words which made her cringe inside. She began to feel seriously sick in her stomach by the thought that she may have been sexually assaulted. Physically she felt fine, but how would she know what her body should feel like? How would she know what the act of sex was like for she had never experienced it?

Ashleigh reassured her that none of this was her fault, not by a long shot. He had considered the blame to rest fairly and squarely on the shoulders of her stepfather, for if it wasn't for him, Josephine would not be here right now and in this situation. But he did have one thing to be thankful for, Dirk had bought her to him. He told Josephine that whoever this Marty was, he was undoubtedly gone by now. The chances of finding him would be slim. He had clearly assaulted his daughter, but to what extent? This was a fifteen year old girl and if she had been sexually assaulted, regardless whether or not it was consensual, the cold hard truth of the matter was, it was rape. Clear and simple, for she was only a child.

The world may have changed since the coming of the Darkness of the Great Despair, but moral justice and ethical standards remained the same. It was wrong then and it was still wrong now. He would have to remove this thought from his mind of the potential harm that may have befell his daughter and get on with their immediate task. He still needed to get her things and get her out of there.

He reached down towards the boys. A shudder gripped them both with fear for they had not known what he was going to do to them. To their surprise, he simply lent forward and grabbed the backpack from the young boy's grasp and gave it to Josephine. In a panicked state, she walked back outside to the kitchen bench and emptied its contents. Ashleigh glanced over to the bench to see what she had been carrying around with her. There were more pictures of her mum and her two brothers, a notebook which must have been her diary, some cosmetics and toiletries, and a small change of clothes. There wasn't much in there.

'Where is it?' she yelled back at the boys.

There was no response and again she yelled out the question, where is it? Ashleigh now rested his hand on the rear of his pistol as the electro-mechanic links securing it to his side disappeared from view. He would be ready for what might come. Suddenly, from out of the corner of her eye, she noticed what seemed to be some cotton protruding out from the top of one of the drawers in the kitchen. When she opened it, she had seen a teddy bear with its stomach ripped open.

Like a bolt of lightning striking the dead back to life, Ashleigh gasped in amazement, he immediately recognised the bear. It had been a parting gift to Evonne all those years ago when he had left her and returned to Melbourne. Evonne must have given the bear to Josephine when she was younger and now it had meant everything to her.

As she picked up her beloved teddy bear, a small rolled up paper package fell out. Ashleigh, so stunned at seeing this teddy bear again, was nearly knocked over as both boys, forgetting their fear, rushed by him scrambling to reach for the small package. Its contents had revealed a bag that contained a small amount of herorain.

It was all starting to make sense now. Ashleigh had surmised that Marty, not wanting to use any of his own possessions for fear of losing or misplacing something that could identify him, had wanted to use Josephine's backpack to buy some drugs. Knowing that she would not willingly give him the backpack because it contained her bear, Marty had doped her up and which is why she couldn't remember the night before.

He had figured that once Marty had seen the teddy bear, he could use this to conceal the drugs. Once they had returned from their buy, the bear and the backpack were obviously useless to them now and forthwith discarded. The bear was stuffed into the kitchen drawer and the backpack was snapped up by the drone that had been holding it when he burst into the room.

Marty all hyped up from the excitement of the buy and proceeding to get high must have at some stage seen an opportunity while Josephine was still knocked out to take advantage of her. Well at least he had tried to as there was still no firm evidence that he had done anything at all. He had hoped that due to Marty's drug induced state, he would not have been able to perform the act of coitus. What a low life coward he had thought. If he ever got his hands on him..... well? He hoped secretly that he would never find Marty. He did not want the sins of his past rising to the surface again. Things he had been ordered to do, things he had to do, in the line of duty and service were buried deep in his soul and he would see that they remained that way.

They had been using the bear to conceal their drugs. The bastards he thought. He would never look at another teddy bear the same after this point. If he did, it would bring back too many unpleasant memories. That was it, he no longer held desires to seek vengeance against the boys for the way they had treated Josephine; it would be pointless and serve no purpose. So they picked up the back pack and left, leaving the two boys fighting over the herorain as they did. They had not even noticed that they had left.

Ashleigh would see to it that Josephine was checked by the medical staff at the Queenstown Central Hospital for any signs of sexually transmitted diseases, other diseases or physical rape. It would be a shame if she had been permanently scarred from this preventing her from being able to bear children of her own one day. But how would he explain this at the hospital? Would she be taken away from him and placed into state care? He still had a lot of questions for her. But his needs were insignificant to that of her welfare and safety. He would take her to the hospital and make sure she was medically fine, while he and Siobhan would see to her mental state of mind.

Josephine was now listening to everything Ashleigh was telling her to do, she had felt very comfortable around him now and had placed complete trust in him. At the hospital, Ashleigh had explained to the nurses and doctors that she had come to Queenstown to visit her father, him. Well that much was true and if they didn't believe him, they could always do a DNA test.

He also explained that she had been out one night and coerced into taking a drive to the old city districts were eventually she was led into a hostel. He continued by saying that she had been drugged and had no control over her judgments or motor functions. All she could remember is a man named Marty talking to her and then seeing his face very close to hers. She recalled that she felt the weight of his body on top of hers and now had fears that she may have been raped.

After describing the drugs that had been used the night before to the medical staff and informing them of the hostel, they had suggested that perhaps Ashleigh's assumption had been correct. Marty would not have been able to do anything. The Darkness rain that now effected the opium poppy also effected the body's function on the person taking the drug. They did however, have grave concerns over other diseases and illnesses that Josephine may have been exposed to. Purely for the reason of where she had been taken. They would run all the tests and check for everything leaving no stone unturned.

Ashleigh had known he had broken one of his sacred vows to the OTD and more importantly to the FCR Corps. He had not told the truth, but he would be taken at his word because of who he was. Everyone knew that the FCR took their duty seriously and the bond they had for their Ranger brothers and sisters. This bond tied them together in unity, trust, honour and courage. But he didn't care about that, he held something higher than this vow, and that was family.

The fact that she had run away from home and that her stepfather was an abusive wife bashing arse, was not mentioned. This would be his alone to sort out and take care of, at least for now. The medical staff at the Queenstown Central Hospital were very thorough, they would ensure that they didn't miss a thing and had made comment on Josephine's obvious lack of nutrition. But one didn't require the skills of medicus to clearly see that this girl had not had a decent meal in quite some time.

Josephine quickly rebutted the statement before her father had a chance to answer. She explained that this was just how she was and that she had never been any different. Ashleigh couldn't do anything now except nod his head in agreement with his daughter. Once again he was taken at his word even though the answer rested uncomfortably in the minds of the medical staff. They weren't exactly lying to them, they just weren't telling the whole truth.

By now the State Division Police had been called in to investigate the matter, although they knew that the assailant would never be found. If a Ranger could not find him, and they had figured that he would surely have tried, then what chance did the SDP have? But they were still required to log and document the processes and findings of their inquiry.

Both Ashleigh and Josephine would now have to answer to the SDP and tell their stories again. They knew that they would both be questioned individually, but there was no fear of reprisal. In their short time together, they started becoming attuned as one. Ashleigh could not understand this, but his sixth sense told him something different. It told him that everything was going to be all right with this.

However, he still had slight reservations that Josephine might crumble under the weight of the lie, but she had surprised him and stayed true. His fears had been founded on her lack of emotional stability earlier that morning at the Queenstown Centre Shopping Village. This, however; was now a different girl that stood beside him. She was teaming with confidence and pride. He figured she had felt safe for the first time in her life and it was all because she had found her real father. She would back him and take his lead on anything.

After a night in the hospital under observation to ensure that there were no delayed signs of physiological or mental trauma, she would be released the next morning and allowed to go home. Ashleigh had asked Siobhan to return to their home in Glassenville with their children while he would remain by Josephine's side throughout the night. Siobhan had been unsure of this, but trusted her husband and would therefore respect his wishes and do what was requested of her and know to be right.

He had spent the entire night awake just sitting and watching over the girl that he now knew to be his daughter. He had watched her as she fell asleep and as she breathed peacefully knowing that her father was with her by her side. As he stared at this gem in the night, he thought about Evonne and recalled how he had watched her sleep when they had been together. They were very much alike. He saw this now and his thoughts turned to what his next move would be.

Come the morning, the Doctor who had treated Josephine the previous day came into the room. The immediate diagnosis had indicated that she was fine, she had not been raped. However, there were still bloods away for tests. She would have to wait a couple of days until the results of the analysis came back. As there were no physical signs of penetration, the tests might still find something that indicated otherwise. The tests would also hopefully clear her of any STDs as well as other diseases she may have been exposed to and therefore contracted.

This came as a huge relief for Ashleigh; he couldn't bear the thought of this innocent girl being violated. There were no signs of penetration the doctor said. She had not been raped. He now prayed for the blood test results to tell him the same. She would hopefully be clear of all disease and remain as pure as she could be.

As they left the hospital, they were reminded that the SDP investigation was still ongoing and that follow up calls and questioning may still be required. Siobhan had fears that her husband might be charged with obstructing an SDP enquiry, or worse still, he would be vanquished from the Rangers. But as he explained it to her, he had actually given the complete truth about what he knew of Marty and the two other drug fiends he had come across. Everything he withheld would have no bearing on the outcome of their investigation.

Chapter Six

S iobhan put the kettle on and prepared a cuppa for her and her beleaguered husband. A glass of lemonade would suffice for Josephine. All of them would now sit down and discuss the issues that had bought her to Queenstown. Alexander and FJ had wanted to hang around to listen in, but Siobhan had told them no. She instructed the pair to take Marcus and themselves outside to the undercover awning that covered the back yard and play while they talked inside. The awning was used to shield them from the sun and the rain but was able to be rolled back during winter.

The first thing Ashleigh needed to do was inform Evonne where her daughter was. As he understood it, Josephine had been away from home for six months. She would obviously be worried sick by now and be turning herself inside out in knots. Josephine advised caution for if Dirk ever found out that she had gone in search of, and actually found her real father, the consequences for Evonne would be severe.

There was a long pause as they all sat quietly and stared at each other. Ashleigh would consider his next words wisely and tried to figure out in his head where he would start. He also struggled with the thought of talking to Evonne. What would he say to her and when would be the best time to call? Would Dirk be scanning all the incoming calls on the home line and did he have control of Evonne's mobile phone?

He decided he would take the chance and he asked Josephine when the safest time might be for him to call her mother.

She informed him that her mother worked from Monday to Friday and usually finished around four in the afternoon. She was not allowed to carry her mobile phone on her while she was in the building because of the nature of her employment with the Consortium of Trust. Her initial training with the OTD as an ISR Ranger had secured work in the Intelligence and Analyst Division of the Melbourne Headquarters. She would have very limited time to check her phone during her lunch breaks after going through a series a security scanning devices as she left and then re-entered the building.

'What time does Dirk finish work?' he asked.

Dirk was fastidious and you could guarantee that he would be home at four in the afternoon everyday on the dot. It was now 3:30pm, thirty minutes prior to Dirk getting home. Maybe if he sent her a text message she would check her phone just as she finished for the day, and while she was walking out of work.

'Evee, its Ash, Pheenie is with me and she is ok. I know. Call me when it is safe please.'

He had wanted to keep the message as short as possible but he didn't want it to be cryptic. His only hope now would be that she saw and then deleted the message before Dirk saw it. Suddenly the phone rang, it was his mobile. That was quick he thought and as he picked up his phone and looked at the display, he confirmed it was Evonne.

'Aren't you at work' he asked her.

'No, I finish half an hour early these days, Dirk doesn't know. Can I speak to Pheenie please?'

He handed Josephine the phone and immediately she started crying and telling her mum she was so sorry for running away from home. She just needed to find her real father and bring him back to help her. He was sure that

Evonne was also crying on the other end of the call and asked his daughter for the phone back. He had to be quick for time was quickly running out. He only had about ten or so minutes before Dirk might catch her in the act.

He explained to Evonne that he would be coming to Melbourne to fix this problem. His wife shifted nervously in her chair as she heard him say this. He hadn't had time to formulate a plan of attack and would have certainly have had no time to have told Siobhan about it before now if he had. He was cuffing this on the spot; playing it by ear so to speak. But this was nothing new to her husband for he had done this many times before during the course of his duty. At work he had planned on the spot and in the moment. He had made split second decisions often in the middle of combat zones and with men and women's lives' at risk. So this came somewhat natural to him.

Just as suddenly as the phone had rang, did it suddenly cut out. He was not sure if it was because Evonne had hung up or whether Dirk had caught her, and if he had? He couldn't think of the possibilities; he had to stay focussed on what he knew was fact. Speculation now would only serve to worsen the issue and create unnecessary worry. He would sit and think for a few moments collecting his thoughts. Once again, all fell quiet around the kitchen table. His wife knew by this look that he was formulating a plan in his head.

By now Siobhan had placed her arm around the young girl that threaten to divide her family. She still knew very little of this girl and all the answers to her questions had yet to be answered. But for now, Siobhan would provide care and comfort for her. If she was her husband's daughter, then she was family, hers included.

Now that Evonne had knowledge of her daughter's whereabouts, he would get to the route of the problem and find out exactly what had been going on. This was going to be hard on Josephine as she would have to dredge up past memories; reliving past events while telling her father and Siobhan what she and especially her mother had been through. After a slight pause and a deep breath, Josephine began. She explained that she was only three years old when her mum married Dirk, he being five years her senior.

It had been difficult for her mother to maintain any kind of long term meaningful relationship. Josephine now understood it that her mother had only ever loved Ashleigh, but this was a forbidden love and she would have to except that fact. It was also hard on Evonne to maintain relationships because she had a young daughter.

Throughout those early years, Evonne was never short of catching the eye of the young men around her. After all, she was a very attractive young woman. Potential suitors would present themselves and given any other time and place, one of them may have become her husband. The problem arose when they eventually found out about Josephine that they would back off and run to the hills. The men that entered her life would tell her that the relationship just wasn't working out for them and that it was their fault and not hers. Yes it was a common breakup line, but this became a regular event until Evonne eventually gave up on love.

It would be another couple of years later when she returned to live in Melbourne after discharging from the OTD that she would meet a handsome and successful man named Dirk. Her mother had finally found someone that loved her for who she was and didn't mind that she had a daughter to someone else. Early in their relationship, Evonne had told Dirk about Ashleigh, but she never told him that she still loved him. She simply explained that she was young and naive at the time.

Evonne had thought herself very lucky, here was a man, a successful lawyer working for one of the biggest law firms in Oceania, and who was going places. Here also was a man that would accept Josephine and stay the course in their relationship. And so just after Evonne's 21st birthday, they were married. The years that followed were blissful and they enjoyed all of which life had to offer. Being a successful lawyer also meant that he was well to do, financially speaking, and well connected. They would live in a fine house and travel on many holidays to many different parts of the world.

Dirk had agreed to become Josephine's father as she was still young enough at the time to believe it. Evonne had wanted a secure life for her daughter believing that she came from a solid upbringing and united family. She would recognise many years later that this had been the wrong decision to make for her daughter. She should have never tried to hide the truth about her real father, but Evonne was only twenty-one. She had to make decisions for the both of them and had thought she was doing the right thing at that time. Dirk had also wanted it so.

Over time and as the years progressed, her relationship with Dirk started to wane. She had only thought it was due to the pressures of his work and he was now starting to drink a lot more than before. She became concerned for the wellbeing of her husband and so she confronted him with it. His response was one of anger and abuse hurled back at her. She had never seen this side of him before and thought and hoped that it was only a one-time event. But there would be more arguments like this in the years to come and with more verbal abuse and throwing of objects around the house.

At this stage, Josephine explained that the violence had yet to become physical and during all of this she would hide herself in a secret crawl space within the walls clutching the teddy bear her mother had given her for protection and comfort. What protection a teddy bear could give was obviously none, but to a young frightened girl, it had meant everything. This was the teddy bear her perceived knight in shining armour had given her mother and it was now hers.

Sometimes after an argument or during an argument with Dirk, he would shout abuse at Josephine. Why? Just because he could. This would usually be after he had been drinking and occur after midnight. She explained that she would be fast asleep in her bed and all of a sudden she would be awoken to the violent sounds of his voice.

Although these outbursts occurred a lot over the years, they were infrequent with their regularity. They would have weeks on end where no abuse would be present at all and Dirk would be the picture perfect husband and father. Just as Evonne and Josephine started to believe the horrors were past them, it would all start up again and Dirk would erupt into another drunken tirade of profanity and abuse.

As Dirk became ever distant from Evonne, a change would come. This would be after the twins, Jeremy and Damian, were born. Evonne had wanted more children before she became too old and her body clock told her that she couldn't, and so during a period of relative calmness and loving between her and Dirk, she asked him the question. She considered that he really hadn't been that bad up until that point and believed that she had been the cause of his rage. She was still very much in love with this man and had wanted to give him a son. She also thought that having a baby in the house and with Dirk becoming a father, it would mellow him. She couldn't have been more wrong.

He, on the other hand, was quite content with the way things were at the present time in their marriage. He didn't like the thought of running around after children and changing nappies, which is probably why he accepted Josephine as his own in the first place. He had virtually found what he coined as, 'a hot chick with a ready-made family'. It meant he could pass all the baby years and go straight to the instant child. Plus the firm he worked for, were very family orientated and thus would only serve to improve his position and standing, both with the firm and the surrounding community. Sometime later, Evonne learnt that Dirk never ever did anything unless he could benefit from it.

But Evonne was coming to her thirtieth birthday and had wanted more children. She had wanted to become pregnant before it was too late. Dirk finally succumbed to her pressures and agreed to a child, but only one. She was overwhelmed with joy and excitement and quickly became pregnant with child. Her first ultrasound though revealed that she would give birth to twins. Dirk, who was with her during the ultrasound at the time didn't say anything, but one could see by the scowl of disdain on his face that he was not happy with this news.

As the months dragged on and Evonne put on more and more weight as her twins grew inside her, Dirk had started to spend a lot more time at the office. His excuse was that because of his recent promotion, it had come with extra responsibility which meant he was required to put in extra hours. His new promotion would also see him travel to Sydneyton to attend conferences and business meetings with the firm's surrogate branch located in the heart of that city.

The love and affection that Evonne had once received from Dirk was now becoming non-existent. Soon Jeremy and Damian were born, but Dirk still remained distant. Their upbringing would have to be the sole responsibility of Evonne. She was not overly happy with this turn of events or that of the behaviour of her husband of late. Again, Evonne would confront him.

Unfortunately and as with the last time she had done such a thing, this would also turn out to be a very bad decision. Dirk responded with shouts of abuse and further profanity, but this time the verbal abuse would be followed with a slap to her face. The force of the slap had been that ferocious that it had flung her across the room and onto the floor, almost knocking her out stone cold.

At this point, as Josephine was reliving her memories and explaining the events of the past to Ashleigh and Siobhan, she needed to take a break. All of this was becoming way too much for her as she was overpowered by grief and sadness to be able to continue. She needed a moment to recompose herself before continuing again. Siobhan just held her tighter in her arms as her motherly instincts began to kick in. All she wanted to do was just spread her wings and protect this poor girl from any more harm. Whatever her husband was going to do, she would support him all the way. Ashleigh meanwhile, continued to hold her hand in his and placed another on her head.

After a short break, Josephine recommenced explaining her life's story up until this point. She explained that this was a side of Dirk her mother had never seen before. He had yelled and hurled abuse at her in the past, but he had never struck her before, now he had. But once again Evonne would place the blame solely onto herself and say it was because of her that Dirk had felt compelled to strike her. She believed she had been the cause of his rage and the cause of the slap had come as a result of their argument.

But the abuse, both verbally and physically, became more frequent. She couldn't dare tell anyone for fear of reprisal and besides, no one would believe her anyway. Dirk had become a well-respected man within the firm and the local community. People would just assume that she was making the whole thing up just because she didn't agree with the late hours he was keeping at work. People would say that she was being selfish and that she should think herself lucky to have a man such as Dirk.

Eventually, Evonne started to suspect he was having an affair at work for which was the reason for all the late hours he had been keeping. She also suspected that he had been having relations with a woman in Sydneyton. There would be many a time when the phone would ring or the VIDCom would alert her of an incoming call, only to answer it and have it immediately hang up after the person on the other end had heard her voice. Dirk also started receiving gifts. He said they were from the firm, but she could tell that these were the gifts that only another woman would choose.

Her suspicions' were later confirmed a year later when she saw and overheard a conversation he was having with a woman on the VIDCom. She quietly went into the other room and gently pushed the receiver icon on the visual display to listen in. She would have to be careful to simultaneously mute the video image as she did, just in case she was found out. The woman she saw was beautiful and at least ten years younger than Dirk. Alluring had not even come close to describing this feline minx. Looking down at her belly and seeing her post baby weight that just refused to be shed, she could see why her husband had drifted from their bed. It didn't mean that she understood though. Didn't he love her anymore?

As she watched the woman speak, the words that escaped her mouth were heart wrenching to Evonne's ears. She had heard the woman's voice telling Dirk that she couldn't wait until his next trip to Sydneyton. She also overheard the woman say that the hotel room was booked and she planned a romantic dinner together for the both of them followed by some hot sexy action in the bedroom. She now knew the truth.

After the conversation ended, Evonne quickly ended the call hoping to time her movement with that of her husband's as he also terminated the call. Unfortunately though, she wasn't as careful as she hoped for and Dirk gave her the thrashing of her life. He usually kept his blows to her stomach or would use an open hand. He had wanted to conceal the fact that he was the monster beating his wife and would see to it that he left no visible marks on her.

However, this time he did not hold back and he lashed out a vengeance of fury with a closed fist to Evonne's face, striking her several times. She would later use makeup and wear sun glasses to conceal the fact that she had been beaten. She would also prepare a story she could tell people in the event of being asked about her bruises. Ashleigh immediately understood it that the photo Josephine had shown him and Siobhan the day before was as a result of this fight.

She was now in a living hell and saw no way of escaping. Dirk provided for her and the children and she also had nowhere else to go; she was afraid to do so anyway. At one stage when Josephine was just thirteen years old, she had tried to stop Dirk from hurting her mother; but this ended poorly for her and she was also struck by Dirk's hand.

For the next two years, Josephine and her mother would be the subject of domestic violence while he now embraced the twins. He would see them become an image of himself. This is something that Evonne feared even more so than the beatings. She couldn't bear the thought of her babies growing up like this and becoming monsters as their father was. She needed to protect them, but this only angered Dirk more. As well as this, he no longer hid the truth of his adultery. He had complete power and will over the people in his life and he was loving it. He had become evil incarnate and Josephine, after learning the truth of her birth, decided to run away from home in search of her real father and seek help.

Josephine finished telling her story of woe and asked Ashleigh if he would help. By now both he, Siobhan and Josephine were all holding each other tight for comfort. Josephine had started to cry again but this time she was joined in empathy by Siobhan. This was a shocking and tragic story and one which he could not turn his back on. For a moment he just bowed his head in stillness and quietness, contemplating what his next move should be.

While Ashleigh was deep in thought, two green glowing eyes appeared from around the corner of the kitchen, it was Marcus. He, Alexander and EJ had all come back inside and guess what? It was lunch time again; their stomachs operated like clockwork. Not even the Swiss made clocks kept time as well as his children. Marcus seeing the young girl in full flight as tears streamed from her eyes, walked over and hugged the girl around her neck. There was a connection here and the longer that Josephine stayed amongst them, the stronger it became.

Siobhan had suggested that Josephine take a nice warm shower and freshen up a little. Her clothes were dirty and her hair was ragged; a shower she thought would do this poor girl a world of good, even for the briefest of moments. When she was finished in the shower, Josephine could wear some of Siobhan's 'around-the-house' daggy clothes and discard the rags she had been wearing. It sounded too good an idea to refuse and Josephine was handed a towel and free reign of the bathroom.

'Well?' asked Siobhan.

'What are you going to do?'

Siobhan had returned to the kitchen after showing Josephine where the bathroom was and had asked him what his next step would be. Her husband looked up from his deep train of thought and with a tear in his eye, told her how sorry he was that all this was happening. He told her that he had been stupid when he was young, not only for getting Evonne pregnant but for also having the affair in the first place. He knew that these events would change their lives forever, but there was no going back, not now. The only way was forward.

Chapter Seven

J osephine looked much better now that she was clean and sat back down at the kitchen table. She asked her father what they were going to do. A question that his wife also wanted to know. The first thing he would do would be to book a flight direct to Melbourne for Josephine and himself. Siobhan would have to remain in Glassenville to take care of their children. After their arrival at the Oceanic South-Centre Airport, he would hire a vehicle and drive straight to his grand elders' home where he would introduce Josephine to them as another thrice daughter. That was going to be an interesting moment to say the least.

The next move would be a call to the local SDP where he would then see what happened next. But as he was still officially on call with the OTD, he would need to inform them of the situation and where he would be. Unconditional leave without reprieve was required and so he would call his Commander requesting to do so.

'Boss, it's me, Ash. I need to take some leave for personal reasons'

Ashleigh knew how fast rumours could spread if not kept in check, it wasn't so much the Ranger Corps he feared, but other corps' within the OTD weren't as disciplined. If the news of what was happening leaked out, it could sully their reputation. He explained everything to date of the last couple of days and reassured his Commander that he had it all under control. His Commander in turn would keep this under wraps within the regiment and offered the assistance of other Rangers to come to his aide if required. The one thing that Rangers held as dear as trust, was their undying support to their fellow brothers and sisters of the corps.

He graciously acknowledged the offer and knew that this would be the case if it came to this, but he remained unmoved in his stance to handle this situation on his own terms. He requested that he be entrusted with this task and proceeded to ask for a two week furlough. He figured two weeks should be enough to see this out. He had also wanted to have this resolved before the 35th coming of the Christmas Union and had hoped that they may all share in its celebration as a complete family.

The next question on everyone's mind was why Ashleigh had not known of Josephine and why he had betrayed his one true love's calling for another. This would take some extreme care in its retelling and he would have to choose his words with wisdom and thought.

He began telling them both that he had only been a young man of seventeen when he first joined the OTD and decided that he wanted to be a Federal Continental Ranger as his grand elder had once been, and who had been so instrumental in its founding. Although the fact that he was young was no excuse, it was still fact. Siobhan was fully aware of his upbringing and it was this upbringing that should have made him see the reason and the subsequent consequences of his actions.

Evonne herself had only joined up at the tender age of fifteen. The enlistment age for training as a Federal Continental Ranger had been between fifteen and eighteen back then. The training would consist of military tactics, techniques and procedures as well as tertiary education in technology and the sciences. The premise being that upon finishing specialist training after three years, even the lowest aged recruit upon entry would then be old enough to be assimilated into the OTD and be legally of age to go to war to preserve the UFTN if required.

He continued explaining that friendships had been forged very fast in those initial three years. The training was tough and all those kids that joined up during those years at such young ages were very susceptible to suggestion. Young minds were still being developed and were now being filled with thoughts of military life and upholding the UFTN foundations of the preservation of peace and unity for all. For some it was survival of the fittest. Those that were not strong of character and will, found themselves on the outer and less accepted by their peer group. Many recruits did not make it past the first six months of training and were either returned home to their families or placed in less specialist corps'.

They had to understand that although these were young Rangers in the making, they were still at the core of it, just children. And just as children would do at school, groups would be formed. The dynamics and demographic would see to it that those who were not strong enough, were simply pushed to the side. It was quite hard on some and especially considering that these children were now, for the majority of, separated from their parents for the first time in their lives.

That first day of Ranger training commenced in Christchurch on New Zealand's south island at the OTD FCR Barracks and would see them all put into platoons and company lots. Those that had joined and signed up in a particular province of Oceania were placed together in the same platoons. There were South Africans, Indians, Australians, and even a select few from the north. Those Ugbees and Traps that enlisted were dispersed amongst the platoons and were a welcomed addition to this highly trained and specialist corps.

Ashleigh explained that on that first day, he saw a young timid girl as she struggled to lift her bag, now fully laden with various items of military clothing and items, struggle with it as she walked up the stairwell to her accommodation. The place where she would call home for the next two years. She was tiny compared to some of her male counterparts that brushed her aside as they too clamoured up the same stairwell.

He thought to himself at the time that she was not going to make it through initial training. She would never be a Ranger. At this early stage right now in their training, it was every person for themselves, a trait that come the end of their training, every Ranger would never think of again.

As that initial year progressed, friendships would form. The old expression of walking in the footsteps of another to truly understand their life was true, for they were certainly doing that. Only another can fully understand and appreciate what a person had been through if they too have also been through that very same experience. Therefore, through common ground, Ashleigh and Evonne, as well as others, now had a bond in which they could only ever know and in which no-one could ever take away from them.

But there was something more. Evonne had struggled through that first year and had found it difficult to make friends. She was always falling behind and others looked down on her with disdain and loathing, resenting her for them always being asked to take up the slack, her slack. He, on the other hand, had decided that she would not fall, she would instead succeed and make it through, and it would be by his hand that this was so. His upbringing would see him compelled by his actions. He would help her and watch over her during those years acting like a big brother to her. She reciprocated his friendship and would forever be grateful to him for his help and offered friendship.

At the end of their two years together in training, they were sent to the Capital of Destiny to finish their third and final year off, gaining some on-the-job experience as they did. As they had both chosen similar fields of endeavour, they would spend another year together where their paths would take them on a course heading, unknown to them at the time, to each other.

It was this year, he explained, in which his relationship with Evonne started to take on a different meaning. They were starting to spend more time together, both at work and after hours. This was the Capital after all, it was a joyous and exciting place to be, especially for a third year Ranger who had now been granted local leave every night of the week for the first time in two years.

This relocation in training, although being made geographically closer to his high school sweetheart, was still located some distance from Melbourne and that of Siobhan. He instead remained, for the most part, in the company of a young attractive girl which he now cared for a great deal. The two of them had spent many nights just watching movies together or going out clubbing together. But it was their final parting that their relationship moved from the platonic to the personal.

It was his last day in Destiny and he was about to say goodbye to all his friends as he left for Melbourne. Up until that point, the two of them had never embraced in a kiss. They had both secretly wanted to several times, but had resisted their urges to do so with uncomfortable silence and then quickly moving on to new topic of conversation. He could not break his vow to Siobhan, especially as the following year would see the two of them married. Evonne had wished she could have Ashleigh all to herself, but also knew as she did, it could never be so.

So that last day as he left her, they had shared their first kiss. It would be like holding the most precious and valued diamond for three years, knowing what it was, knowing how beautiful and enticing it was, but never being able to have it, touch it, or feel its slender smooth surface, forever being barred from it, and then suddenly being allowed to reach out and make it your own. It was like the two of them had reached perfection in one single moment.

How could he have felt this way? How had this kiss affected him so when for the last three years he had constantly thought of embracing Siobhan? But over the last twelve months he had also thought of embracing the young girl in which he had now just kissed. He continued explaining to his wife and Josephine that he was a very confused and tormented young soul back then through time and circumstance. He continued to say that unfortunately back then, that kiss led to Evonne and him sharing a romantic moment together. It was unfortunate then, but he quickly expressed to Josephine that he now considered that moment a blessing in disguise because it had bought him her.

The reason he had not known of Josephine's birth was simply because Evonne had never told him. Would it have been different if she had? Would he have still left? The answers to those questions would never be answered, but he did explain that his relationship with Evonne was born out of lust, and time and place. Yes he did love her, but he knew that his heart had always been and truly belonged to Siobhan. He just needed to be reminded of that.

The last couple of days had been very hectic and emotionally tiring for all concerned, especially for Josephine, and she soon settled in for the night. Even with her stay in the Queenstown Centre Hospital, this would be the first night that she had felt safe for a very long time. It would also be the first time in six months that she slept in a decent bed. She relished the moment and curled up under the pristine white and feather downed soft duvet, clutching her now fully restored and cleaned teddy bear thanks to the talented efforts of Siobhan as she did.

She had been treated well by her new self-adopted parents. She had food in her belly, a nice warm shower, and a comfortable bed to sleep in. She would not be watching over her shoulder for her things or worry about what might happen to her during this night as she slept by people she really didn't know. Although she had only just met Ashleigh and Siobhan the day before, she felt very secure and knew in her soul that she could trust them and that they would never harm her in any way.

Later that night and just after Josephine had gone to bed, Siobhan expressed her concerns over whether or not she could be trusted in their house while they slept. Siobhan had now given into the reality that Josephine was indeed his daughter, but what if because of how unstable she was, she decides to get up during the middle of the night, rob them and leave?

'She wouldn't do that.' Ashleigh stressed to her.

'I trust her.'

Siobhan had also revisited that evening's telling of how her husband and Evonne come to have a child together. She thought that the story he told was for the benefit of Josephine and that some truths were still hidden. She knew that if there was more to this story that he had only chosen to hide these facts to save her from more hurt. Now that Josephine was out of ear shot, she would press her husband for more answers.

'Would you have stayed with Evonne had you known of the child?' she asked him

He simply could not answer that question with any level of certainty that would appease his wife's question. He had always been an honourable man and had taken his vows to others and to life very seriously. She knew and understood that once he gave his heart and soul into something or someone, he was fully committed. It would be a question that she would have to accept would never be answered.

These revelations that had threaten to tear at the fabric of their marriage had done nothing of the sort. After the initial shock of the moment and after sitting down at home and discussing it further, it had only made her love for Ashleigh grow stronger. She couldn't just put behind and forget the last sixteen years of their marriage. A marriage which had remained strong and loving even with his time spent away. This one event that happened so long ago wouldn't change the man she loved. She knew he had been foolish in his youth, but she forgave him for that and she was now proud of his actions and how he was handling this current situation.

For a time, Ashleigh just laid there in bed unable to go to sleep, but eventually did. Siobhan however, was still awake and as she had done many times before, laid on her side facing her husband and just stared at him while he slept. This had only been his second week home from the AN Uprising, twelve long months he had been gone with her not knowing if he would return to her or not. She considered every passing second spent by her husband's side as a blessing and still considered herself very lucky to have this man in her life.

In the pale moon light that shone through the void made vacant by the curtains being left ajar before they both entered their bed, she could see the tops of his eye lids flicker as his eyes moved beneath them. She watched as his chest rose and then fell with his every passing breath he took as he slept and gently placed her hand on the side of his face to brush his cheek.

He stirred for just a moment, but long enough to instinctively place his hand a top of hers. Usually he would have jumped up and sprung into a state of readiness. Never wake a sleeping Ranger unless you are another Ranger, but he knew the tender loving touch of his wife. He was familiar with the sensuality of her soft skin and the gentle way her fingers moved as they caressed his cheek and ran over the top of the lips of his mouth.

She shuffled her body closer to him, just close enough so that her lips were in reaching distance of his. As she leant forward, he could feel her breath on his face and knew what was coming next. Ashleigh then opened his eyes and the two embraced with a passionate kiss. He would place his arm around the curvature of her slim waist and pull her closer to him.

As they each pulled away from the kiss as it finished, they gazed into each other's eyes with a longing for the other. They would spend a night in each other's embrace solidifying the love they shared. After the last couple of days they just had, they needed to feel each other's warm embrace and feel safe in the knowledge that their love for one another had not suffered.

Come the morning's sunrise, Josephine awoke with a slight spring in her step. She must have had a solid night's sleep for she looked totally refreshed. There wasn't a sound out of her all night. Her appearance of liveliness must have been born out of a tinge of excitement, as she would certainly have been thinking about the oncoming day's events with anticipation. She also knew her excitement could turn sour at any time and realised that the coming days would hold many more emotional moments for her. But for now she was just glad to be in this place with this family and would cherish every second of it.

This was the start of a brand new day, would it also be the start of a whole new life for her and her mother? Would life change now that she had found her real father? All she could do was hope and pray for it to be true. Her mind started to wander into the future and began to fantasise about life with her mother and father together. This is what she had been praying for, for a very long time.

Her dreams however, were quickly bought back to reality as she heard the sound of Siobhan's voice and she came to know that her mother and father would never be joined as one. Josephine maintained her smile anyway for she was just happy to have her father back in her life and she was also starting to be fond of Siobhan.

The morning's coming would also provide a busy hive of activity. The plane for Melbourne wasn't leaving until midday so Siobhan decided she would take Josephine shopping for some new clothes. The one's she had were all but worn through. Josephine had only originally packed very little when she ran away from home. In fact she had only possessed two long sleeved shirts, a set of jeans and a pair of shorts with some underwear.

Siobhan would see to it that Evonne's daughter would look presentable and well cared for when next they met. So after a hearty breakfast, one in which Josephine had not had in a very long time, they travelled back into the Queenstown Centre Shopping Village for a new wardrobe. This time they would drive the XCV into town due to the previous day's weather causing damage to the main auto lane that joined Glassenville to Queenstown. The XCV, otherwise known as the Cross-Country Vehicle, would be perfect for the journey. Josephine gave Siobhan a gentle smile with a look of admiration as she climbed into the vehicle. She had started to feel a bit more at ease with her father's wife and hoped that she had gained a new friend.

Meanwhile, Ashleigh packed their bags and rang his grand elders along with his older brother Andrew to let them know he was coming to town. He also let them know that he would be bringing with him a surprise and would ask for their support when he arrived. He decided not to inform his grand elders of Josephine just yet, but he did tell the story, so far as he knew it, to Andrew.

Andrew and Ashleigh were close as brothers, there was only two years between them and through their younger years they had been known as the double A's. Action and Adventure, Assertive and Admired, Athletic and Agile, or whatever took the meaning of the A's at the time. He knew he would have undoubted support from Andrew and had wanted him to be present at their grand elder's home when the news was broken. He also knew that although Andrew would support him, he would also give him a stern talking to about getting into this situation in the first place. The brothers never missed an opportunity to have a go at one another if the opportunity presented itself.

Siobhan and Josephine arrived back home just as Ashleigh was placing the last of the bags at the front door ready to be packed into the Public Service Transport or PST when it arrived. Josephine burst out of the XCV nearly tripping down the running board with excitement when she saw her father. She couldn't wait to show him the new clothes that Siobhan had bought for her.

'Well that looked like a successful shopping trip.'

'It was daddy, wait to you see what Siobhan bought me.'

With that, she quickly brushed him by and went inside to change into her new clothes. When she re-emerged, she looked a million terra marcs. The clothes that Siobhan had bought weren't over the top, but they were very fashionable and acceptable of the current attire girls her age wore. Siobhan had always taken pride in her appearance and had always known what clothes would suit for which occasion. She quite often bought the clothes her husband wore when he was not in uniform.

The next stop would be Melbourne and the PST soon arrived. So with that, he and Josephine said their goodbyes to his children. Ashleigh gave his wife a long heart felt and loving kiss as he wrapped his arms around her in a tight embrace. He reassured her that he would not let his emotions or feelings get the better of him. This would be a matter for the SDP and he would be careful not to put himself in harm's way. Just in case though, he still had his Beretta if called upon to use it.

The FCR of the OTD were given certain sanctions to be allowed the carriage and concealment of their service weapon. It had been bestowed upon them at the end of the Terran Wars for their unwavering dedication to duty to the UFTN. Such was their sacred vow that no harm would ever come to the citizens of the UFTN. They would protect the weak and helpless, offer assistance and aid to the poor and unfortunate, never be the instigators of unwarranted aggression, provide unquestionable duty of service to the UFTN, and defend and stand shoulder to shoulder with their brothers and sisters of the FCR.

Their creed being based on the tenets of Saint Michael the Archangel. The foundations of protection, courage, strength, truth, integrity and plain old mateship. The last creed being taken and adopted from the old text. They never left a mate behind, be they alive, wounded or dead. All came back, even at the expense of their own lives in the process if needs be.

Ashleigh released his hold on his wife and Josephine quickly moved in after him planting a sly cheeky and nervous kiss on Siobhan's cheek. She would be hoping for a look of approval and was unsure how this peck on the cheek would be taken. Siobhan did give her the look she was hoping for and Josephine rushed back in to her with a big hug and to say thank you for all she had done.

As the PST pulled up, he and Josephine got in and left. A longing look of worry however, remained on Siobhan's face as she watched it drive off down the road and onto the airport. It had been a look she had given so many times in the past as her husband had left to preserve the UFTN, and it would be a look she would undoubtedly give many more times again in the future. But each time the look was given, each time he returned. She knew her husband would remain focussed and considered, she just didn't know however, what Dirk's reaction would be. If he was as bad as Josephine had described, what was he capable of? She would just have to wait and see and pray to God that all of them would return safely.

Chapter Eight

During the flight to Melbourne, Josephine had fallen asleep and had rested her head on Ashleigh's shoulder. Again he watched her as she slept, peaceful and quiet. She did indeed have many features that were his, but she also looked like Evonne. Evonne he thought, how could he have done this to her? If he had not have slept with her during his final days in Destiny, she would not have fallen pregnant; and if she had not fallen pregnant, she would not have been in this situation now. She would not have had trouble finding someone, other than he that loved her, and she wouldn't have had to settle on Dirk.

The more he thought about it, the more he blamed himself. He also considered that it was his fault that Josephine had run away from home and had found herself in trouble. He had been relieved to hear the doctor tell them both that there had been no sign of sexual assault, but there were still blood tests away being analysed. What would they reveal?

Ashleigh had always taken things personal and had given his heart so willingly. It was his curse and now this flaw of his had cursed others. He considered the events that could have been if things were different and he had his time over again. The answers he could not tell his wife or his daughter rested uneasily and heavily on his mind.

Would he have stayed with Evonne if he knew she was pregnant? Yes he would have. This would have broken Siobhan's heart as it would have broken his. But they were young, they would've surely gotten over it and moved on given time. He knew as those thoughts entered his mind that they were untrue. He would never have gotten over the love he felt for Siobhan, but he would have lived with it regardless.

Somehow he knew deep in his heart that Siobhan also knew the hidden truth behind his words, and although she had asked him and had received his answer the night prior to his departure, she would not press him again with it. He realised others around him, especially his family would also know the truth about what his actions would have been if he had known of Josephine. This whole turn of events had been the doings of one man's actions, his.

Ashleigh continued looking at the daughter that was now sleeping beside him. It had been such a shame that someone so young and beautiful had been exposed to so many horrors in her short life. No one deserved this he thought. All have a right to live a happy and free life, and not be subjected to the wills of angry and violent men. This is what he had fought for his entire adult life. This was the freedom he would give to others while sacrificing his own. This was the Ranger way.

He loved his daughter and would protect her at all costs no matter what it took. He would also protect Evonne with every fibre of his being. He had loved her once many years ago and had never forgotten that. Even now after so many years and before he learned of Josephine's existence had he still cared for her in his heart.

Josephine stirred a little when the plane hit some turbulence as the pilot negotiated the oncoming storms of that afternoon's rains. She remained asleep though and readjusted her position slightly as she placed a hand on his shoulder and underneath her head. She continued dreaming about better days to come when all this was over.

The plane trip would only be about two and a half hours, give or take a couple of minutes either side depending on if there was a tail wind or not. He would have ample time to sit and think about the events of the past. He had time to think about the events that had unfolded and which had led them here to this point. He was always a believer that things happened for a reason. If God had wanted it this way, then it was because he was required to find the answers, but the answers to what. What more could come his way?

—∞— ✝ —∞—

He thought of that time when he had left Destiny and said goodbye to Evonne. They had gone to an end of year function and were celebrating the completion of their training. They had faced three long arduous years of intense rigor and now they had earned their Ranger Clips. It was a special time for a Ranger as these Clips were pinned on to their uniform. The Clip, an image of Saint Michael the Archangel with fiery sword in hand, showed their devotion to duty, to the preservation of all life, and to each other. It was no easy feat becoming a Federal Continental Ranger. On average, only about a third of each intake succeed, the rest are either transferred to other branches of the Peace Keepers or sent back into civilian life.

There would be much cause for celebration. Many of their class mates would head to Queenstown for the sub-tropical conditioning they would require if deployed to the trouble zones along the equator. While others would be headed west to provinces along Australia's coastline. A few would remain in the Capital, but he would be the only one returning to Melbourne. It was getting close to his departure time and he wanted to say his goodbyes to Evonne in private, but the opportunity was becoming increasingly difficult to come by.

There had been laughter and drinking for most of the afternoon and there was always one of his mates hanging off his shoulder telling him something. As with how his school years were, so too had been the last three years, he continued to attract attention and people just seemed to gravitate towards him. Many also knew of his grand elder's prestige within the corps.

During the course of that afternoon's proceedings, he naturally had not had anything intoxicating to drink at all that day. He needed to be clear of outside influences and sound of mind if he would be able to ride later that evening. The nights during the summer months were deadly if one did not have their wits about them. He would be riding south to Melbourne with very little rest before he left and would have to consider his safety and that of others on the road.

Evonne herself had only had a few glasses of Vodka and blood limeorange and had caught sight of Ashleigh trying to leave. She too had wanted privacy for their parting. The look on his face suggested that he would meet her outside in the vehicle lot. This was not the place he had wished for such a goodbye to take place. But it was the only option that had presented itself.

He eventually said farewell to his mates inside the tavern and left to walk towards his Overlander X-Trail. He was alone at last and he soon spotted Evonne leaning against the side of his OXT with her rear resting on the edge of its seat. As he got closer, he saw an uneasy smile on her face that grimaced with sadness at the same time. Her eyes were glassy and she reached out a hand making a gesture that she had wanted to hold his, and then dropped it again. He too was also smiling and knew at last he could say goodbye to her the way he wanted to.

As he reached her, Evonne stood up from the OXT and placed both her arms around his waist as she looked up at him into his deep blue eyes. He returned the gesture with his arms around her.

'This is it.' he said.

'Time I was leaving.'

He placed a hand on the side of her face slightly cupping her head as he did and proceeded to tilt it back. Looking deeply into her eyes, he told her that he had cared for her a great deal. Her friendship had meant the world to him and he would always remember fondly the times they spent together. The parties they had gone to and the night clubs they had been to together. But he would cherish and remember most of all the times when it was just the two of them alone watching a movie or two.

He told her that he had felt a special connection with her over the last couple of months, in fact it had really been ever since arriving in the capital twelve months ago, but he didn't want to cloud this goodbye with too many thoughts which could upset things. He would also want to keep it rather short and brief. He didn't need this to linger too long, it was hard enough as it was already.

He told her that because of his feelings for her, he had always wanted to share a kiss with her, just once. He had wanted to feel her lips against his and taste of their sweetness, and now was the perfect time. He asked her if he could have this one final request, after which he would leave. He knew she had felt the same way but she never gave into temptation, not even when they were alone watching those movies together.

'I feel for you too Ash, but it would be wrong and you know it.'

Yes it would be wrong but they couldn't deny their feelings for one another any longer. The expressions on their faces said it all. Besides that, he was leaving, she would probably not see him again for many years. She was scheduled to spend the next three years remaining in the capital working at the Central UFTN Intelligence and Analyst Section, while he would have the next three years in Melbourne specialising as a Federal Continental Ranger Scout. So what harm could one kiss do? What harm indeed?

While still cupping her head, he bought her face up to meet his, she in turn, now with her hands pressed on each side of his face, brought his face down to meet hers. Their lips suddenly met; it was slow at first for he had not wanted to rush it. He had waited a life time for this moment and he was going to savour it. Gradually the pace and intensity of the kiss increased with each precious second as the two of them finally let go of their feelings of passion and lust for each other. Evonne pressed against his lips harder and harder as he, now with his arms back around her waist, pulled her closer. He could feel the beating of her heart against his.

Eventually their passion subsided as Evonne lowered her head and as a result removed her lips from his. They knew that this would be all they would have. But it would be remembered for a lifetime. That one moment when both of them left this world and travelled to a completely different time and space, a place of serenity and bliss. They had not wanted the moment to ever end, but it had to.

Evonne then turned her back slightly on him; the two of them still holding hands, but then paused for a moment. She was about to walk away and Ashleigh was going to let her, for what else was there left to be said? Anything after this point would only taint the moment. She took another pace to walk while still holding his hand, their arms now outstretched as the distance between them increased ever so slowly but gradually.

Suddenly she turned to look at Ashleigh over her shoulder. He was about to say something, but she just gently shook her head in a gesture to tell him not to. She smiled at him one last time and released her grasp on his hand. Their fingers now the only part still touching in a hooked grasp, and then she walked away letting her finger slip from his. That was it, no more words, no more looks, no more temptations; he would soon be on his OXT and on his way. At least that is what he had thought.

As he rode his OXT down the road and prepared himself for the 1000km plus trip that awaited him, he couldn't stop thinking about Evonne. The lingering taste of her lips still residing on his from their recent embrace. His mind was jumping all over the place and his heart was pounding with an irregularity he had not felt before. He kept jumping between his thoughts of Siobhan and the thoughts he had for the girl he had just left. He had been sixteen years old when he first met Siobhan while at secondary college. She had completely blown his mind by her beauty and sensuality.

He was now nineteen years old and although still very much a boy, he was also a young man that had been through the rigorous training of the FCR Corps, as well as facing all of life's challenges along the way. He had been around the stupidity of young foolish minds who could think they were invincible only to find themselves dead on the side of the road in a motor vehicle accident.

He had seen a lot in his nineteen very short years. It had only been eighteen months ago when he buried his best friend at that time because he agreed to get into a vehicle driven by another who had been drinking. Such a waste of life he thought. A life is not to be taken lightly, we only get one so make the most of it. Oh he had his moments of foolhardiness of course, but he loved being alive too much to see it gone.

One life to live he thought to himself, and again he repeated those words in his head over and over. One life to live. Was he making the right choice in marrying Siobhan? He couldn't believe the thought that just entered his head. He loved her, didn't he? Or was it just the teenage romance that all around him at the time had said it was? It was only his brother, Andrew, which told him to stay the course and be true to his feelings. Don't let anyone stop you little brother he remembered Andrew saying to him.

Ashleigh thought that given chance, Andrew may have gone after Siobhan for himself. But the two of them were too close to let a girl come between them, and it is something that he simply would not do to his little brother.

'AH KNUCKS!'

Ashleigh panicked as he heard a loud noise and saw another vehicle coming his way. It was the sound of an alert horn coming from another transport telling him to get out of the way. When he had looked up, he realised that he had very nearly ridden head on into a Heavy Transport Wagon that was travelling in the opposite direction to him.

His soul was in agonising pain and he continued to struggle with his thoughts. What he thought he knew about love was now unravelling all around him. Confusion set in as love became lust and lust became love and so on and so on until he had no choice but to pull off to the side of the road in order to clear his head. He was clearly not thinking straight and had become a danger to himself and to others on the road as was evident with his close encounter with the Heavy Transport Wagon.

One life to live, again these four words filled his thoughts. He needed to find out for sure if Evonne and he could ever have anything between them. They had never openly revealed their love for each other, but deep down they both knew of it. It had been six months since he last saw Siobhan. She had flown up for the weekend from Melbourne to see him. But every other night over the course of the last twelve months, Ashleigh had saw and spent time with Evonne.

His mind was clear again and he would turn his OXT around and go back to the ISR & TacCom Specialist Barracks and wait for Evonne to return. He knew she would be of sound mind to talk to him for she had agreed to be the designated driver for that day. Maybe it was because she was already feeling upset at the thought of Ashleigh leaving and thought that alcohol would only make her feel worse. So she had chosen to keep her drinking to a minimum.

He parked the OXT out of sight as he did not want others knowing of his intentions, and then waited near her accommodation for her to return. It would be another two hours before the first of them started to arrive back at the barracks. Suddenly, there she was, walking down the pathway towards where he was standing.

'What are you still doing here?' she asked him.

'I've come back to tell you something that you need to hear and that I know you are already aware of.'

She did indeed know what was coming. He confessed that his feelings for her were deeper than he had led her to believe. There would be no holding back this time. He told her that he cared for her more than anything else and that he now wanted to be with her. He explained to her that his feelings for her began to change from the very moment they arrived in Destiny to finish off their training together. She had become more than just a friend to him and each passing day as they spent more and more time together, his feelings for her grew deeper and deeper. Evonne knew this to be true and a tear formed and fled from her eye.

'Ash, you can't be having those feelings and thoughts about me, it's not right and I won't have it.'

The sound in her voice as she spoke those words she knew were false, were filled with a bitterness and loathing of one who regretted saying them. These were the words of someone who was in extreme emotional pain. She wanted to have him, she needed to have him, but she knew it was not possible. She just felt like she was being tortured by his reappearance.

'Evee, you know that I have wanted you for a long time, I need to be with you, you must understand.'

Again she denied such things and this time she started to storm off in anger. He was not going to let her go and he raced after her. By now, others that shared the same accommodation complex could hear their argument and had started to watch as events unfolded. Ashleigh told her to please stop, but she just kept on walking. This time he yelled at her to stop and she turned around looking him squarely in the face with a determination in her voice.

'WHAT? You and I have had our moment back at the farewell. I gave you that kiss you always wanted. Isn't that enough? Why come back now and torment me over something that could never be?'

But it could become possible Ashleigh explained to her. If it was right then it would be right. He had told her that he had nearly ridden head on into another vehicle because his mind was distracted with thoughts of her. A look of concern filled her face at the sound of hearing this from him and she asked him if he was alright. Ashleigh told her that he was prepared to give up everything just to be with her. He would break off his engagement to Siobhan, he would try and get his assignment changed to remain in the capital, and he would give her everything he had to offer.

Evonne's face was now covered in tears and she pleaded with him to stop. She couldn't bear to take any more of this for it was breaking her heart. She was hearing the words that she had secretly wished for and had longed to hear. But this was all too late, he couldn't change things now. She just wanted him to leave and told him as much. She told him that enough was enough and that this was the end of it. She instructed him to stop being foolish and go back to Melbourne to be married to Siobhan. Get married she said and raise a whole heap of little Maynard's. With a stern voice of authority she would turn to him and say her final words.

'Stop being stupid, leave and don't come back.'

With that she again stormed off, this time there was no tears, just the sight of an angry young woman who wanted to get on with her life. Ashleigh stood there with his head lowered in one hand as he cupped his forehead and the other resting on his hip. He thought that was it, what else could he do?

'Evee!' he shouted, 'I love you!'

Suddenly she stopped dead in her tracks. Could it be true, had he said the words that she had wanted to hear, the words that she needed to hear? He had skimmed around the edges of it but up until that point he had never actually said it. She turned around and looked at him. This time in more of a gentler and caring way. It had been the same look that she had given him back at the farewell gathering where she was leaning against his OXT. She couldn't hold back her emotion any longer and she rushed to him throwing her arms around his neck, hanging off him.

Evonne settled herself with a calmness and moved her hands from around his neck and placed them once again evenly on each side of his face. She smiled as tears re-emerged and she informed him that she had always wanted to be with him. In fact she had prayed for the day to come when he finally told her that he loved her. She told him that she had dreamt of the time when they would share an intimate passionate evening together and had imagined what it would be like the first moment he pressed his naked body against hers in a loving embrace. But time and time again she resisted these thoughts and was stopping herself from allowing it to ever happen.

She had respected his love for Siobhan and had respected him too much to let go of her inhibitions by releasing her desires of passion upon him. In those final months leading up to his departure, she struggled as she fought back the urge to just throw herself upon him.

'Why didn't you ever tell me? He asked.

Evonne had told him she had believed it to be the right thing to do. She couldn't bring herself to let her real feelings be shown. She would not be the cause of a break up between two people that loved each other. Ashleigh, still tormented with his feelings for both girls, his love for Siobhan, but also his love for the girl standing in front of him, knew he was treading on dangerous ground. He needed to know where his feelings would take him. For him, who was to be married the following year, had wanted to confirm where his heart laid. All this time he thought, he could have explored his feelings for Evonne further, but was it now too late? He at last had confessed his love for Evonne and hers for him.

'I love you too.'

Chapter Nine

A shleigh felt a sigh of relief that in one part, his feelings for Evonne were now known. Unfortunately, they were also known to all the people who had witnessed the two of them declare it. On the other hand, his sigh of relief also turned to despair. How was he going to inform Siobhan about this recent development? The two of them realised that this was far from over and that their next move could have very severe consequences for the both of them. In fact, this was only just the beginning. They moved inside into Evonne's room closing the door behind them as they went.

'This is still very wrong.' Evonne explained.

Her worry was well considered. A lot would have to change if the two of them were going to be together. Ashleigh thought of his family and the years of nurturing and guidance he had received off his grand elders. They had given so much to him and his brother after their own parents had been killed in a terrorist attack by Trap extremists still clinging to the old ways. Their mother and father, Catherine and Marshall Maynard were out celebrating the fifth Christmas Union while their sons, seven year old Andrew and little five year old Ashleigh were being baby sat by their grand elders. Since then, their grand elders had assumed the role of parents and had raised them as their own and as they knew how.

He knew the sacrifices of his Elder mother and father and held honour to thy family very high above all else. He also held honour to the people around him that he would serve with. He thought of the honour he held for Siobhan. She had been sorry and sad to see him leave that day for the corps three years ago. He remembered as the tears filled her eyes as the All Purpose Transport pulled away, and although she did not want him to leave, she would not stop him and she watched as the APT drove off. She respected his decision and would stand by her man.

However, his time spent with Evonne had now outweighed his time spent with Siobhan. One year was all they had when he had said goodbye to her. One year to meet, one year to fall in love, and one year to declare their intensions to be one under God in marriage. He had even changed his religious beliefs to satisfy the wishes of her father just so he could be with her. Was this all now a lie? Of course it wasn't, as with anything else he did in his life, he took this seriously as too did he take his love for Siobhan. He had never stopped loving her and still yet loved her as much as he did when they first met. It was just now, he also loved another. But he couldn't give his heart to two women.

Evonne could see the look of distress in her man's eyes and offered comfort by cuddling into him. She told him that if he still wanted to be with Siobhan, thus leaving her, she would be fine with it. Her words, although unwanted, had seemed unsure when spoken. It would be extremely hard on her she admitted, but she would respect his wishes and learn to live without him. She would know that as time passed and the distance between them grew, she would eventually find and fall in love with another. Though right now, it was very hard for her to see this and believe in her own words. The thoughts that filled her mind were firmly planted with images of the two of them in a life spent together.

Evonne moved away and again considered her next move. She sat on the edge of her bed, a place where the two of them had laid many times before as they watched those movies together. This time she sat alone as he remained standing. He was pacing the carpet space in her room nervously thinking about what he would do. He had made his intensions clear, he wanted to be with Evonne; that was it. Everything else he would deal with later, his family, Siobhan and her family, and the many looks they would receive off their colleagues and friends.

Evonne however, was having second thoughts. As she sat there alone on the bed, she had asked him to stop pacing for a moment so that she could tell him something.

'Ash, I know you love me and I know that it is real. I love you as well and I desperately want to be with you, however; and it pains me to say this but...'

'Please don't!'

Ashleigh couldn't bear to think of what was coming next and interrupted her in mid speech.

'You must hear me. We cannot go through with this. Please don't be angry, just except it to be true.'

She was making perfect sense, she had always made perfect sense. He knew she was right, but he couldn't deny the thoughts of what could be. He told her that he didn't want to leave, not now, not after what he had just put himself through. She told him that she would forever love him no matter what. If she was to find love again and marry one day, her love for Ashleigh would still be there. He possessed everything that she had wanted in a man. He held love for her, he was generous and kind to her, he watched over her and protected her, and she always felt safe when wrapped up in his arms. But still, regardless of all these things she saw in him and the fact that she loved him, she couldn't go through with it.

He knew by the look on her face that she would not be persuaded to change her mind, but he still tried. He reached out to kiss her again, the one earlier, the only one to date, still burned in his soul, but she moved away. He grabbed her arms, but still she turned from him. As he released his grasp on her, he considered his future. Would he do as she commanded?

He knew that if he returned to Melbourne to be with Siobhan, he would be happy. He would be extremely happy and there would be no doubt that they would share a great and loving life together. But there would always be that doubt in the back of his mind of what could have been, and as she had just said to him, he too would always carry a special place in his heart for her. He would always love her.

Three hours had now passed since he was supposed to have been on the road travelling south. He should have crossed the border by now and been in Victoria, but instead here he was, still in Destiny tearing his heart out over the love he felt for two beautiful young women. Eventually, he decided that he would leave, but before he left, he would try in one desperate final attempt to change her mind.

'I've booked a room in the city. I'll be leaving tomorrow morning at seven. If I don't see you tonight, I'll know your answer.'

He then handed her the address of the hotel along with the room number. He gave her one final glance as he slowly exited her room to leave. She was now on her own. What would she do this night? Evonne struggled for the next few hours with her emotions and sense of reason. It was no use trying to go to sleep, her mind was racing a million miles an hour. The man she loved was only a very short drive into the city. He was there, he was waiting for her, he loved her.

Later that night as he sat on the balcony drinking Scotch on the rocks, he peered down in the street below, wishing against all hope that he would see her All Purpose AutoMobile pull up. Wishing upon wishing that the doorbell would ring and when he opened it, she would be standing there in front of him. An hour went by followed by another, and then another. By now he had finished almost half a bottle of Johnny Walker's finest when a knock on the door could be heard ever so lightly. Did his ears deceive him? Could this be true?

It was now eleven at night and he moved to the door of his apartment to see if indeed Evonne had changed her mind and had shown up. As he reached the door, his nerves began to take hold of him. He just decided to stand there for a moment as if stunned with fear. This would be a pivotal moment in their lives if she was indeed on the other side of the door. Although he was not entirely intoxicated by the drink, he was a little off balance and this may have helped plant the seeds of uncertainty that he was now feeling. He had waited this long and had poured his heart out to her. Could he change his mind at the eleventh hour?

He would have another sip of whiskey and place the glass down on the table by the door. Slowly he put his hand on the cold alloy steel handle when again came a knock. His heart was now racing, it could only have been her, who else would be knocking so quietly he thought. He released the security latch on the door and turned the knob to open it. Not a word was spoken; not a sound. He just looked at the girl standing in front of him, a picture of perfection; an angel that came down from the heavens just to be with him.

Evonne looked at him for a moment and smiled. She then walked straight passed him and into the apartment closing the door again behind her as she went. The rear of her long cherry red gown flowed from behind her as it naturally hung off her slender hour glass figure when she walked. Ashleigh, in his excitement, had almost forgotten to re-lock the door, but suddenly remembered.

The lights had been turned down low and Evonne moved into the bedroom where she stopped and turned to face her man. Still, silence ensued as not a word was spoken. Slowly she unzipped the rear of her dress and slid one of her straps down over her shoulder. This was quickly followed by the other strap and her gown gracefully fell to the floor as if in slow motion. What he saw next revealed the beauty of her almost naked body that now stood in front of him.

He had never seen her like this before and now that he had, she had gone out of her way to make the occasion special. Black sheer stockings covered her slender legs and were held in place by a black pair of lace suspenders and belt. The dress she had been wearing meant that when it fell, revealed her sensuous bare breasts. Her ensemble had been completed by a frilly lace black thong. He could not believe what he was seeing. She was only two months away from her eighteenth birthday, but her image showed that she was much more woman than girl.

He moved closer to her removing his shirt as he did and placed his hands around the small of her waist. He would not rush this. He knew that she had only been with one other which had been her first. He had also known that it had not gone so well. He would be gentle and considerate with his touch, and he would love her as she deserved to be loved. The two then shared their second kiss. It tasted as sweet as it did the first one. Next he gently lowered her onto the bed and removed her panties as their uncovered bodies met for the first time.

Her hands were shaking with the anticipation of what was to come and her breathing became heavy and shallow. This was the moment she had dreamed of so many times and now it was finally here. He reassured her that everything would be fine as he stroked her face down its side following the contours around the outside of her ear and finally letting his hand come to rest around the base of her neck. Moving her head closer to his, they kissed again.

The following morning, he had awoken before her and had propped himself up on one elbow. He laid there just staring at her. When she opened her eyes, she gave a little smile as she looked up at him. She reached out her hand placing it around his neck to pull him in closer for a morning kiss. They were content and they were happy, but Evonne had something she was hiding. Last night she had not spoken a word when she entered his apartment. Instead, she had led him to the bedroom where the two of them had made love. She had not wanted to spoil the moment of that evening, but now it was time to come clean.

She struggled to bring words to form so she decided that for now, what she had to say could wait. She would enjoy the moment for what it was and would always remember last night as her first time. She would erase the memory of her previous disaster and think of this moment instead. Ashleigh placed his arms around her and the two remained in bed for another hour. But time was getting on and she had to let him know why she had changed her mind coming to see him last night.

After she had showered and changed, she greeted Ashleigh in the kitchen who had just finished making coffee for the both of them. He turned to her and told her that he would still go to Melbourne, but only to inform Siobhan in person that he was breaking off their engagement. She was owed at least that much. Evonne quickly interjected and told him not to. He was amazed by this, had he heard her words correctly? What did she mean? Evonne then repeated her words and explained that she loved him more than anything else, however; she just couldn't be with him in a permanent relationship.

It had been like someone had taken a knife and had driven it straight through his heart. But why he kept asking, why? She explained that she had wanted to share a moment with him of pure love. She knew that no matter who she would eventually marry, she would always only ever love him. She had wanted to make love to a man that truly loved her and had wanted to feel what that type of love was, at least once in her lifetime. For she knew that she would never experience such a feeling of euphoria and passion like this again. If she had revealed her intensions to him the night before, his passion and intensity for her in the heat of the moment would have been tainted.

But because she was still only young and with a lot left to learn about life, she had told him that she had needed to do this on her own. For his best course of action now was to return to his one true love. She knew this to be true in spite of what he had told her. Over the last three years and especially before he had developed romantic feelings for her, Siobhan was the only thing he would talk about. She told him that once he again laid eyes on her and held her once more in his arms, he would remember the reasons he fell in love with her in the first place, and all this would seem like a dream from a distant past.

She was right of course, yet again. This young girl who started out so naive and uncertain, had found a maturity and understanding beyond her years. Evonne reached for his wallet and pulled out a photograph of Siobhan and handed it to him. She was definitely right about this, she had been right about things all along. And just like her, he would always remember a time when the two of them became one, even if it was for just one night. An hour later, he would be on his Overlander X-Trail and heading south.

—ɯ— ✝ —ɯ—

Ashleigh looked over at Josephine who was still asleep on his shoulder as they were coming closer to Melbourne. She was just fifteen years old, the exact age her mother was when he had first met her.

How ironic he thought. How had she been born without his knowledge? The only logical answer that stood to reason was that Evonne's contraceptive medication had failed. They had conceived a beautiful child in the name of love, but he should have taken more thought and care to share in the responsibility of taking precaution.

He knew that she would not have deliberately gotten herself pregnant; not at such a young age and not with her life about to start in a career in ISR analysis for the OTD. It had been him that had decided for the absence of any protection. It had been a foolish decision which had now come back to haunt him.

He continued looking at Josephine and reconsidered his last thought. It had been a foolish decision then, but he now had a sweet and caring teenage daughter that only wanted to be loved. Her life, her wellbeing, now meant as much to him as anyone of his children. Josephine shifted again in her seat and he could see the teddy bear that was firmly clenched under her arm. This bear had obviously remained a symbol of love and hope for Josephine over the years, just as it had been for her mother. He still remembers the moment when he first gave Evonne the bear.

About a week before he left Destiny, they had travelled down to the carnie district to visit one of the adventure parks for the last time as a group. During the course of the day, he had won this teddy bear in a game of chance and luck. Evonne immediately took a liking to it and so, he gave her the bear. He told her that every time she would look at it, it would remind her of him. He also told her that this bear would have special powers and would protect and keep her safe when she needed it. Of course he was just fooling around, but she must have told a similar story to Josephine.

Little did he know at the time that this bear would end up back in his hands fifteen years later. Josephine stirred once again and opened her eyes.

As she began to awaken, she let out a very tired sounding yawn. It had been made clear to him that she had not slept very well since running away from home. As a matter of fact she had probably never slept soundly in her life. It was almost as if she was catching up on six months' worth of sleep in the three days she had been with him.

With her yawn, she stretched out her arms and as if like natural instinct, she grabbed hold of the bear so as not to let it drop and fall to the ground. She must have had this bear every moment of her life he had thought.

'Are we there yet daddy?'

They were nearing there descent and were lucky they were coming into the southern part of the country. The further one headed south, the more one was safe from the harmful effects of the Great Despair. The environment was nowhere near as harsh as it was in the north. The sub-tropical rains of the north were at their worst along the equatorial land masses that occupied that zone.

Melbourne was now the second largest city in Oceania, on par with Johannesburg in South Africa and Delhi in India which had all initially formed part of the Oceanic Triangle, now known as Oceania. These cities however, paled in comparison to the capital, Destiny. But Melbourne was his home, this was his lands, his territory. He felt safe here and knew these lands like the back of his hand.

His brother and he had spent many hours, days and even weeks upon weeks exploring this landscape when they were just children as young as ten. This land to them was full of adventure and excitement. They had hunted wild boar in the mountains of the north east wilderness together and stalked the cunning deer. By the age of fourteen, they were both expert trackers and marksman and could live off the land for months at a time if needs be. A trait of his which had made him most suited as a Scout in the Ranger Corps.

Although this had been against the wishes of their elder mother, their elder father had different thoughts and would allow it. In fact he encouraged the boys to go out on their own. He had said that it would toughen them up and make them both into strong independent and wise members of a harsh environment and new society centred on the UFTN. It would have mattered not if they had of both been born female, his decision would have remained the same. All needed to learn the ways of this new terran world. This was not a time that they lived in where one could be soft. Otherwise this world would swallow you up whole.

Both their grand elders had come from a time since before the coming of the Darkness and had known what life was like before the Great Despair. They both knew that this life that now greeted them with each morning's sunrise, had become a world of danger with trappings. It would be hard to survive in such a world if one did not quickly learn the ways of it. The boys had already lost their parents to the new world, their elder father would see to it they were not lost to it as well.

Over the course of their upbringing, their elder father would teach them everything he knew. He would see to it that his boys would gain all the years of his knowledge and wisdom that he had to give. They learnt a lot from the old master, he who had fought in the War of the Great Despair. Their elder mother realising that her husband's will in this matter would not be broken, decided that she too would pass on her valuable years of experience in the field of medicus. Her years as a military theatre nurse during the War of the Great Despair would also serve the boys well to their advantage.

This was something that Josephine was clearly lacking. Her domineering step father must have either had her locked up behind the confines of their home or he had wanted to shield her from the harsh reality of life. The answer was clear, Dirk was a monster. He would surely have kept her locked up excluding being allowed to attend school. This girl that new very little of the real world was an enigma to him. How could she have survived for so long on her own? Those six months she spent searching for him must have been the longest six months of her life. But yet she did survive and she did succeed in her mission.

But then again she had a sub-conscious way of self-protection. He had seen this of her when answering questions at the Centre Hospital in Queenstown. How confident and sure she had been, and the initial courage she had displayed in finding him, her real father. People around her seemed to feel uplifted by her presence. He himself had felt a sense of well-being at times but didn't know why at the time. Now as he sat and stared at his daughter, he felt it again, but lacked its understanding or meaning. Whatever it was, it was a shame that her stepfather hadn't felt it as well. Maybe things would have been different if he had, but he always knew there was a reason for every action and every action had a purpose.

'We're just about to land.' He replied.

The look on Josephine's face was one of excitement as he told her this, but it quickly turned to anguish as she feared the confrontation that would soon be. This had all been a painful necessity; the running away from home and the dangers she had faced on her own. What had she been exposed to in Sinton with a man named Marty. Ashleigh told her that he did not believe in coincidence or chance. Things invariably always happened for a reason. He told her that there was a reason they were put here on this earth, there was a reason why the Darkness of the Great Despair had come, and there was a reason why she had been born and was made to suffer. That reason may have very well been for his sins, but that too would also hold reason.

He explained that we must have faith in God and in our moral and ethical guidance that challenges are put before us. Not to taunt us, not to make us give up, but to make us stronger and make us search for the answers to our questions through knowledge and wisdom. These things were very close to our grasp, we just had to reach out for them. Was there an answer why the Great Despair befell earth? Was the planet they called home forced to collapse in on itself it an attempt to make them reach out beyond the stars? To the heavens?

He continued informing Josephine that her stepfather's ways had also been for a reason, one which he was certain he knew the consequence of. Dirk would soon be bought to answer for his sins and crimes against human life. These things they hold true that all life is born free and they must maintain the rights of freedom and respect for all. But it must be earned before it is given. Dirk's judgement day would soon be upon him and he would not like what would be waiting.

Josephine nodded with uncertainty of her father's meaning for she had never heard such talk before and was unfamiliar with its content. She had the teachings of her mother, handed down from generation to generation as each matriarch of her family line passed down the ways of their beliefs. It had been this way since before the Coming and beyond. The old text that Evonne had kept, told stories of rituals from earth's ancient times when the world held faith not only in one god, but for many. Hers had been a journey of discovery as her mother had tried to pass on her teachings and so protect her from Dirk. However, even this she did not fully understand. The only real faith she held above all else was that of family unity.

Josephine had come from a violent and hostile environment in which she believed all life was based on. She had now just recently witnessed what life could really be and how a family can live. She wanted this more than anything. She yearned to have its loving and tender embrace. She relished the thought of being able to go to sleep at night knowing that when she awoke, she would be greeted by two loving parents. She had tasted this and now lived for its coming.

She would wish that she could learn more of her father's ways and also that of her mother's. But now was not the time, so instead she would listen intently to his words and try and understand the context they were put in. She knew a time would eventually come when they could all sit down together and go over the new and old text. More pressing matters would take her attention for now as next it would be time to meet her father's grand elders. She had never met anyone before who had fought in the War of the Great Despair and she wondered just how old they would be. She would hope to gain further insight into the man which was her father by seeing and understanding how he had come to be. Was his elder father, William, like him, and what of his brother, her uncle, were they similar?

Chapter Ten

William Maynard was already a veteran of previous conflicts due to the 9/11 attacks on the United States when he entered the War of the Great despair. A graduate from the Royal Military College of Duntroon in Australia, he quickly rose through the ranks and in the fifth year of the war in 2018 and at the age of twenty-nine, he was handed command of a new regiment. He was promoted to Lieutenant Colonel and was made the Commanding Officer of the 6th Continental Ranger (CR) Battalion.

This was one of nine new battalions raised at the time, all being formed from other regiments and battalions from across the Coalition of Western Continents Military Armed Forces. It is also the same battalion Ashleigh was assigned to after his initial three years of training. However, after these battalions were re-raised after they disbanded when the War of the Great Despair ended, the initial nine battalions that made up the 1st CR Regiment had now expanded to become a corps. This corps would also be given the added prefix title of Federal after federation took place when the Consortium of Trust formed the UFTN.

Two years earlier during the summer of 2016, William had been seriously wounded and temporarily blinded with flash burns from a medium impact stun grenade that went off during a building clearance. Holding the rank of Major at the time, he and his men were tasked that particular day with the clearing duties after a major siege had taken place. Their job was to go from building by building to search out and eliminate any REAMAN soldiers that were still in hiding.

Unfortunately, for William, he entered a building that had been marked as cleared and instead of being empty he found a young REAMAN soldier of sixteen or seventeen holding a grenade. The young REAMAN was shaking and obviously very frightened. Instead of shooting the poor boy, William tried to reason with him. By this stage, William could speak most REAMAN dialects and asked the boy to put the grenade down.

There were quite a few other CWC soldiers that would have shot the young boy on sight, but William still held compassion and believed that all had a right to life. He held true the belief that one day when the war was over, what were once enemies would become friends. He saw it as the only way that the human race could move forward. Mistakes like this had been made in the past in previous wars. It was one thing to be the victor, it was quite another to heal the wounds of fallen foe.

As he shouldered his weapon, he reached out his hand in offered friendship and informed the young boy that he would be taken care of in a prisoner of war camp. Other CWC soldiers were still clearing buildings around them when some came across a small group of defiant REAMAN soldier's intent on making a stand. The sound of yelling and shouting along with the unmistakable sound of CWC weapons being fired could be heard. In a panicked state, the young boy pulled the pin and dropped the grenade. William had no choice but to bring his firearm to bare, killing the boy only seconds before the grenade exploded.

This particular type of grenade was designed to maim and incapacitate its victim rather than kill, and it achieved just that. William had been too slow to avoid the resulting blast and was struck with tiny shards of fragmentation to his legs and arms. The bright flash of light that accompanied the blast, created by the small addition of white phosphorus had caused William to lose his vision of sight. Some of this white phosphorus had also penetrated his skin and was now burning away in a fury. If this had been a full incendiary grenade, William would be now dying an agonising death, but this was a medium impact. The small amount of white phosphorus contained in the fragmentation would burn themselves out before going too deep into the body.

The combat body armour he wore at the time was designed to protect the vital organs such as the heart, lungs and head. He would survive if medical treatment was forthcoming. His men hearing the blast, immediately rushed to his aid and casevaced him via helo back to an aid station. It was here that he met a young sweet twenty-two year old nurse by the name of Jocelyn Armstrong. Initially, she took no particular notice of him. He was just another patient that deserved as much care and attention as any of her patients.

The wounds had been severe and would leave lasting scars to his face, arms and legs. It was doubtful if he would make it through the next twenty-four to forty-eight hours. But William was a tough old bugger, it would take a lot to keep him down. He was often first of his men to enter battle and the last to leave. He was a strong believer in leading by example and the only way to do that was from the front. Though he was not careless in this mantra, due diligence and well thought out plans would be executed while he had command. He would not lose his soldiers to stupidity and fool heartiness. But he knew one important key element which must be portrayed every single time when going into combat, that is, his men need to believe in their leader.

If he was going to ask men to risk and possibly give up their lives for the cause, he would have to show courage, tenacity, integrity and trust. It is a hard thing sending a man to his death, but sometimes the cause is greater than the life of one man, even that of his own life. He still believed with what the CWC were fighting for, that it was a righteous and honest cause. The threat of nuclear extermination was real and the REAMAN had to be stopped. That didn't mean, however; that innocence had to be lost along with it. It was this innocence that had bought him here to this aid station; it was what had bought him to Jocelyn. Cause and effect had always filled his life, and had now done it again.

As the days past and his wounds healed, his eyesight would continue to be the cause of concern for the doctors and nurses that administered his care. Jocelyn up until now had only said a few words to him and had been the first to hold his hand and tell him everything was going to be fine when he was first bought in. Those few words and her touch had a lasting effect on him and he yearned to hear her voice again. When it came next, he immediately pricked his ears up and reached out aimlessly for her touch. The doctors had noticed that his will to live had been fading and was only picked up when Joselyn entered the room. So they suggested that she sit with him on regular occasions.

It was getting to be that she didn't have to say a word for him to notice that she had entered the room. He recognised her smell and it was alluring to him. After a few nights of the two of them talking, she started to learn more about the man, of who he was. In many ways, he held the same beliefs and opinions as she did. And although, to date, this had been a five year veteran of this war that was laying on the recovery bed in front of her, she started to see a softer side to him.

She was amazed at how much he had kept his sanity and hope of better days to come. Most others that had come through the aid station had either given up on life all together or were itching to get back to the war to kill more REAMAN. This was a vile thought to her as her mantra had been the preservation of life, all life.

William eventually told her the story of how he came to be blinded with flash burns. Again, this amazed her as anyone else she believed would have instantly shot the boy. Gradually their conversations moved to life after the war and of having a quiet little piece of land in the country. They would raise cattle and have many children to help them in their daily chores around the farm. Of course this was only in jest as the talk of children and of owning a farm together was a distant dream to them both, but deep down, they each believed that this jest could be real and one day turn to fact.

Jocelyn continued to nurse William back to full health night after endless night for almost five weeks until his bandages were removed from his eyes. A specialist eye doctor in his mid to late twenties and not much older than he had been flown in to assess his condition. As the bandages came off from around his head, pads were removed from his eyes. He was nervous at first, but slowly he opened his eyes and with a few more blinks, a vision started to appear. Standing in front of him was the doctor and just off to one side was who he had surmised must have been Jocelyn. He was then asked what he could see.

'My god.' He said, 'You are beautiful.'

He had regained his vision and the young specialist had told him that was no way to act as an officer and a gentleman of the CWC towards a fellow officer of the CWC Nursing Corps. But William didn't care and he took a step forward past the doctor and planted a kiss on Jocelyn's lips. The young doctor was aghast with disbelief by what he was seeing, but a senior medical officer told him to forget it and settle down.

After all, it had been the doctors who suggested that she take an interest in him in the first place and besides, there was enough hatred that filled the world they lived in already, a little bit of love would be a good thing. The senior medical officer instructed all in attendance to leave the room so the two of them could be alone. That was the start of their relationship, one that would see them survive the war and be married.

As the War of the Great Despair progressed for what would seem to be a never ending conflict, both sides were becoming desperate to see its end. The People's Republic of China had recently turned on their former ally and were in the process of invading mainland North Korea. William however, now a Brigadier General was given complete command of the 1st Continental Ranger Regiment and was ordered to march on the west REAMAN contingents in the Middle East and North Africa.

His orders were to put down any and all opposition to the CWC, including those that harboured REAMAN forces. Towns and villages were to be destroyed as they made their way into the heart of the Middle East. After nine long hard years of fighting and now that the tides had turned in their favour, the high command of the CWC had wanted to make an example of those who would challenge the free world of the west.

Quite a few high ranking officials and diplomats of the CWC disagreed with these tactics at the time. There were already strains on international relationships with the Russians and the South American governments over matters of opinions and decisions, this would only serve to add more fuel to an already smouldering fire. One could only hope that this fire could be contained, even put out.

William also disagreed with the high command and saw these orders as futile and pointless. He would question their strategic advantage, especially now as masses of REAMAN soldiers were laying down their arms and surrendering to the western forces as they moved through. The catalyst that swayed his final decision not to attack mercilessly the enemies of the western world had come when he reached the Iranian border, hundreds of thousands of displaced refugees and surrendered REAMAN soldiers were lying in wait for CWC forces to help them and to provide much needed care and assistance. Instead of making an example of these people as he was ordered, William instructed his Regiment to provide medical care and protection for those requiring it.

Decades later and after federation of the UFTN, this moment of compassion and the ideals forged that day of protecting the weak and helpless would be one of the tenets the FCR Corps would adopt. Though his decision had been admired by some, not all agreed and the powers that be, set upon the refugee camp with an arsenal of might and force. Intelligence reports had been doctored to state that a counter attack was imminent. Many thousands were killed along with scores of his own men. It would be a dark day for the CWC and one which would later see those decision makers punished when the Consortium of Trust formed the UFTN. There would be no place in this world for people like that.

William also suffered extensive injuries from the attack and once again found himself in the arms of an angel, Jocelyn. Her admiration and love for this man grew immensely. After he had returned back into the fray of battle after their first meeting, her thoughts have constantly remained of him. She dreamt of a life together, a peaceful and quiet life beyond this one, beyond all this death and destruction. This was a man she believed was good at his core and a man she would want to be with.

Much to his surprise, evidence of the last time they were together, was starting to show. Jocelyn had tried to keep the fact that she was pregnant with his child a secret. Their passion and emotion had obviously gotten the better of them a couple of months ago and although he was happy at the thought of being a father, he would not bring a bastard son or daughter into this world.

Finally in 2022, William and Jocelyn were married by a priest in a small ceremony by his hospital bed. She could not obviously continue as a theatre nurse at an aid station in her condition and he's injuries were too severe this time to see him returned to the war. William had also been stripped of command for his actions in Iran and was to forfeit his place amongst his brethren as a Ranger. He had been stripped of all titles and former honours.

With that, they concocted a plan for their return to Australia using his injuries as the mechanism. His recovery would take place back in Australia and he would need someone to accompany him on his way home and attend to his medical needs. Who better to do this than Jocelyn?

He had removed himself from danger, but much more important than that, he had removed his new bride and child to be from the danger as well. They were now home and relatively safe from the war in the northern continents. The following year, the Chinese military invaded North Korea and the first of many nuclear warheads were detonated around the planet. Their son, Marshall Maynard was just one year old when the war finally came to a close. He would be bought up in a world ungoverned and uncertain of its future until federation.

The Consortium of Trust recognised William's achievements and moral convictions and had him reinstated as a Ranger and promoted him to Corps Commander of the newly formed Federal Continental Rangers. Now a three star Lieutenant General, it had been Jocelyn who suggested they should adopt Saint Michael the Archangel as their Corps patron symbol. Saint Michael she said, represented everything that a Ranger stood for.

—m— ✝ —m—

Knock! Knock! The door opened and there stood an elderly woman with crinkly old skin who must have been in her eighties. A voice from behind her somewhere inside the house sounding withered and crackled asked the question, who was at the front door. Suddenly another voice spoke up and asked if she was going to let them in. What did the second voice mean by saying them? The woman at the door then sighted a figure of a young teenage girl that stepped out from behind Ashleigh's solid frame. Immediately the elderly woman could see the resemblance, she was gifted with that talent.

'What have you done?' she asked.

'Mum, just let me inside and I'll explain everything.'

Although she was not actually his mother, he had always lovingly referred to both grand elders as mum and dad. He was too young to remember his natural parents, so for him, referring to William and Jocelyn as mum and dad was natural and made sense.

Jocelyn could clearly see that the girl was somehow connected to her twice son and after giving her a kiss and a cuddle, he entered the house with Josephine close behind. Inside the house they saw an older man sitting in a chair, his face was covered with a mask which was feeding him oxygen. Around the living room were pictures of him as a young man when he was married and more photos that displayed the vigour of one in his early twenties dressed in military uniform. Though this uniform looked unfamiliar to Josephine. It was obviously a uniform worn by soldiers from before the time of the Coming.

In another corner were some military honours and awards; medals he had earned for his time in past conflicts. As she glanced closer, she could read the inscription on one that read, 'International Security and Assistance Force – Afghanistan 2011' and another which simply read 'IRAQ 2009'. Josephine found it hard to believe that a time could ever exist.

She whispered into her father's ear the question as to why there were no pictures of her twice grand elder in the War of the Great Despair, as she had heard it mentioned back at his home in Glassenville.

Ashleigh told her that his elder parents refused to recognise that period in history. It is one in which they had wished never happened. The only good thing to come from it had been their meeting and eventual marriage.

Josephine had surmised that the oxygen mask that he now relied upon for extended life may have been as a result of his time during that period. It would be later explained that proof of this was never confirmed. Things, events, times and places and the kept archival records of such were all lost from that period. He could not prove that it had been his own coalition forces during the battle of Iran that resulted in him returning from the war with an illness. One in which would slowly end his life in agonising pain with each passing year.

The world had been subjected to nuclear fallout and it would be by this that the government of the day would lay blame for many of the population falling ill and dying. Even though in the last year of the war before the nukes were released, William had been removed from the conflict due to wounds his sustained at the time. This placed him back in Australia, now Oceania, where the fallout was minimal. The maths simply didn't add up. The man had never smoked a cigarette a day in his life, then how could it be that for the last forty years, he required the aid of a breathing apparatus to help him live and extend life?

Though one must say, for ninety-two years of age, he was doing extremely well. Especially considering that many lost their lives during the actual war and many more would die during the twenty-three years of unrest immediately succeeding it. Ashleigh's elder father had always been stubborn when it came to death, particularly his own; somehow he just kept going when all around him were not, regardless of what ailed him. Unfortunately, due to his deteriorating health, he and Jocelyn found it difficult to maintain the home estate. They would have to either sell up and move into old aged care or receive some external assistance.

The boys knew that this day would eventually come and had decided when they were just teenagers, that because Andrew was the eldest, he would manage and take up ownership of the property. By the time this had come to pass, Andrew was flying Nighthawk attack helicopters in the OTD Southern Hemisphere Aviation Corps. But just as with his younger brother, he too considered family first and he soon discharged from the service to return home. It was here that he first met Constance and here they still are.

Ashleigh quickly walked over and gave his elder father a kiss on the forehead and a huge cuddle telling him how glad he was to see him again. Andrew also gave his brother a manly hug, quickly followed by a sharp punch to the arm as the two began to playfully wrestle. They were evenly matched regardless of their age, neither of them ever gaining the advantage over the other. Jocelyn told them both to settle down and to stop being silly. William in turn looked at the young girl which was now sitting next to him and kindly told her in a weary tone not to worry about these two fools, as they were always horsing around like this every time they got together.

Ashleigh introduced his very young companion to his family, including Andrew's wife Constance and their two children, Marshall and Catherine-Lee. The children were named after, and in honour of, Andrew and Ashleigh's real parents who were no longer of this world. Although Andrew was the elder brother, he had been wed to Constance sometime after his brother had married Siobhan. Therefore, his children were somewhat younger than Ashleigh's and because of this, they struggled to comprehend the situation that now fronted the Maynard family.

Jocelyn invited them all to sit while she put the kettle on. Josephine had yet again found herself in the company of strangers, but this time she was not as reserved and as timid as before. She felt comfortable in this home and wondered to herself if this is what a normal family was. Was this how a normal family behaved and was this what she had missed out on all these years? She could tell that they were very close and immediately formed an attachment with the old man sitting in the chair.

The photographs around her confirmed her previous knowledge that her twice grand elder was a war veteran, but she could also see that a kindness and gentile streak flowed through his soul. Was this where her father had picked up his kindness and gentle nature? As the coffee was bought into the living room and all these strangers around her were chattering away, she had also noticed that Andrew was a lot like her real father. He too seemed gentle and caring, and especially kind and loving to Marshall and Katie-Lee. Josephine had seen her father with his own children and now she was witnessing another man behaving in the same manner. She was quickly coming to realise that not all men were like her stepfather. This new revelation was breaking her heart as she now understood what she had been missing out on over all these years.

Ashleigh had sat them all down as he revealed that the surprise he had mentioned to them on the phone was this girl, and that this girl was his daughter. William and Jocelyn were taken aback momentarily by this statement but suspected as much by the young girl's appearance as she walked into their home. They were also somewhat disappointed in him. They had not raised their twice son to be so foolish when it came to this kind of thing.

They were especially surprised because of all the trouble he and Siobhan had went through to be together. They remember this like it was yesterday. How could he have committed such a foolish act? But unlike Ashleigh's response when he initially found out, his elder parents and assembled family were a little more sensitive to the feelings of the young girl that sat before them.

William gingerly reached out his hand in immediate acceptance of Josephine and she willingly accepted his offer, cupping his with the two of hers. He was so kind to her that she had found it hard to imagine that this man who had obviously fought in past wars, had likely killed others in the undertaking of his duty. Jocelyn knew that her twice son would not make up such a fanciful story and could see by her resemblance that she was of Maynard blood; that much was true. But she wondered as did they all, was how this all came about.

Ashleigh had asked Josephine on the plane to Melbourne if she minded if he could repeat her story to his family. It would be a compressed version but none the less, her story would be told. She had agreed and as Ashleigh was about to begin, a tear formed in Josephine's eye and ran down her cheek. Jocelyn got up from her seat and sat down beside the young girl placing her arm around her. This would obviously be tough on her yet again, but it would be just one of the many times that she or someone else would have to retell it. So she prepped herself as her father asked her if he could begin.

William and Jocelyn were beside themselves with sadness for this poor girl when they learned the truth and the horror behind her life and that of her mother's. William was proud in the fact that although his twice son had made a foolish decision when he was younger, he was now taking the honourable path in seeking its justice. Andrew who had known part of the story and who now knew the rest, offered his assistance to his brother for anything he needed. They would stand together again side by side as the double A's and as they had done when they were teenagers on the sporting field, in the school yard, or out camping together. They had always stood together as one.

'So what's your plan of attack son?'

William struggled to produce words as the effects of his illness and age were clearly painful with anything he did or said. Ashleigh asked his elder parents if Josephine could stay at their home while he travelled into the local State Division Police precinct to inform them of their situation. There was no question about it, of course his elder mother and elder father would take care of their thrice granddaughter; she was family. He knew that they would stand by him as they had always done. He hadn't known it at the time, but it was actually Jocelyn who had spoken to Siobhan's mother, Lucienne, that convinced her father to allow the two of them to be married.

He arrived at the local SDP precinct that was responsible for the south side on Melbourne's outer suburbs along the bay. He had informed the SDP of his daughter's plight and that of Evonne's and explained that he had wanted to approach them first without Josephine being present in order to protect her. He knew that she would have to be called in for questioning, but he would delay this for now.

He also explained what had happened to Josephine in Queenstown and what they had told the SDP there. Both he and Josephine would maintain their stories, not for fear of reprisal from the law, but rather that of his Ranger family. The Melbourne SDP had no jurisdiction in Queenstown anyway, so that particular matter would remain up north.

They instructed him to come back with Josephine where they would interview her to get the story from her own mouth and in her own words. Not that they didn't believe him or anything, how could they not? He was a Ranger. They explained it was just part of the course. Josephine now sat in a small room with two Senior Detectives, one of them a female. Beside her was a woman in her mid to late sixties dressed in clothes similar to what she had seen in her mother's family archives.

The woman was very caring and tender to her touch. She had sensed a familiarity in Josephine, but her judgment of her was clouded with questions of doubt that were emanating from this young and very confused girl. She introduced herself as Anne Phillips, but had informed Josephine that she may call her Auntie Annie if that was more comfortable for her. Anne had continued to say that although she was not employed by the SDP, she provided assistance to them as a family grief counsellor, specialising in domestic violence and abuse, including rape cases.

The moment Josephine shook her hand she sensed a feeling of motherly care and protection, very much like the touch of her own mother. Josephine quickly became confused about her feelings. She had been hidden from the world for so long that she didn't know what to do next. Anne's touch had soothed and eased her emotions, this was her skill, her talent. It was almost as if she could reach into Josephine's mind and tell her everything was going to be alright. This is the same type of feeling she had received every time her own mother had held her in her arms, only the strength of her mother's touch was much less impacting than the one she just had with Anne.

Josephine looked at her father with uncertainty; she did not want to go through with it. A look of fear again formed on her face as she kept her gaze on her father. She had been looking for some sign of guidance and comfort from him, which he gave.

'It will be alright baby girl, you're safe here.'

They proceeded to position themselves in the interview room. As she sat down at the table, facing her were image recording cameras, one directly pointing in her direction and another which set behind her seat facing the SDP Detectives. On the table also sat two microphones. All this ready to start recording and capturing the proceedings of the interview.

They had informed Josephine that her father would have to wait outside while they questioned her. As she was legally still a minor, her rights would be protected by her counsellor, Anne. Josephine did not like this at all and for the first time in three days, she panicked with tremendous fear. Since finding and meeting her real father, he has not left her side, not once. It had been strange that in another first for her, she now found herself running towards a man instead of away from one. She had run to her father's side putting her arms around him. He told her again that everything was going to be alright and that these people could be trusted. These were the good guys and she had nothing to fear.

He would just be outside. In fact the Detective had said he could use the room adjacent to the interview room. In there was a two way mirror where he could watch and listen, but would not be seen or heard. Josephine would of course not be aware of this for if she had, she would have spent the entire interview staring towards the glass and her answers may not have come naturally, thus retarding the truth. It broke his heart to see her go through all this pain and agony of retelling her story again. He now felt a real emotional attachment to her.

On the plane down as they travelled to Melbourne, he recalled as she had fallen asleep and nuzzled up close to him, resting her head into his shoulder. He knew that he would love this girl for the daughter she was and see to it that no more time would be lost or wasted between them. When all of this was finally over, they would all take a very well earned and extended holiday. It wouldn't matter where, just as long as they were all together, his family, her, and Evonne.

After the interview, Ashleigh was allowed back into the room and once again Josephine rushed to her father's side. There next step was one of immediate action. Evonne had been trapped in an abusive relationship for years and with no way that she saw as an out. Dirk had to be stopped and removed, and now. The senior lead Detective organised a warrant for Dirk's immediate arrest, along with search papers for the house so that they could gather evidence against him. They would search for any visible signs of violence and collect it; whether it by bag and tag or by photograph.

Anne would also accompany the SDP, something in which she very rarely did. But there was something about this girl that required her attention. She was ninety percent sure she knew what it was, but she needed to confirm it. If it had been the struggle she imagined it was, it would require her guidance and teachings to help both her and her mother.

It was soon time to go and the Detectives assembled a team from the Tactical Special Operations Division (TSOD) of the SDP to accompany them. Against their wishes, Ashleigh would follow behind in the All Purpose AutoMobile he had hired at the airport along with Josephine. They had no power to stop him anyway as his clearances and privileges as a Ranger granted such actions. He would still however, listen and heed their concerns. He had known that if he had become involved, it would most likely be the end of Dirk's life.

Ashleigh informed the SDP that he would stay well clear so as to not inflame the coming confrontation or to place any one of them at risk, especially Josephine. He explained that he would park the APAM just around the corner out of sight and when Dirk was removed, only then would he declare his presence. He was not going to delay the union of mother and daughter any longer if he could help it.

Chapter Eleven

Panic and curiosity engulfed the residents of the street where Dirk Van den Berg resided. His neighbours were bewildered at the thought that all these police in special protective uniforms were here in their quiet little colder sack. They had all thought Evonne had been the reason for the presence of so many SDP TSODs in their street. Just like they had also all thought that Evonne had thrown one of her temper tantrums again. Not one of them thought for a minute that the SDP were there to arrest Dirk.

They had all known of Evonne's stories but none of them ever believed her. They considered her to be a moocher and not worthy of a man such as Dirk. They blamed her appearance, as in her manic depressive state, she had failed to rid herself of the post pregnancy weight and had let herself go. It had been this, as just one of the reasons that Dirk had become so distant from her. He would often go to neighbourhood barbeques alone and tell stories that is wife was ill again or she didn't feel like seeing people. He had painted her out to be a cold selfish woman that turned away from friends and from him, no matter how much he would try and convince her otherwise.

Evonne had tried to approach some of her neighbours, but they simply would not listen, even when she had the black eyes and bruises to prove it. What once were her circle of friends had now turned against her because of Dirk. She had considered these people to be superficial at best. They were spiteful, mean and cruel and only ever thought of themselves. Eventually, other than leaving the house to go to work, she just stayed in and became a recluse. She was trapped with no escape.

On occasion when Dirk went away to Sydneyton on his so called business meetings, Evonne would sneak out of the house with the children to visit her mother. She would have to take extra special care not to be seen by anyone because she knew her neighbours would undoubtedly inform Dirk upon his return. She was lucky enough that her mother had taught her ways around this and time again she succeeded in keeping herself hidden from view.

Every now and again the thought of leaving her husband entered her mind and filled her thoughts, but this she realised she could never do. For if she ever tried, his reach would be far too great and he would eventually find her. Dirk had very powerful and influential friends.

Ashleigh had done as he promised, he had parked out of visible sight of the house and Dirk. He would keep himself hidden from view along with his daughter. Suddenly a man appeared on the front yard to their home, it was him; it was Dirk. He had said something along the lines of get inside please, and that he would handle this. He must have been talking to Evonne, where was she? He couldn't see her. His heart began to pound as if it would burst through his chest. It was then that he had realised he was not just here to help Evonne and Josephine to rid themselves of an evil man, but now, standing here in this place and with Evonne literally only twenty metres from him; he was here because he wanted to see his Evee again.

The men and women of the TSO Division could be seen moving closer when a woman came screaming out of the home.

'HELP ME! PLEASE!'

It was Evonne, she knew that Ashleigh would not let her suffer any longer at the hands of this man as was evidenced by the presence of so many SDP Officers. She had thought this must have been by his hand and saw an opportunity and way out now. Evonne believed that the people in the street would surely have to believe her now, but as she ran to the officers, Dirk lurched forward to restrain her. A TSOD Officer quickly held him back while other TSOD Officers held taser guns pointed towards his direction. They would not draw their lethal firearms unless absolutely necessary.

Ashleigh who was caught up in the moment had been caught off guard by the sight of the girl he once loved with a passion and still cared for. So much so that Josephine upon hearing her mother's voice had jumped out of the APAM and was now running towards her mother. He quickly grabbed her to keep her out of harm's way, but it was too late, Dirk had spotted her and him. He quickly realised that Josephine had found her real father and it was her who was to blame for the SDP being here now.

This enraged Dirk and soon the neighbours and the entire street would see just what he was capable of. He broke free of the TSOD Officer restraining him and lurched for Evonne calling her a fucking bitch and a slut whore. He had managed to grab her arm swinging her around connected with fist upon face as she was hurled backwards by the force of the blow. Ashleigh immediately and instinctively reached for his service weapon. This time it would be Josephine who had the clarity of mind to persuade him not to use it.

'Let the SDP handle it daddy, please?'

Dirk was about to launch another attack on Evonne when suddenly two metal darts carrying 50,000 volts pierced his body and sent electricity surging through it. He was instantly stopped in his tracks and dropped to the ground thrashing around violently as every muscle in his body tensed up. Ashleigh usually didn't like seeing people in pain, it was against the Ranger creed, but even he had to admit feeling a brief moment of joy and satisfaction as he watched Dirk receive just a fraction of what was yet to come.

Evonne, being released from his grasp and wiping the blood that now fled the cavity of her nostrils ran to her daughter. The both of them threw their arms around each other as they were again united. They were overcome with a flood of tears of emotion and happiness at being back together again and finally realising their dream come true, that at last they were free of their tyrannical overlord.

Evonne had looked a mess, she was battered and bruised, and the years of living with Dirk had aged her once attractive features. Ashleigh had to put this in perspective, they had all aged since they were last both together, and later as Evonne had been cleaned up with the aid of the paramedics, she was as pretty to him as she had always been. But that was still yet to come. For now he would bask in their joyous reunion.

The rip in the back of Evonne's dress had shown more years of abuse as she turned around while continuing to hug her daughter. Ashleigh was mortified by what he saw. Not only were there fresh marks from a recent beating, but there were the scars left behind by past beatings. From a distance they had looked to have been raised welts. Closer inspection would show that these were the result of receiving a whipping by a cane or something similar.

Ashleigh would see to it that she would receive only the best medical care and using today's technology to completely repair her skin. When finished it would appear as if she had never been whipped at all. But although medical technology can heal physical scars, it would take some time to heal the psychological ones. He would help her deal with this in good time. Right now though, he had also wanted to embrace her.

As he stepped forward and as their eyes met, Evonne looked up and simply mouthed the words thank-you.

Meanwhile, Dirk was being handcuffed and forcibly placed into the back of the Urban Tactical Assault Vehicle and was yelling out words of profanity cursing her and her daughter along with Ashleigh, vowing that he would not be stopped. He shouted out that he was a big time city lawyer within the country's biggest law firm. He boasted that he had powerful friends in high places and vowed he would beat these charges and that he would seek vengeance on her for being such a bitch to him all these years.

This man, Ashleigh thought to himself, was completely insane. But he was right about one thing, he did have powerful friends in high places, but so did he. His elder father had finished off as a Lieutenant General in one of the most respected branches of the UFTN Peace Maker Division and had maintained a lot of contacts within the UFTN inner circle. Ashleigh was also highly placed reaching the top of the enlisted personnel's rank of Chief Sergeant Major. He had been decorated many times for his service to the UFTN and it didn't hurt their cause for the fact that he was a Federal Continental Ranger.

If Dirk thought he was the only one who had powerful allies, then he was sadly mistaken. For him to think he would escape conviction would only be but a dream. Once all the evidence had been produced and the truth behind his sinister ways revealed, not even his friends would be able to save him. No judge, no matter how much he knew the person, could possibly let him off.

The crowd of people stood in unison as silence over gripped them. Was it true, had poor Evonne been right all along? How ashamed they had all felt. How could they have ignored the signs for so long and let this continue? Evonne displayed her back to the crowd of people amassed in the street. There would be no way that she could inflict these wounds to herself on her own. It would be a physical impossibility.

'See! See what he has done? This is the person you thought was kind; this is the man that you protected, and I am the woman he beat and tortured, and you failed to help!'

Ashleigh echoed the sentiments of her words. Some would stand in ignorance and defiance against them both until he removed his jacket to place over Evonne for comfort and cover her exposed back. It was then that the tattoo on his inner forearm could be seen by the mob. A figure of a powerful man, flaming sword in hand and wings outstretched. Yes, it was Michael the Archangel and it was then that they knew this was a Ranger standing before them.

He was completely disgusted by the attitudes and the appearance of these people. The fact that they lived in such an upper-class society was bad enough, but to have turned their backs on this situation for so long was despicable. Because of their reputation they had become known as the SnoSose by the lower classes. The SnoSose stood for the Snobs of Society and most of them were. This was a class standing of the past since before the Coming and which some had wanted to cling to this way of life. While some gave back to society, most did not and would only do things to serve their own purpose.

Living classes of human kind was one such endeavour that the UFTN had tried to abolish. It had been one of the tenets laid down upon its founding and came directly from the heart of the Consortium of Trust. All were considered equal, Ucusee, Ugbee, Trap and the AN, even though the peoples of the AN still needed to be reminded of that. This division of classes had also been part of the reason why Ashleigh was sent to fight in the Terran Wars against the RFN. But different classes of society did still exist, even in Oceania, the most peaceful of the six Territorial Continental Divisions.

This was an environment where people looked down their nose

at you. Whereby if you didn't have a certain vehicle or wear a certain dress or suit, you were considered of lower standing. This was not Evonne he thought; these weren't her type of people. Yes it had been a long time since the two of them last saw each other, but he knew her. He knew who she really was. You cannot change the core of a person, you are who you are. Deep down, those beliefs and those values that we all possess, will always define us. Evonne was no different, she was simply caught in a world never wished for and which was foreign to her.

He embraced Evonne as a father would embrace a son or daughter, as someone who loved and would care and protect them. He told her that he was going to take her away from all this. He told her that she didn't belong here and that he would provide a new, better, life for her and the children. And he told her that he loved her still. Maybe that was the wrong thing to say at the time, but being caught up in the moment, his thoughts were resting squarely with Evonne and Josephine. It was true anyway, he did love her, but not as a husband would or should love a wife. His meaning behind his words may have set Evonne on a path which if misconstrued, could lead her to more disappointment.

'Come on, let's go.'

One of the SDP Detectives that had interviewed Josephine earlier that morning had walked up behind them to lead Evonne over to where the paramedics were. She was in desperate need of medical attention. As her adrenalin had kept her going, she hadn't felt any pain through the entire ordeal. She was just happy to finally be rid of Dirk, but now as things began to settle, the pain from the fresh welts on her back and the bruise to her jaw started to take effect. She remained focused on her daughter and the man that had come back to save her as she walked to the Paramedic Casualty Transport or PmCT. And although she was in agonising pain, Evonne maintained her smile.

There was still a lot of work to be done now that Dirk was in custody and still sitting handcuffed in the back of the Urban Tactical Assault Vehicle. The Detectives and Ashleigh both asked about Jeremy and Damian of where they had been through all this? As it turns out, the twins were with Evonne's mother. That had explained the reason why she had a fresh batch of welts on her back. After receiving Ashleigh's phone call the day before, she knew this would be the day of reckoning for her and Dirk. The twins were still young, just three years of age, but they were still susceptible to their surroundings. Evonne would place them out of harm's way.

This had angered Dirk when he found out and he began asking her questions as to why she had done this without his permission. If anything, she should have sent the twins to his parents if she wanted some time to herself. Why her mother's? Dirk didn't have much time for Crystal, in fact he despised her. He had hated the way that she kept filling her daughter's head with nonsense about being one with the earth and all living things. Throughout the latter part of their unhappy marriage when things started to become violent, Dirk had forbade Evonne completely from seeing any of her family.

The Detective had asked her why she too didn't also go to her mother's and stay there when she had the chance. Why wait for Dirk's return from work only to feel the wrath of his rage? It was simple and as she put it, she had wanted to be here to see the look on the bastard's face when he realised his reign of terror was coming to an end. She had wanted to see the look on her neighbours faces when they realised that they had been wrong for all these years. What's another bashing she thought? She had survived others and she would survive this one as well for it would be worth it to see him taken away.

By now the other detectives on the scene had started interviewing the people in the street. They had already known who to seek out due to the information that Josephine had given earlier. These stories she had told the SDP detectives should provide some very interesting results. They would expect that there would be a vast difference of opinion once all the information had been gathered. The detectives new that from the people they would interview that their natural instinct would be to try and save their friend, but as the truth would slowly start to hit them, their stories would start to change. It would take quite a few interviews until the truth would finally surface.

These people were also cowardly and any thought of being publicly disgraced or the threat of doing prison time would be enough for most of these people to quickly tell the truth. It would be the hard core ones the detectives would have to press. These would be the ones with varied degrees and masters in higher education, who thought they could outsmart the people around them, especially the SDP. They would eventually be proven wrong.

Evidence was now being collected from inside the house as paramedics continued to tend to the wounds on Evonne's back and her face. A forensic photographer had come over to her and had asked her to remove her blouse so he could take photos of her back and arms. There would be plenty more photographs to come once she arrived at the hospital and had been examined by a doctor.

The detectives had identified the weapon used on her back. It was a riding crop that he kept by the side of his bed. Evonne had said he had always carried it. She explained that he needed it nearby for he never knew when he might be in call of it. The riding crop would later confirm the presence of tiny fragments of dried skin and blood. The DNA results would later prove that this body tissue and residue had belonged to Evonne. It was a good find by the SDP. It had been foolish of Dirk to use such a coarse object and to not have it cleaned as it would later become one of the centre pieces of evidence which would see Dirk convicted.

As the police searched through the house, they had come across many more items that could be used in a court of law as evidence. One detective in particular had come across an unsuspecting find of surprising and strange objects. As this junior detective searched what had previously been Josephine's bedroom, he noticed what looked like to be salt on the floor. As he traced the salt it seemed to have been laid in a circle but it was very messy and unclear whether it had been placed that way or not.

When the trail of salt reached the end of the bed, just underneath the end of it, the detective noticed a loose floor board which was slightly ajar. When he had investigated further and finally opened it, he called for support. But instead of other SDP Officers coming to his aide, Anne appeared at the door.

'You don't need to look at this.' She said.

Unbelievably, the detective replaced the floor board and left the room. Anne had to act fast for she knew the contents under the floor would incite unwelcomed questions. Quickly she knelt and removed everything from the cavity under the floor and placed the contents into her bag.

'What's the matter?'

Two more officers entered the room just as Anne was standing up from being on her knees. She had told them that the young detective must have seen something strange from the bedroom window and that he was now in the rear of the yard searching for it. True to her word, the detective was indeed in the back yard searching aimlessly for something that wasn't there.

Anne's assumptions had been correct. That feeling she received when she first met Josephine back at the SDP precinct had been confirmed. It was now apparent that Evonne and Josephine needed her help. Evonne was about to be taken to the Melbourne Centre Hospital when the PmCT was halted. Anne opened the rear of the transport and was shocked by what she saw.

Up until that point, Anne had not seen Evonne's face. Now she had, it had explained everything. Anne told Evonne that she had collected some personal objects of hers which she might need. She then handed Evonne a necklace which had a small five pointed star made of silver hanging from it. The look on Evonne's face told her everything she needed to know. Anne had discovered her secret.

Chapter Twelve

Later that evening at the hospital while Evonne was being treated, Ashleigh called his wife and filled her in on all the events that had happened since arriving in Melbourne. She was relieved to hear his voice and know that he was safe. It had been a bit of a struggle to remove Dirk, but at least it had been done. He told Siobhan that he would spend the next couple of nights in hospital by Evonne's side for support and comfort, and that he would call her again once she had been released and allowed to return home.

Evonne had suffered severely at the hands of Dirk. Her back required extensive treatment and there were signs that she had been drugged over the years. Not only had Dirk kept her locked up, he had also knocked her out, medically speaking, so she wouldn't be a disturbance to him. So severe were her injuries that she couldn't remain on her back. She had to lie face down in a specially designed bed. It was heart wrenching for Ashleigh to see her this way and he recalled the times when they were younger and the way she used to look at him. All he could do now was continue to provide moral support and care.

When he returned to her hospital room after talking to his wife, Evonne and Josephine were having a long discussion about the last six months. Where she had been and what she had been up to. Evonne had wished that she had prepared her daughter for the outside world a little better when she was younger. She had hoped that Josephine had known a little more about the ways of life before jumping head on into it.

The Clip of Saint Michael that had been bestowed on her years ago after completing her training as a Ranger had been the same as Ashleigh's. But whereas he now stood tall and strong, she did not. Why hadn't she fought back and why didn't she pass on her years of experience to her daughter? It was a tradition in their family that the matriarch always passed on their years of knowledge and wisdom from mother to daughter. It had been that way since as far back as she could remember. The truth was, Dirk had simply broken her will and spirit.

Ashleigh asked them both if Josephine's story had been completely revealed. Evonne responded with a quizzical look on her face that indicated that it had not.

'I was just getting to that. I wanted to break it softly.'

Ashleigh told his daughter that she was fine. Siobhan had received an earlier than expected phone call from the Queenstown Centre Hospital. The doctors had told her that Josephine's blood results had come back negative for all tests. She was free from any sexually transmitted infections and her body was clear of any foreign toxins from drugs and other diseases. The blood results also came back negative for any evidence of foreign bodily fluids or matter. She was still pure and this had answered his earlier unasked question of whether or not she had turned to the sin of the skin trade to get by. He felt relieved that he never had to ask this question of her.

Evonne, still with a look of confusion on her face, again asked the both of them to explain what had happened. She was horrified when she learned of what her daughter had been through but had been grateful that Ashleigh had been there to help. All the questions that had filled his mind three days ago were now being answered as rapidly as they had been originally asked. There was a lot of catching up to do. Josephine and he now knew why Evonne had kept the existence of her daughter a secret from him all those years ago.

Their little reunion in the hospital was suddenly broken with sounds of another woman and two very restless little boys coming down the corridor and then entering her hospital room.

'Mother.'

Crystal had entered her daughter's hospital room with Jeremy and Damian in tow. Now her family was complete. All the people she had cared for most in this world were now all together in one room. The boys were very excited and rushed over to give their mother a cuddle, but Josephine stopped them, telling them that their mother was still very sore and that they had to be very gentle with her. Damian heeded his older sister's words and gently placed his arms around Evonne's neck to give her a tender cuddle.

Jeremy as usual didn't listen to a word anyone said and continued to rush in before Ashleigh had picked him up with one hand in one fluid motion. You have to be gentle he explained again, but Jeremy just shrugged him off. He had always been a bit of a handful ever since he was born. As far as twins went, these two were worlds apart.

Next it was Crystal's turn and she bent down to greet her daughter with a motherly kiss to the top of her head. She would look at Ashleigh and thank him for being the man he was and for coming to help. She had known that he was the father of Josephine but never held any malice towards him for this. At the time he had loved two very special people in his life, a choice was made and that was the end of it. At least it had been then. As he believed, she too held true the belief that things always occurred for a reason, and always knew that one day he would return.

'It is very pleasing to see you once again Ms Taylor. You are looking very well.'

'Stop that, you know you can call me Crystal.'

Josephine looked at her Nan and would just know what awaited her. Crystal had been bitterly disappointed by her twice daughter's actions. She had put herself at extreme risk and danger by running away. Although she had shown courage and would be praised for that, she would also not hear the end of it. Her Nan would ensure that she learnt a valuable lesson by this and see that she would never make the same mistake again.

Crystal may have scorned Josephine for what she did, but she loved her more than anything else on this planet. If she was hard on her, it would be for a very good reason. Evonne had always told her daughter that she was destined for great things. Crystal echoed those thoughts and told her that she must always be cautious of getting herself into situations that she may not be able to get out of. Her life was too important.

Josephine had been told numerous times that she was a special little girl. She had thought that this was just words that nans and mums said to their child because that's what all nans and mums must have said. But now she felt like these words hid more than what they were actually saying. Josephine hadn't seen her nan for quite some time and as she looked at her, she recalled that she always wore outfits that were somewhat different to most people. She had not really given this much thought until she remembered that Anne had been dressed very similar.

As per usual, Crystal had bought her special broth for them to feast on. And as usual, it went as fast as it was served. Ashleigh had tasted her cooking before and it had always been superb. He often asked her all those years ago what her ingredients were. There was always something, that one ingredient that he couldn't quite put his finger on, but knew that without it, her food would be as normal as anyone else's.

The next day, Evonne was allowed to lie on her back. The doctors had done some fine work and the scars on her back were healing very nicely.

Ashleigh had stayed with her that night while she slept and had instructed Josephine to return to her Nan's home where she would be looked after. At first, Josephine had not wanted to comply with his wishes, but eventually she did. Josephine had learnt to listen to her father. She had complete trust and faith in him. Plus she held the same faith and trust in her Nan. She was at last safe.

As Evonne slept throughout the night, he had watched her and remembered the morning he woke up beside her all those years ago. He remembered how she opened her eyes and as they kissed each other gently and passionately. He was not having thoughts of romantic intensions, that was in the past now, but as he had said to her then, he would never forget their time together and he never has.

The doctor entered the room for his morning rounds and was quickly followed by the SDP Detective that had been in charge of events the day before. The Detective informed them both that unfortunately, Dirk had been released on bail. Evonne's blissful awakening had suddenly turned to dreaded fear.

'Don't worry Evee, we always knew that there would be a chance of him getting bail. I'll be here by your side until he is safely put behind bars.'

Ashleigh's words provided comfort, but she wanted this to end and thought about the onset of the court trial. She thought about the lies he would tell and how he would try and twist her words to once again make her out to be the bad person. The Detective told her not to worry, they would have men stationed around her home when she returned. He would not get within throwing distance.

For the next couple of days, Evonne recovered in hospital and on the seventh was allowed to go home. She dreaded going back to that house, the place where she had been kept as a hostage and slave to her husband's every whim. How would the neighbours treat her when she returned?

Most of which had now come clean with the truth as they knew it. Only one remained defiant, but Ashleigh would soon make him come clean as well. Truth was one of the Ranger's creeds and he always had a special talent for getting it out of people.

Back home in her house, she could see the two SDP Officers conducting surveillance of her surroundings. How had she lost so much confidence and self-esteem? Dirk had been a domineering presence in her life for so long that she had buried all her past Ranger training and became completely subservient to him. She had been an ISR specialist, surely she could remember the basic principles of surveillance, or least remember how to set up the equipment.

When she entered her home, the remnants of her last fight with Dirk and the beatings she received were still very visible around the house. Crystal had not wanted her to return to that home at all and insisted that she come and stay with her. But Evonne told her mother that she had to face her demons so she could move past this. The only way to achieve this would be to return to that house of sin.

As they entered, a noise could be heard coming from within the house. It was a very big house with lots of rooms and dark corners to hide in. Now that it was empty, sounds could reverberate through passageways and open doors giving false indication as to the origin of their source. The house contained twenty seven rooms in total, anyone of which could harbour the doings of a dangerous man. Surely Dirk was not in the house waiting for them. How long had the SDPs been watching the house for?

Ashleigh drew his weapon from the electro-mechanical holster underneath his trench coat and placed Evonne behind him. As they both slowly moved further into the house and down the long corridor, suddenly there came a voice.

'Put that thing away young man and come into the kitchen.'

He knew immediately who the owner of that voice was. There was only one person who would know it was them and who would talk to him that way. When they entered the kitchen, they were greeted by two older and very similar looking women. One had been Crystal who had spoken to them from down the end of the corridor and who was nursing Damian on her lap. Sitting beside Crystal at the kitchen table had been Anne, who was struggling in vain to nurse Damian's twin brother, Jeremy. The little boy just didn't like anyone holding him, except that is for his father, Dirk.

Josephine was standing behind the two women and was still in the dark about many a curious thing. Why was Anne at their home and why did her mother squeal with excitement when she laid eyes on her? Evonne had already seen Anne when she had stopped the Paramedic Casualty Transport and had opened the rear hatch. But she showed no emotional attachment then, so why now?

'Auntie Annie, it is so good to see you again after all these years.'

Anne had previously instructed Josephine to call her Auntie Annie back at the SDP Precinct and thought it just to be a name used for a calming and more familiar affect. Was Anne really her auntie? They all sat down at the table where Crystal would explain all. Crystal and Anne were in fact sisters; Anne being the elder by four years and was born in San Francisco, the home of their mother. Crystal, however; had been born in Melbourne after their parents and Anne, who was just two years old at the time, had relocated to Australia in 2019 to escape the War of the Great Despair.

Their known history goes back as far as medieval England. But it was during the early years of Australia's infancy, when the country was still used as a penal colony for Great Britain that the first of their kind was sent there to live, as punishment as it would turn out to be.

Much to Josephine's surprise, she was informed that she was the direct descendent of convicts sent to this land, and that she was in fact the tenth generation of, what is now referred to as, the Graceline. Her namesake, Josephine Annabelle Grace, had been tried and convicted for stealing a loaf of bread in London and penalised for her crime and was sent to the island prison in the year 1859.

Story has it that Josephine Annabelle Grace did not actually steal that loaf of bread she was accused of, but rather it had been her husband who had committed the deed. It was just unfortunate that they had both been caught red handed with the loaf when the constabulary found them. Times were very different back then and the separation of social classes vast, extremely vast. Her husband had been without employment; there wasn't much on offer for a one armed, one eyed veteran of the Crimean War. They were homeless, they were hungry, and she had been six months pregnant with their unborn children.

While trying to defend his wife from the lawmen, Josephine's husband, Aneirin Grace, was shot and killed. There was nothing that she could do except weep over the body of her now dead husband; his blood running red in the damp wet streets of London's East End. So called justice was swift and three months later, just before her twenty-eighth birthday, Josephine Annabelle Grace gave birth to triplets on Australian soil. Out of this three daughters, only one would survive to continue the Graceline.

The first to be born died three months after birth from Cholera Infantum, whereas the second of the triplets died aged seven when the Master of the house she served at the time lashed out in a rage killing her. It had all been over a ring mark left by a brandy glass that had stained the Master's solid mahogany sitting table. It had formed overnight by the man's excessive drinking and the following morning he had blamed the child for not cleaning it off. The young girl's body was never found and the Master of the house was never charged with her murder.

The Master, being of some considerable stature and standing within the colony, had said that the poor girl had slipped and fell into the property's local water hole. This was a billabong that lay just a kilometre south-east of the main homestead and where the main supply of drinkable water was fetched. Back then there was no such thing as dredging equipment or rescue divers, therefore; no evidence could be found to either deny or confirm his story. He was taken at his word.

But Josephine knew better; she was not about to lose her third baby girl to this country or to this man. Some say Josephine cursed the Master as he remained childless and alone to his dying day, his seed dying with him. There would be no more offspring that would hail from his loins. Years later Josephine Annabelle Grace was released from servitude and granted her freedom. She would reinvigorate her past customs and traditions and henceforth became the first matriarch of the Graceline.

That had all been very interesting to Josephine, but for a fifteen year old teenage girl, what intrigued her more was the contents of the box. Anne positioned the box on the table in front of them. It was a pretty run down looking sort of box and Anne looked at Crystal with dismay.

'You were supposed to teach her our ways Crystal.'

Yes it had been Crystal's job to pass down the ways of her mothers and her mother's before that. Unfortunately with Dirk's constant interfering, this was almost impossible to do. Evonne was in the Ranger Corps by age fifteen and by twenty-one had been married to Dirk. Josephine was intrigued by all this and impatiently asked if she could open the box. But this right was only for the privilege of women, not even the children were allowed to know of its contents.

Ashleigh accepted his fate and took the twins outside into the back yard to mind them as they played. The box was soon opened and the first item to be removed from its rustic interior was that of a leather bound book which seemed to be very old. On the front of the notebook and carved into the leather were the initials A.R.G. Upon opening the book and just inside the front cover, an inscription could be read.

'For all the women of Hope and Grace'

Signed Agnes Rose Grace.

Who Agnes was, is the question that Josephine was about to spill from her lips when Anne answered. Anne now took the lead as she was the eldest and it had been the way of it. It was unfortunate that Anne was cursed with the inability to bear life; a task she knew had been reserved and gifted to her sister, Crystal, by the higher powers that be. You see, Anne was born when her mother was just twenty-three years of age and not the required twenty-seven as all the previous matriarchs had been before her. All previous matriarchs had also borne only daughters. As Evonne had given birth at just eighteen years of age, what this had meant for Josephine not even Anne could foretell.

Agnes Rose Grace had been a great spiritual Celtic princess during the time of legend and making. It was estimated that she lived in the time of 1250 AD and had come from a society rich in worshiping Mother Nature and the land around them. Her faith revolved around the beliefs of not just one God, but that of many. Like many of her kind living in a world in which science had yet come to prominence, all believed that life was a result of the gods. Her faith had been one of Pagan worship and Druid life. She held sacred the elements of earth, wind, fire, water and spirit.

It was a tradition that the knowledge and wisdom from each first born female, or the first sister to bear a daughter, would be the keeper of the book. It wasn't until the 1960s that their twice grand elder, Diana, who was roughly the same age as Josephine is now, started to realise that more could be gained from their beliefs. Through their respect and honour towards the gods, they would apply the art of white magick or wicca. The practice of which was taught by mother to daughter.

Another page in the old book was turned and there held the signatures along with the year of their births of all the matriarchs that had been the care takers of the book. The most recent being Diana Kay Reynolds b. 1940, Summer-Rayne Clarke b. 1967, Paige-Rose Phillips b. 1994, Crystal Taylor b. 2021, and Evonne Van den Berg b. 2048. The next name in the book would surely belong to her, Josephine thought to herself. But she would have a lot to learn if she was going to continue the tradition and the Graceline. How would she learn with only two elder matriarchs left alive and her mother who was a novice at best?

Josephine wondered what had happened to previous Graceline matriarchs and ask her mother the question. Diana had been born in Australia and had met a US sailor on shore leave when his warship had pulled into Sydney Harbour. The warship at the time was undergoing some minor repairs after seeing action in South East Asia during the time of the Vietnam War.

Later after his period of service had ended, Diana had moved to the United States to marry the man she loved. Meanwhile the war in Vietnam had now become a bitter and unpopular conflict and this would see Diana and her husband join the peace movement of the 1960s in protest against the war. The years following would see them give birth to a baby girl by the name of Summer-Rayne; her name being a reflection of the times.

These women and their history was never spoken of while under the rule of Josephine's stepfather, Dirk. They had sounded like fascinating people and she was very sad to hear that both Diana and Summer-Rayne had lost their lives during the War of the Great Despair. It had been when the battle for California was being raged and subsequently lost, that Summer-Rayne had returned to their home in San Francisco to care for her mother, Diana, in her later years. However, as the battle grounds shifted and the REAMAN entered mainland USA, San Francisco and LA were the first two cities to fall.

Diana was 81 years old and Summer-Rayne just 54 when the bombs hit. Summer-Rayne had left behind a daughter, Paige-Rose, who was now living in Australia with her husband and two daughters, Anne who was four years old and Crystal who had just been born. Paige-Rose however, would also fall to a similar fate just twelve years later. But instead of her body succumbing to the ravages of war, Paige-Rose would suffer the effects of radiation poisoning and eventually die of tropical pneumonia and malnutrition in the far north reaches of Australia. She was just 40 years old. Anne was now the leading matriarch of the Graceline and had charge over her thirteen year old sister. How would they learn the Graceline ways and pass on their knowledge and wisdom at such a young age?

Chapter Thirteen

H er family history had been confronting to say the least. The Graceline women had suffered tremendously over the years and now here she was, in the same age bracket her elder-mother and elder-auntie had been when they had to learn their ways on their own. At least she had them for they then had no-one. The book was handed to Josephine for her to peruse through as the remainder of the box was emptied.

The myriad of fascinating items that Evonne continued to remove from the box was more intriguing then the last. Some of these included a small bell. Anne had explained that the bell was a symbol of femineity and was used to evoke positive energies. Various crystals and stones were revealed that contained old rune markings. Evonne had only known very little of the markings and was unsure of their application. In fact, because of her limited teachings, she had been unsure about a lot of things. She feared that if Dirk had ever found this box it would surely spell the end for her and her daughter.

When the sight of a double edged blade appeared from the box, Josephine immediately thought the worst. She knew her mother was unhappy in her marriage, but she never thought that she could kill someone over it. Josephine had not known much about her mother's training as a Ranger and had found it difficult to understand how she could have been a soldier, but believe in peace and tranquillity at the same time. What she failed to understand is that Rangers also wish for peace, but will also defend it and uphold it. It had been something that Evonne had desired to do. To think otherwise would have resulted in Josephine never being born. So was this meant to be?

Josephine's mind was quickly filling with questions, but these were questions that would only be answered in time. She knew and understood this and would have to wait for her time to come. What she did not realise though, was that she was already learning. Was her father right when he told her everything happened for a reason?

She still had a lot to learn about both her parents and would seek to ask her father at a later time about such things. And what did the tattoo on his arm mean? It was obviously a religious symbol, but she was confused as to how this applied to a soldier. At the hospital during her mother's examination, Josephine had seen the same tattoo imprinted on the inside of her mother's arm as well.

Evonne had been careful to conceal all this from Dirk all those years as she was enslaved to him and under his control. It had been another one of his demands to have the tattoo removed, but Evonne would not have it surgically done. Her faith and commitment was still as strong as ever to the Ranger Corps, no matter how much she had strayed from it during recent times.

The knife was handed to Josephine and Anne explained that this was no ordinary knife. This was not the instrument to be used in anger or violence. The handle of the blade was quite decorative upon closer look and the blade dull to the touch. Anne called the blade an Athame and said it was used for directing energy during ceremonies. Her mother had tried, sometimes in vain by all accounts, to ward off her husband's evil temperament. But maybe at last, she had actually succeeded. As Ashleigh and Crystal had always said, these things happen for a reason. Was it Evonne's doing that put thought into plan and plan into motion that bought Ashleigh to their rescue?

There were so many strange items that had come from the box, but there was also still so many more to follow. Josephine started to realise and understand that as each item was explained to her, she too would someday have to learn all this. She had missed so much already. Training usually begins after the time of spotting in a young girl's life where the female form is ready to create the gift of life. The pressure and overwhelming sensation gripped her as some of this was at last starting to sound familiar to her.

As she listened to her elders speak, she continued turning the pages of the book; each contained what appeared to be incantations and information about various gods and goddesses. They had all been entered in different hand writing; obviously by the book's many previous owners. There were scratchings of writings and drawn pictures and diagrams of cooking directions and rhymes. The notebook also contained pressed flowers and herbs. Suddenly she stopped turning the pages when she came across one particular page that contained words she recognised. These were words familiar to her, words that she had heard before but thought them to be from a dream.

'I invoke thee, Aradia, goddess of protection and healing, protect me from all attacks, now and forever.'

Anne nodded towards Crystal indicating that this one would be for her to explain. But Josephine, being a quick study, already knew the answer when the remainder of the box was emptied. Photographs of her and her mother, blue and white candles, essential oils, sage, acacia leaves and tourmaline stones just to name a few. She referred back to the book and saw that this was the listed ingredients. This was obviously a spell that Evonne had recited over her bed while she slept in order to protect her from evil people. Evonne had replaced the word 'me' with 'Josephine'. But as Crystal explained, the spell is only effective by one who is reciting it for themselves, not for others.

There may have been some truth in her words, but Evonne had felt that it had worked from time to time. Maybe it had and maybe it hadn't. Maybe the vile and evil attacks from her husband Dirk, were sometimes thwarted. It was hard to tell at the time because of his sporadic behaviour.

But consider being a young runaway, away from home for the very first time on her own, away for six months and on the road. Consider a young and attractive girl who could appear older than her years. Consider this girl has been hidden from the realities of the real world and therefore know very little of it and its dangers. Now consider that nothing extremely terrible actually happened to her. The question remains, did it work? Both Josephine and Evonne had thought it must have.

Sure, Josephine was surrounded by lowlife scum, drugs and violence. Sure there was an attempted rape against her, but that failed. There is no evidence to prove that she had been sexually assaulted at all, not even once. Was Marty's inability to commit coitus hindered by the herorain or was he stopped by her mother's magick? Much of which she didn't know herself.

'What's this?'

Anne had picked up the last item in the box, a vile which contained a blue illuminescent liquid. She had not seen such liquid since her elder-parent, Summer-Rayne, had been alive. And then it had only been in conversations with her great elder-parent Diana. Anne, now angry and worried at the same time, quickly recognised the substance and warned Evonne of its consequences. Only one with years of experience and teachings knew how to manipulate the liquid. For anyone to use the liquid would be unwise, and at worst case, could be fatal. Evonne made no apologies as she believed her actions to be correct at the time.

'How long have you been taking this daughter?'

Crystal also knew of its dangers and stressed caution with its application. Josephine was anxious to know what it was and what on Terran Earth they were talking about. Suddenly she realised when she glanced down and had seen the page that had been opened in the book.

'To sun and moon, through day and night, fire, aqua, wind, and terra.
Thy spirit guide my heart's desire for thy soul's rebirth from afterlife.
Live now and let these tears of hope wash away all kinds' of anger and not fight ever.
Let Lacrimis Speiv heed my way and guide thy light with Athame thy knife.
Hope brings life and lifeblood's energy through thy will and compassion.
Let Jovis forgive Caput, and let Aequreus and Labos unite.
Titan among us have Medius return, for thy balance and peace with all enthusiasm.
For Proletarius no longer serve any and all, and be no more hidden from sight.
Pietas, Sophia and Carman of life, death and rebirth, have thy Lacrimis Speiv to ration.
Bring Lacrimis Speiv, share Lacrimis Speiv, partake of Lacrimis Speiv, and
bring back Titan to protect.
Show by divine light.'

What did all that mean and what was Lacrimis Speiv? These names used, who were they? Were they more gods and goddesses of their faith? But they weren't mentioned anywhere else within the book except for here. The 'Lacrimis Speiv', Anne explained, was an ancient term used to refer to the 'Tears of hope'. But even she did not fully understand its meaning and never dabbled in such things, neither did Crystal for that matter. It had only been that Evonne had read the passage in the book and considered it to either be dangerous or helpful. Seeing that that there was no other information in the book about it, except for how to produce the Lacrimis Speiv, she had banked on the latter.

The Lacrimis Speiv was said to have been a potion sent by the three goddesses of Pietas, Sophia and Carman. Although, who these Goddesses were, had been anyone's guess. The making of such a thing was dangerous just in itself, let alone the actual taking of. One had to collect the poisonous rains of the Darkness and then distil the liquid in order to produce the correct amount. Too little and the Lacrimis Speiv would be useless, too much and the Lacrimis Speiv would contain too much of the Darkness rain and would therefore be poisonous. It was a great gamble Evonne had taken, but she thought the cost outweighed the potential good. Said with the right words and the Lacrimis Speiv could be their salvation.

With that, Evonne decided to make and take the Lacrimis Speiv. She was desperate to rid herself from Dirk's anger and violence, so she took it herself and laced Josephine's food and drink with it. All in the room were shocked by this revelation including Josephine. How could her mother give her a substance without telling her? That wasn't right, plus the untold effects it could have on the young. But what was even more worrying was, that she had been taking it while being pregnant with the twins. No male had ever taken the Lacrimis Speiv to their knowledge, what effect would this have on the boys?

Evonne had obviously made mistakes, but what else could she do? If Evonne was going to relearn the ways of the Graceline and if she was to regain her independence and freedom from all fear, she would need the assistance of both these elders. Anne and Crystal agreed that together they would lead them into the direction of light and hope. But first things are first. Evonne no longer needed to take the Lacrimis Speiv and there was also the matter of the house; Dirk's centre of evil.

During Evonne's stay in hospital, Anne and Crystal had let themselves into the house and started removing the presence of all evil. Everything that Dirk owned was boxed up and sent to his parents' home in the outer suburbs of Sydneyton. His forbearers once hailing from Holland, now also call Oceania home. During the later parts of the War of the

Great Despair, swarms of Dutch children were sent to the southern continents to escape the ravages of war torn Europe.

Dirks father Daan Van den Berg and his mother and Emma Heidermann were just infants when they were sent to Australia on their own. Years later, Daan and Emma met while in their early twenties and Dirk was born three years later. It was just as well for Dirk's sake that his parents were forced to flee their homeland because the birthplace of his elder-parents finally succumbed to the coming of the Darkness and is now deep under sea level from the rising of the oceans.

Anne and Crystal had started their cleansing once the SDP had finished collecting all their evidence. They needed to wash away all impurities. Josephine learned quickly and lent assistance to the task. Quite often she had started of her own accord and without guidance. It was almost as if she knew what to do despite her years of isolation. Something inside her told her what was required, and so she just got on with it. They had hoped to be finished by the time Evonne returned home but had unfortunately missed one room. The very room they had entered right at the start.

—ᗰ— ⳇ —ᗰ—

At last they were alone, Jeremy and Damian were fast asleep in their cribs and Ashleigh had just sat down to open a bottle of wine. He would share this with Evonne and Josephine, but only one glass for his daughter. He had said it was a special time to sit and reflect and that Josephine was now a young lady. She had endured hardships and every challenge thrown at her. Throughout it all she has shown courage, strength and integrity. Many of his and Evonne's sworn creed. Josephine had earned this.

This was it, at last it had all come true. The stories she was told as a child, her mother's protection, and the truth of it all was out. It was such a strange feeling, here they were, Ashleigh, Evonne, and Josephine all together in one place on their own. Josephine could not hide her excitement and she leaped up from her chair and gave both parents a kiss and a huge cuddle. Her family, her real family were together at last.

There was an unearthly silence as Josephine pulled away.

Evonne looked at the man she once loved and still loves now. It was the same look of grimaced happiness she had given him the first time he left her. She knew as she did then that they could never really be together, but she was still happy to just have him by her side once more. Josephine too understood the situation, as the realisation came to her that he had a family waiting for him back in Queenstown. A family which has only seen him about two weeks since his return from the AN Territories. A place he is due to return to in just under twelve months.

There was no way that Josephine could deny this or be angry with any of it. She had come to love and respect Siobhan, for it was she who offered the olive branch of friendship and caring. His own children needed their father just as much as she needed him now.

'Do you still love me as you told me that day you came to save us?'

He recalled that yes he had actually said those words to Evonne when Dirk was finally apprehended. He did of course love her, but he explained that it could never be any more than the love a brother has for a sister, or that of which a child loves their father or any member of the family for that matter. She knew this to be true but it didn't stop her mind racing with thoughts of what could have been. It had been a very emotional ride up until now and she finally had a chance to sit in her own home with her feet up without the fear of Dirk bursting in and hitting her.

The three of them remained on the couch, the glow of electronic candles flickered around them and the wine was an excellent vintage, a 1990 from the Barossa Valley to be precise. Dirk was at least good at one thing. He had an excellent pallet when it came to fine wines and the cellar was stocked to the brim. As the night wore on, Josephine closed her eyes and curled on the couch next to her father with Evonne resting her head on his other shoulder.

'Look at what we did. She may have been born out of sin, but she is our angel. She has done very well for herself.'

Ashleigh agreed with Evonne that yes she was definitely special.

Crack! The house sounded like it was coming down around them. Crack! Again and this time they saw a flash of bright blue light and sparks fly. As he woke from the ear penetrating sounds that seemed to be right on top of them, he noticed Josephine was no longer by his side. Evonne immediately wrapped her arms around her man with a look of fear in her eyes as he reached for his weapon. His weapon he thought. He didn't have it. Where was it? Crack! This time the few lights that were still left on, had now all gone out. The house and the street was in a complete darkness and Evonne ran to the twin's room grabbing them both, one under each arm.

They hadn't seen weather like this for quite a few years in Melbourne. Up north in Queenstown and further still closer to the equator, it had been somewhat normal, but not usually this loud or violent. However, this type of weather here in Melbourne was a scarce rarity. Lighting shot down from the sky at breakneck speed with such veracity and purpose. The dust clouds of the Darkness engulfed the entire city and the Terran Division Emergency Services were called out from all locations. His weapon, that's right, he had put it in the cupboard above the fridge, out of harms reach and the little hands which may find its deadly resolve. But it wasn't there either and there was still no sign of Josephine.

'Pheenie, where are you?'

He hadn't held this type of panic since his first experience to war. Back then his fear had surfaced on the eve of his first major engagement with RFN Rebels during the Terran Wars. That was the first time he lost fellow Rangers to enemy action.

'Daddy, I'm in here.'

A sigh of relief was felt by both he and Evonne. After everything that has happened, he couldn't lose her now. She was at the front door holding his 9mm Beretta. She explained that she had woken up during the middle of the night and had looked at her mother and father sleeping peacefully next to each other. She had wanted to preserve the moment and so reached for his service weapon to watch over, and protect them. Dirk had been released on bail and could be capable of anything. He told her the thought was appreciated but it was he that should be the paranoid one, not her. His paranoia however, was more calculated due to his years of experience and more often than not, found to be substantiated.

Ashleigh peered through the curtains and outside into the street. The SDP Officers were still at their posts. Their dedication to duty and to their task was above reproach. The Darkness storm lasted for three days and three nights, at which time, no-one was allowed to leave the safety of their homes. Only Terran Division Emergency Services and the OTD military forces could venture out into this kind of weather. All knew of the damaging effects these storms could have and also knew how long they could last for. Therefore, most residents were well supplied by their prior preparations for such an event.

Gradually the Darkness storm dissipated but not before creating an eerie deathly silence. Ashleigh climbed into his PARTNAR Suit and ventured outside. The sky was a mass of thick swirling dust and vapour clouds with streaks of blue and green tinges and shadowy effects throughout. Then a hole opened up above him in the sky as the dust clouds began to fade. Ashleigh removed his hood and mask to let the sun's rays be again felt upon his skin.

The Darkness storm was over and it had been a bad one. Some houses in the street had been struck by lightning and were now in a fiery rubble burning out of control. Coincidence or not, but the houses that had been struck, were ones belonging to close friends and supporters of Dirk. Dirk he thought, this would be a perfect opportunity to succeed in seeking vengeance. As he said those words, he once again scanned the area for the two SDP Officers. This time they were nowhere to be found and he rushed back inside to see where Evonne and the children were.

Service weapon drawn and at the ready, he proceeded back into the house to find they were gone. This time he did not yell out for their names. Instead he quietly searched the rooms where they had been. There was no sight of them and he continued moving through the house, room by room. Wait, stop, could he see the silhouette of a person? His eyes were generally good in the dark due to his past experiences as a Ranger Scout, but not as good as his Ugbee counterparts. He had trained them to adjust very fast in varying light conditions. But he still wished he had his mini NVGs.

'Don't shoot.'

The words whispered quietly and coming from one of the SDP Officers.

'My partners been killed, sliced open with some kind of sword.'

Sword? A look of concern filled his expression and the features of his face. These had been the favoured weapon of choice for a special outfit of the RFN during the Terran Wars, used in close quarter combat. They were stealthy and very effective. People wielding these swords could gain entry and egress from secured areas and quietly achieve their deadly mission without being noticed. But these swords had been abolished, it was now illegal to carry or own these weapons.

Where were they? The two of them continued to search the house when suddenly the power was restored and the lights came back on.

If anyone was hiding in the shadows, it would be bad luck for them now. With his vision and focus returning to him faster than that of the SDP Officer, he sighted a torn part of Josephine's dress that Siobhan had bought her prior to leaving Queenstown resting on the floor.

However, he did not panic at the sight of this, the time for that was over. He was now in full Ranger mode, professional and precise with every calm step and decision he made. He was an excellent marksman and could react very quickly in aiming and firing his service weapon in any direction, and hitting his target.

'Wait! Stop! Don't!'

Evonne had warned him not to shoot when suddenly there came a loud noise of the sound of crashing furniture and fittings as they fell to the ground. The activity of all this commotion had come from behind him as a figure in a dark outfit fled the house going out the front door. However, it had been the mysterious figure who had pushed Evonne out into the furniture in order to create a diversion.

The dark figure had hoped that the noise would incite Ashleigh or the SDP Officer to fire their service weapons at Evonne instead of him or her or whoever the stranger was. Ashleigh had been in similar situations before and knew exactly how to handle the moment. Much to his pleasant surprise, so did the SDP Officer and instead of shooting, he took after the assailant on foot.

Here was Evonne, but where were the rest of them? Evonne explained to Ashleigh that she had told Josephine to look after the twins and hide from danger, meanwhile she would create a distraction and be the bait. She refused to be a passenger and take the back seat any longer in her life. She decided that she would take an active part in the events that shaped her life, an active part where she was in control, not someone else. Her plan had been to reach Ashleigh quietly and without being seen. She had hoped to do this in time to stop the intruder from causing any harm, but she had been found and now her life was once again at risk. Much better her own than that of her children. She would do anything to protect them.

As much as Ashleigh had wanted to know the identity of who the mysterious person was, his main concern was the safety and well-being of Josephine and the boys. He would let the SDP Officer deal with the hidden figure.

'Pheenie, it's ok, you can come out.'

Josephine knew that her father would not just be saying these words under duress, but would be saying it because it was true. They revealed themselves from a small closet that had a false back built into it. Her mother didn't even know this existed. It had been crafted by Josephine when she was about ten years old and was a place of solitude and sanctuary. Josephine often hid in this small cavity to escape all the violence and rage of Dirk's fury. Sometimes she would stay in this space for hours, crying with fear until she fell asleep. There was no need to keep this place a secret anymore and she stepped out with the boys.

When the SDP officer re-appeared, he explained that he couldn't run down the intruder, he was just too fast. It was clear that his partner was dead and upon closer inspection, Ashleigh confirmed that the killing had all the hallmark traits of an RFN Black Ops Rebel. Something that concerned him greatly. This type of assault has not been seen since the end of the Terran Wars. Usually if there was one Black Ops member, there would be more and he decided to inform the Oceania South East Group high command of the OTD; this would be the Australian Command Headquarters or simply AusCom HQ. These events in his life were no longer a personal matter, the revelation of a Black Ops Rebel posed a threat to the Federal security of the UFTN itself.

The next day, Dirk was again under arrest and bought in for questioning. Had it been he who attacked them last night? If it had, he could now add murder to his list of charges. It would be an ill-conceived plan of his if indeed he had. Even if it wasn't him that actually committed the murder, but was rather the orchestrator of it, murder carries a severe punishment of life in the mines. Although it wasn't the death penalty, it was considered as much, as people who were sent there either died in captivity or were killed trying to escape.

Whoever it may have been, it couldn't be proven that Dirk had anything to do with it and he was once again released on bail. The house and the society Evonne was living in was just not the place to be for her recovery and self-healing. This environment was negative and it only served to hinder her self-rediscovery. She would finally heed the words of her mother and go live with her.

Chapter Fourteen

The trial was set for two weeks' time and the 35th Christmas Union was only days away. Ashleigh was desperate to spend the Christmas Union with Siobhan and their children, but he made a promise to Evonne that he would not leave her until Dirk was behind bars. He had missed Christmas Unions before with his family and would chalk this one up as another.

But no, not this time, he wouldn't, he wanted this year to be special. If he couldn't return to Queenstown to be with his family then he would bring Queenstown to him, well at least his family that is. It was also abundantly clear that the initial two week furlough he had previously requested would not be enough. This time he would request an open ended extended leave, one in which he gratefully received. He was committed and needed to see this to its conclusion.

Crystal agreed that they could all stay at her home on the beach front. Her house was a classic Victorian era double story building that had survived the ravages of all the years it beheld, and most recently that of the coming of the Darkness. It had been, of course, restored over the years as each owner passed their way through this life. But as this home was reborn time and time again, it had lost none of its charm. Once situated inland by about 200km and residing on the south side of a ridge, this seven bedroom home was now only a couple of hundred meters from the coastal water line due to the rising of the ocean.

Ashleigh had thought the idea to be sound and had initially agreed with Crystal from the start as to where Evonne and the children should now live. Crystal's home was perfect for him, it was secluded and easily defendable. It would also be a great location for all them to unwind and relax as well. Upon arrival, Ashleigh concerned himself with matters of defence and security for the safety of his charges. Evonne insisted on assisting him with this task. This was part of her re-emergence from her years of servitude; she needed to get back into the game. From that point onwards, he would see her return to her glorious past self by involving her in all decision making and active work.

What a strange turn of events that have unfolded? Here they were on Christmas Union celebrating this holiest of holy days and the day of the founding of the UFTN. They all sat around a huge antique dining table crafted from Tasmanian Oak and enjoyed the delights of a traditional Christmas Union luncheon. What they feasted on that day was possibly the best meal any of them had tasted for quite some time. It was remarkable, Crystal's cooking just seem to get better and better with time.

Siobhan and the children had never met Crystal before and were fascinated by the décor of her home wears. Pentacles hanging down from windows, three nails deceivingly hammered into door frames and the smell of incense burning throughout the house amongst other things. These were the sights and smells that none of them had ever experienced before. It was quite different from their own home being bought up on the Catholic faith and the ways of the Ranger Corps. Although Ashleigh was the Ranger, he installed the Ranger Creed and ideals into his children. One of the most important ideals was the acceptance of others. It was the same for Crystal and her brood.

Everybody seemed to get along really well, especially the children. EJ loved the fact that she was no longer the only girl in the family; she had a sister, albeit from another mother. The two of them immediately found common ground and their friendship and love towards one another was without comparison. But this was the ways of the women in Evonne's family. Their nurturing and protective nature were prominent in every generation. It came natural to them. This had also created a bond between the two women at the centre of Ashleigh's life.

Evonne thanked Siobhan for the way she looked after Josephine in her short stay with her. Josephine had told her mother how much she looked up to and admired Siobhan since meeting her. Siobhan would also return the mutual admiration and feelings. The events of fifteen years ago were pushed aside as they all learned to accept life for what it was. It may have been the calming effect of their surroundings or the years that past that had made them all more understanding and considerate. Either way, it had been one of the most joyous Christmas Unions that any of them had forgone in decades.

For one day, all their immediate problems and fears were washed away. The thought of all the past evils emanating from Dirk and the coming of his trial along with Ashleigh's coming return to the AN Uprising, were all but forgotten. That evening, Anne and Crystal along with Evonne and Josephine, secretly blessed both families and prayed to the goddesses for their continued protection. It had been some time since three generations of Graceline women all stood together as one in the circle of trust and unity. Now Josephine was learning what it was all about.

However, their power to evoke the goddesses had felt a little off this evening. Something wasn't quite right and the women feared the uncertainty of its aura. Evonne and Josephine had felt it too, but due their lack of training failed to understand its meaning. However, Anne and Crystal knew exactly what it had meant. The women in these families were still not safe, including Siobhan and EJ. They couldn't be sure of how or when or by what, but they did know that one, possibly two would soon suffer a great pain one day and perish.

Anne and Crystal decided to keep this fact to themselves as Evonne and Josephine had enough to contend with. As they were also novices, they didn't have the Wiccan maturity to deal with such knowledge and power. This would only come with time.

With everyone now fast asleep, Ashleigh checked out the last of the sensors he had placed out earlier that day and crawled into bed beside his wife. He was so happy to be back in her arms and staring once again into her brown coloured eyes. Just as everyone else had felt safe in his arms or in his presence, he only ever felt safe in the arms of his wife. It had been that way since they first met and it had been the thoughts of her that had him succeed and remain safe during his time in the Terran Wars, and again during the AN Uprising.

The hour had just clicked over to 3am in the morning when Ashleigh's phone started ringing. The Detective from the SDP had called to inform him of the results from an autopsy conducted on the fallen SDP officer, and that these results had yielded some strange findings. Because of his knowledge and past experience with the RFN Black Ops, he was asked to view the findings. He was far too distant from the city to travel in, so instead he excused himself and went into another room that had contained a VIDCom unit. Locking the door behind him, he inserted his FCR identity encryption chip. This would be a secure connection.

Their questions had revolved around the way the fallen SDP Officer's body had been cut by the sword. The cuts were obviously made with the skill and precision of a Black Ops member, but it was the residue left behind that sparked their interest. Under the gamma light, the residue reacted as if it were alive.

Quarantine the area immediately and call a city wide contamination lock down. NOW!'

He had not considered this at the time of the officer's death, but it stood to reason that if a sword was used in the way of an RFN Black Ops specialist, that this would be the result. Evonne and Josephine had affected him in more ways than he had realised, blurring his judgment and commonly clear thought. He looked at the image of Saint Michael the Archangel on his forearm. His professional way of business had been over shadowed by his thoughts for Evonne's and Josephine's safety and possibly more on a subconscious level. He would never forgive himself if others died because of his oversight. Saint Michael he thought, I am supposed to protect the people, not be the cause of more harm.

The examiners did what they were told. By now the women in the house had all awoken to a sense of despair and the presence of ill will in the house. Ashleigh informed everyone that he had to travel into Melbourne to follow up on a few questions the SDP had. He would not tell them what was really going on as he did not want to worry them.

Although the truth of it would horrify them, it would only be Siobhan who knew and understood the full extent of what this meant. She had been with her husband when he had returned from the Terran Wars. She had slept beside him as he woke in cold sweats and screaming in terrifying pain from the nightmares of what he had been witness to. Ashleigh would eventually tell her everything about the war.

How terrible had this been in its time and who could have thought of such a way to kill? If it still existed now, more would surely die. A complete quarantine zone was now in place around the entire city of Melbourne. The OTD Military Forces had deployed and were in full control by the time he reached the city. Soldiers in specially modified PARTNAR suits, not seen since the Terran Wars, now filled the streets and ushered people into temporary mobile medical stations to be cleared from infection. Once confirmed as posing no threat, the people were rushed to waiting helicopters to be airlifted out of the danger zone. It was the only way to be sure. Driving was out of the question for fear of coming into contact with potentially infected persons.

Ashleigh was granted access through to the autopsy room where he met and greeted his long-time friend, Chris Parker. They had gone through basic together and had served side by side in every theatre of conflict until recently. While Ashleigh still belonged to the enlisted ranks and holding the rank of Chief Master Sergeant, Chris had been commissioned and now outranked him as a Captain. Despite this, they were still the very best of friends. There had been quite a few times where they had each come to the other's aid. They quite literally owed their lives to the other. But that was all part of the job and one they accepted and never spoke of.

Chris asked him how a man that was holding such a dangerous weapon had come to be involved in his personal life. All the biological chemicals and agents from that time had been found and destroyed, so how was it possible that some of it still existed? And was there more? It had to be Dirk he explained. It was the only possible answer to all of this. But why hadn't he killed Evonne when he had the chance?

'Chris I need a team sent to the coast, I think Evee may have been exposed.'

He proceeded to inform Chris of the last few days and the events of two nights ago. But it had been past 24 hours, if she had been exposed, she would have been dead by now. No doubt about it. Ashleigh examined the corpse and the area under the gamma light. It was as he suspected, Xialm. Chris escorted his friend into another room where medical professionals along with Major General Paterson and his staff from the OTD AusCom HQ were waiting. They had all been seated around a large conference table.

Ashleigh had not been bought in for questioning as an accused, but rather for his involvement and the information he may contain which could assist in their investigations. The Xialm had been developed by the RFN during the latter stages of the Terran Wars in an attempt to turn the tide back into their favour.

Designed and developed by Doctor Freesensuede, Xialm is produced by the bacteria necrotizing fasciitis and mutated by the effects of the Darkness rain. The result is a biological flesh eating living bacteria that is transmitted via blood and through the skin. Those infected would normally suffer an agonising death as their body was slowly taken away from them, being eaten as they still breathed air. Many were euthanized and died within 24 hours of becoming infected.

RFN Black Ops Rebels would lace the blades of their swords with the deadly contagion so that when the bodies of their victims were recovered, the contagion would spread. The plan by the RFN was that for every UFTN soldier killed by the sword, many more would die by the Xialm at the medical aid stations and body collection points.

The RFN new that UFTN soldiers always recovered their people, dead or alive, no matter what. It had caused such a panic at the time and more than 27 million people died as a result of Xialm, many of which were innocent civilians. How could such a thing have happened in the light of the War of the Great Despair? Hadn't people learned the lessons of the past?

As they left the conference and made their way out of the hospital, they passed a room where victims were already starting to pile up. At last count, ten were dead and another thirteen confirmed as infected. The only way to stop the contagion was to cut it out. That meant having limbs removed, but this had very little success. The Xialm travels through the blood stream and within four hours would be in every corner of the body. If people were to survive this, it meant that they had four hours to confirm infection, find and isolate the infection and cut off the offending area.

Ashleigh decided to give Crystal a call so he could speak to his wife.

'Ash, a Central Division Medical team arrived and started testing Evonne. Is it the Xialm?'

He answered his wife yes and a cold terrifying shiver crept all the way down her spine from top to bottom. Ashleigh asked Siobhan if he could speak to the doctor on site. Tests were usually confirmed as either positive or negative within about five minutes, he wanted to rest his mind at ease. They were indeed negative, as too were the rest of Evonne's and his families. He told his wife that souls had already perished to this. He would remain in the city until it was clear and he knew that his family and Evonne would all be safe under the protection of Anne and Crystal. He was now on duty and back in uniform.

Their investigations had again led to Dirk's arrest. This time he was being questioned by the OTD instead of the SDP as it was now considered a crime against humanity and came under the war crimes act. Ashleigh himself would be leading the interrogation along with Chris. Rangers had a special way of persuasion and getting those they questioned to divulge information. It was only a short time before Dirk's case would be heard by a Judge of the UFTN Council of Elders. Ashleigh and Chris would hope to add murder and humanitarian crimes to the count.

It was now four days after the initial outbreak with no new cases being recorded in the last 24 hours. This was a good sign that the contagion had run its course, but there was still the unknown question of where it had come from and did more exist. 48 hours later and the city was declared a safe zone again. People were allowed to return to their homes and places of business.

Xialm and the perpetrator of such an atrocity had claimed the lives of thirty-three Oceanic citizens. It was a good result considering; from past experiences the count could have been far greater, plus they had also contained it to Melbourne thus stopping it going worldwide. This had been the result of one man initially being infected. Had more suffered the fate of the blade, the numbers would have exponentially compounded.

Over the course of Dirk's questioning, little snippets of information, a word here, a phrase there, indicated that he knew of the inner workings of the RFN. Though he never actually stated as much. He was very well versed in subterfuge and deflecting questions. He had obviously received training and everything was pointing at Dirk being an RFN Black Ops Rebel in his past life. The only thing now was to obtain concrete proof. The UFTN did not believe in the death penalty and the Council of Elders that governed and who passed down such laws and judgment, would require solid uncompromising fact if they were to pass sentence and administer the severest of penalties.

There were the mines and other such work camps around the world, but there were levels within these camps that escalated in severity. Their ideal was based on the fact that if a citizen did not want to contribute to society by their acts of violence, then they would be forced to, thus forfeiting their right to freedom. In a world based on unity and peace, all served one cause. To prosper through knowledge and wisdom.

They knew that time was running short, answers needed to be found and quick. Ashleigh suggested that they search his house again. Although it had already been searched by the various departments of the SDP, as their investigation had evolved from physical assault to the murder of one of their own. Ashleigh and Chris had both searched buildings and homes of suspected insurgents during the Terran Wars and knew the signs to look for. This house was vast, it contained twenty seven separate rooms.

It hadn't occurred to Ashleigh to search the house when he had stayed there with Evonne, but now he held suspicions that more could be found just under the surface.

He now bought into question that even on Dirk's income as a high profile lawyer and on the verge of entering the Council of Elders, he could not possibly afford this house or the area he had been living in. Dirk had been that well placed within the firm that he was in fact being primed as an elder and would gain such an honour on his fiftieth birthday, just twelve years from now.

There must have been others assisting him. Was he really having an affair with a woman in Sydneyton going by the name of Wanda-Mae Bell, or was this just a cover he created to overt others from the real truth. Ashleigh surmised that he had allowed Evonne to catch him and listen in on his conversation so as to deflect her from other thoughts. In her emotional and depressive state, she would believe in the lie without question.

The OTD military were soon knocking on the door of his so called lover in Sydneyton to bring her in for questioning. Her house would also be searched. The other piece of the puzzle resided with Dirk's good friend and neighbour, an Ugbee citizen going by the name of Emerson Harris. He had remained the only one of all his neighbours' to remain defiant against the SDP and still stuck by his friend Dirk. Was he too part of what was becoming a sleeper sect, and was it the goal of this sect to gain entry into one of the most powerful organisations on the planet? The Council of Elders? Which only stood second in ranking to the Consortium of Trust.

The task was underway and OTD Military Forces surged into Dirk's home and the residences of both Wanda-Mae's in Sydneyton and Emerson's in Melbourne. This included any other persons of interest who had ties with these three key individuals. It was a coordinated raid which proved to be fruitful. Writings and manuscripts were found in all three locations.

These contained the teachings and beliefs of Richard Henning, the founder and leader of the True Peoples of Trust, an opposing organisation to the Consortium of Trust and the orchestrator of the Republic of Free Nations.

Biological laboratories for the production of Xialm were found at the homes of Wanda-Mae and in an underground secret chamber of Dirk's home. There was very little of the substance that remained and it was quickly taken away and destroyed. The evidence they had would have to come from the testimonies of Federal Continental Rangers, their truth held sacred. Photographic proof would also be entered as evidence and archived for the records. The Xialm was just too dangerous to be stored in a quarantined safe lockup and used as physical evidence later. They had their proof at last and to cap it all off, the offending weapon was found. This sword would serve as another key piece of evidence in the conviction and sentencing of Dirk and his comrades.

A further five more people were arrested and convicted as sleeper RFN agents. The conclusion of their findings detailed that the sect was isolated in its origin as it was the only one of its kind in existence. Emerson had garnished idealistic dreams and intensions of raising the RFN back to its former glory. Misconceived and ill thought out plans painted a picture of a man that was cleverly insane.

Emerson could portray the image of a well-educated man who was caring and devoted to his family, but behind this laid the seeds of cruelty and sinister intent. His wife and two older boys were key members of the sect and when he learned of Dirks past as a member of the RFN Black Ops, he drew him into his fanciful wild plans.

It was revealed during the hearing that Emerson had assumed a fake identity and was actually a Kommandar Brigadier General in the RFN wanted for war crimes of mass murder to civilians and POWs. In those days, he went by the name of Emery Horus. It had been revealed during the trial that it had been he who attacked them that night and was he who had killed the SDP Officer with Dirk's sword. A sword which he laced with Xialm. Because Emery was a native of the northern hemisphere being born an Ugbee from the Eurpasian Islands, he had the natural ability to stalk around in complete darkness. Dirk was under constant surveillance and Emery would lend his aid to his protégé.

In all, eight people were found guilty and all were sentenced to serve the remainder of their lives in the mines of Western Australia as punishment. The levels of punishment were varied, as Dirk, Emery and Wanda-Mae received the worst of it. Evonne was amazed about how blind she had been all these years not to know that this was happening under her very roof. How could a Ranger trained as an ISR specialist miss the signs? Dirk had achieved great strength over her and possessed the power of suggestion. She would have believed anything he said, but not now and at last she was finally seeing the light of this as her confidence was quickly returning.

She now knew what Wanda-Mae and her associates were, they were terrorists clear and simple, but behind every lie held a touch of truth. Once Dirk had been accepted into the Council of Elders, his plan was to take the twins and be joined with Wanda-Mae. The plans he held in store for Evonne and Josephine however, were much darker. They would simply disappear without a trace, but all that had changed and their plans undone. She looked up to Father Sky and as she felt the light shining down its beaming rays of hope and grace, she once again held the self-belief that she could achieve and do anything. It would still be a long road to recovery, but at least now she had made a start.

Their ordeal was now over and they could all move on with their lives. The much thought of a holiday was now theirs for the taking. But as much as Evonne wanted to share with them this holiday, she would give Ashleigh back to his wife. It wouldn't be fair on Siobhan if she was to tag along. Evonne suggested that the holiday might be a good time to get to know his new daughter and for Josephine to do the same with her real father. She would have two families now and two mothers. Siobhan agreed and said that it was a great idea. Meanwhile, Evonne would stay with Crystal and Anne to catch up on all the training she has missed out on.

But before all went their separate ways, Evonne would collect the last of her things from her previous home and put the house up for sale. She never wanted to see that place again. Ashleigh had kept true to his word, he had remained level headed and purposely minded. He had not taken matters into his own hands until it was called for and Dirk was sentenced to life in the mines. He, Siobhan and family would spend another week with his parents and Andrew before returning to Queenstown to plan out their holiday.

Chapter Fifteen

A shleigh was about to leave for the AN Territories when he received orders from OTD AusCom HQ. In the period he had been away from the AN Territories, a lot had changed. The signing of a new peace accord looked very likely within the next couple of months. Concessions were being sort on both sides and the AN Territories appeared that it would at last sign the charter granting their admission into the UFTN as the sixth Territorial Division.

However, there were still hard line radicals who would stop at nothing to thwart the peace process. Because of this and because of Ashleigh's current skills and recent commission to Captain, he would be part of a new OTD Group being formed in South Africa. This was to be the Federal Continental Ranger Airborne Division.

Eleven months had passed since Evonne's mad husband had been convicted and punished. During this time, Evonne had developed into a Graceline Proficient, capable of guiding and teaching her own daughter in their ways. Both families now knew each other very well by now, but it had still been difficult for Josephine to spend time with her father because of distance. However, she was much better versed in the ways of both her parents now.

Upon hearing that Ashleigh would remain in the Oceania South West Group of the OTD after the AN Uprising was eventually put down, Evonne stressed concerns about continued relationships. Ashleigh suggested that she and Josephine come and live with them in Pretoria, South Africa. Siobhan was also agreeable to this suggestion and they were soon off for a new life.

Crystal had advised against such a move believing her daughter was placing too much reliance on Ashleigh. How was she to continue her re-emergence and independence around a man that had always protected her? The other reason she didn't want her daughter and twice-daughter leaving was because of self-want. She had lost years of family quality time due to the controlling power of Dirk and now she had it back, had not wanted to lose it. It meant that she would now be separated from the both of them. But Evonne explained to her mother that Josephine's relationship with her father came first, besides, she could always visit them in Pretoria.

Siobhan, on the other hand was excited to go, she hadn't seen two of her three brothers for such a long time. It would be good to catch up with them again. Her brothers would also be the source of their protection in the event they required it while Ashleigh was away. Deaglan and Sean Kelly were SDP Detectives assigned to the Oceania South West Group.

Deaglan was only two years her junior while Sean had been the baby of the family, being eight years younger. She still remembers when she was seventeen and first started dating Ashleigh, Sean would follow them everywhere. Out of all of Siobhan's brothers, Sean had been the closest to her husband. Ashleigh had often treated him as a third brother to himself and the two of them would support each other unquestioningly and unconditionally.

With a month prior to his return to the AN Territories, they packed up their belongings and headed off. After arriving, they were driven to a large house on the outskirts of Pretoria; this would be their home for the next three years. The home was ample enough to house all nine of them. Evonne would have one of the two identical master bedrooms to herself. Each was furnished with a king sized double bed, own private ensuite with spa, and large robe spaces for all their clothes and other items. On the lower levels contained a large entertaining area that backed onto the dining room and meals preparation area. Adjacent to the dining room and close to the entry was the family room.

Each of the children would have their own bedrooms. But as time would pass, EJ would find herself sleeping in her sister's bed, as Josephine would tell her bed time stories. Josephine enjoyed having a little sister and she would re-invent the stories her mother told her when she was young about a knight in shining armour. And just as Evonne had done, she too would embellish the story. Gradually, both would fall asleep and that's where they would stay until morning's sunrise.

The time had come for Ashleigh to return to the front lines. Chris had come to collect his friend; both would be headed to the central AN Territories where the last remaining forces of the AN Uprising were based. Although there were still isolated pockets of AN insurgents, the vast organised majority now resided in the Congo. It was a hard thing saying good-bye, this time he had two women to say his farewells to. Siobhan would understand that her husband would say his farewells to Evonne first. Ashleigh placed his hands around her and gave her a big cuddle.

'You're safe here, you are part of this family now. I'll return soon.'

Next it was the children's turn to say good-bye. All were sad to see him leave except that is, for Jeremy. The twins had just celebrated their forth birthday and although still too young, possibly too young to comprehend the situation, Ashleigh always felt a negativity surrounding Jeremy. His last good-bye would be reserved for his wife, Siobhan. The night before they had made love with their usual intensity and passion. For last night, there was no tomorrow, only the moment of then and there.

Now it was the here and now and as with many times before, she accepted the destiny of his calling. Saint Michael would protect him as always, but the cold hard truth was, Rangers died, and sometimes in terrible ways.

As Chris and Ashleigh drove off in their Federal Peace Maker Vehicle, Evonne turned and looked at her house mate. Tears escaping from her eyes. This was the first time that she had ever had to say good-bye to a man that she truly loved and cared deeply for.

'Is this what it feels like every time he goes away?'

Evonne had contained herself while in the presence of Ashleigh, but now that he had left and was out of sight, she had lost all control. As she tried to hold back her tears, she struggled to ask Siobhan that question.

'Yes, now you know Evee. That's exactly what it feels like – every single time. But we stay strong, if not for us, but for them and the children. We tell ourselves that everything will turn out for the best and tell our children that their daddy will returned safe and sound back to us; although, deep down in the pit of our souls, we know that this may not always be the case.'

Siobhan continued to tell her that they both needed to remain on task and focused, not only for Ashleigh, not only for themselves, but for the children as well. With that, Siobhan placed her arms around Evonne and walked her back inside the house.

Ashleigh and Chris parked the Federal Peace Maker Vehicle and made their way into the African Command Headquarters of the Oceania South West Group based in Johannesburg. The Council of Elders at the UFTN Central Command had placed the African Command Headquarters, AfCom HQ, in charge of putting down the AN Uprising. After a short briefing, they re-joined their regiment. Once again and as they had done so many times in their past, they were again serving together, side by side.

The Terran Wars had taken a huge toll on the FCR Corps and there were quite a few new younger faces. Most of the veterans from the previous conflict were now promoted into positions of authority and commanding their own men and women. The Corps virtually had to rebuild itself at the end of the Terran Wars.

Although Chris had already been the Officer Commanding (OC) of his own company, this would be Ashleigh's first time with such a large body of troops. In the past, Ashleigh had mainly operated in, and been in charge of four man teams. In his earlier years he had often operated alone or with Chris by his side. Both were highly trained FCR Scouts. His elder-father had always taught him to put the safety of his men first, for their lives resided in his hands. His own life would be secondary.

Ashleigh would soon find out just how much his elder-father's words would impact on him. Some of these kids were just eighteen and were yet to experience the horror of war and death. And although they would have Saint Michael at their side, they would be looking towards him for guidance and inspiration.

They travelled north via air transport; some would peer out the small windows and see the land waste of previous battles, some still smouldering from the most recent campaigns. All could feel the effects of the sub-tropical weather as they neared their destination. This was nothing new to the Rangers as most had received conditioning training in the far north reaches of Australia and southern parts of India. But it was again another summer and yet again it would prove to be severe.

Electromagnetic particle clouds formed and the Darkness rains soon engulfed their air transport. Turbulence shook the plane from left to right as it sporadically plummeted fifty or so meters before again reaching altitude. The pilot continually struggled to bring the craft back to a safe flying height even with the aid of electronic counter magnetic stabilisers.

As they began their descent, the sounds of gunfire and battle could be heard off into the distance.

'Easy lads.' Ashleigh told them.

'This is nothing new, all in a day's work.'

His Rangers watched and observed as Ashleigh kept a cold steal hardened expression as he walked the length of the inside of the air transport. They looked at him, but he didn't look back. They watched as he maintained focus with determined resolve. The battle they were hearing had been from a minor skirmish on the north side of the Forward Operating Base or FOB. Insurgents had endeavoured to expose a weak spot within the inner defences, but they were pushed back.

'Ok, this is it Rangers, Truth, Strength, Courage, Integrity and Protection of the less fortunate. Let's go!'

With their blood up and adrenalin racing, they all yelled out Saint Michael's name and exited the rear of the air transport. They had literally only seconds to vacate the inner hull of the transport as the pilot would not want to be on the ground longer then what was necessary. The insurgents still maintained an arsenal of munitions and attack from IDF remained a real threat. Air transports were always prime targets for AN insurgents. Only a year ago had one been hit by a Terra to Air Missile or TAM rocket, killing all thirty four occupants as it came into land. Although this was a rare occurrence, the possibility still existed.

His troops took up their positions immediately and assisted in the ground defences of the FOB. Other branches of the Federal Terran Forces controlled by the high command of the UFTN Peace Makers also occupied this and other FOBs within the Area of Operations, known in military terms as the AO. Most notably, the Terran Armoured Carbineers commonly referred to as TACs. These were the conventional troops of the UFTN Peace Makers operating anything from the All-Terrain Light Armoured Vehicles to the All-Terrain Heavy Armoured Vehicles and everything in between. In support were the Terran Logistics and Technical Support Corps who maintained life support systems and equipment.

UFTN forces were made up of contingents sent from the Eurpasian Islands Group, the North Americas Group and the Canaan Group. But AfCom HQ had supreme command and had tasked the special branch of the Federal Terran Force to spearhead the assault on the AN insurgents stronghold of the Congo. Most TACs admired the Rangers, but some thought them to be arrogant and self-righteous because of the mantra they held. It must be noted though that some who thought this had themselves once tried to join the FCR Corps, but had failed in their attempts.

Amongst his own troops, were terran beings from all walks of life: Ucusee, Trap, Ugbee, Asian, and Eurpasian; all. It didn't matter, they were all equal under Saint Michael and that of the UFTN. Soon they bedded in for the night, for the next day would be arduous at best. They had a long march ahead of them and although they would travel in their Light Armoured Tactical Assault Vehicles, the LATAVs couldn't take them all the way. The jungle and sub-tropical environment was just too dense and severe to take the vehicles all the way in. They would travel to a designated staging area of de-embarkation point where the TACs would stand guard over the vehicles and heavy equipment until the Rangers returned.

They had now reached their first staging area at FOB 32B. It was now 11 o'clock at night and he had received his orders for the coming day's task. He was about to bed in for the night when he decided he would VIDCom home and talk to his wife. He wanted to let Siobhan and the rest of his extended family know that he had arrived safely.

Their mobile accommodation they were stationed in had been built from hardened steel at least four inches thick. It had been just as well because as he was about to start talking to Siobhan, AN insurgents had fired artillery shells into their positions. As usual the Air Projectile Alarm Warning System was triggered, warning everyone of incoming IDF. And as usual he had thought them to be far off, but not this time.

Not knowing that Ashleigh was on a call to his wife, Chris had opened the door to where he was and was about to enter the room to go over a few of the minor details for tomorrows trek with his friend, when suddenly the ear shattering noise of an explosion filled their space. The concussion from the blast immediately hit them and they were lurched rearward. The air around also became thick with smoke as the toxins from the explosive ordinance filled their breathable air space.

Momentarily dazed and confused from the shock wave and being unable to focus through the dust and debris, each were unsure of the other's condition. Siobhan, meanwhile had been instantly cut off from the VIDCom connection and worried about what might have happened.

Other Rangers were now rushing to the aid of their commanders. They would hope they were both still alive for they needed their leadership in the days to come. When the smoke cleared, Ashleigh put his hands up towards his face and felt a warm wetness dripping from his jawline. The force of the blast had perforated one of his ear drums and he was now bleeding profusely from the canal. This wasn't much to worry about for they had the medicus expertise and technology to implant artificial synthetic organs, thus repairing his hearing back to a hundred percent capacity.

'Sir? Sir? Can you hear me?'

It was his Company Chief Master Sergeant, one of the first to come to his aid. A position he had done many times before when he held that position himself. Ashleigh slowly answered that yes he was fine, but he asked about his friend Chris. As his vision and composure reasserted itself, he saw his friend laying on the ground with a large piece of shrapnel protruding from his rib cage. This was something he thought he would never see. Chris and he had survived everything that had been put in front of them. He couldn't lose his friend, not like this.

'No! Not Chris! Not now!'

In complete disbelief and now completely oblivious to his own injury, he brushed aside the Chief Master Sergeant and crawled over to his friend's body. The accommodation may have been four inches thick, but the deflector plating had been less. The impact of the High Explosive shell had veered in on a trajectory path completely on the vertical plain. It had shattered the armoured deflector plating causing shrapnel to fly off in all directions and it had been unfortunate that Chris was now embedded with one of these pieces. Ashleigh called his name hoping against all hope that his friend was still with the living.

Chris's face was covered in blood by the tiny shards of steel fragments that had also sheared off from the explosion. As medics worked on his wounds, Chris opened his eyes and struggled to brings words to form with sound.

'Damn that hurts.'

Although Ashleigh laughed at his friend's statement, he knew this was far from a jovial matter. The shrapnel in the side of Chris's chest cavity could be very well preciously sitting against or in a vital life giving organ. It would take all the skill of medicus to have it removed and save his life. Gently, the medical team lifted Chris onto a stretcher and evacuated him to the mobile medical aid station. Ashleigh himself would also be seen too for his injuries.

Tomorrows planned operation would still go ahead, even though the 2nd/14th Company had lost their commander. Ashleigh, who by mornings light had made enough of a recovery to re-join his troops and lead them, had felt compelled to be care taker of the 2nd/14th. He knew in his soul that this was not required as there were enough Chief Master Sergeants within the Company to get the mission done. But he went back to his elder-father's words.

'Your men will look to you for guidance and leadership. You have to ask them to do extraordinary deeds and feats of courage against overwhelming odds. You will only succeed if you lead by example.'

Being placed in charge was nothing new to him as he had done this many times before, only on a much smaller scale. The added pressure came from the fact that this mission they were about to embark on could seal the fate for the end of the conflict. It had come down to this, they either succeeded in their task, or face more years of insurgency and attacks against the UFTN. They would have to succeed, for there was no other way. He knew that Chris would not want his soldiers placed in harm's way unnecessarily. Ashleigh would see to it that they weren't.

The morning of their departure, Ashleigh resumed his conversation with Siobhan. She and Evonne had not slept at all that night, staying awake all night, sick with worry as to what had happened. Now that he had called back, both breathed a sigh of relief. They were so glad to hear his voice and see his image on their VIDCom display. But they noticed the medicus bandage covering his left ear and asked if he was alright. He would have to wait until the mission was over before seeing to its full repair. He explained what had happened the night before to both the women in his life. Evonne had secretly cast an incantation the night before for his continued protection and safe return.

Siobhan had asked about the condition of their friend, Chris. He had been a very close friend of the family over the years and had been made EJs god-parent. Ashleigh explained that he was alive but he was still in a critical condition. Doctors has stated he would live if the next 72 hours passed without incident or complications. When the danger period had passed, Chris would be evacuated from the FOB and be returned to Johannesburg. There he would receive further medical care and treatment and it would also be the place that would allow him to make a full recovery. Siobhan and Evonne would join Chris's wife and children at his side in the hospital when he returned.

Before closing the VIDCom call in progress, Siobhan would inform her husband that she received a message from his brother, Andrew. It had appeared that Ashleigh's elder-father, William, had taken a turn for the worse. This again would be a life defining moment for Ashleigh. This had been the man that had raised him from childhood, the man that had given everything to him, the man he respected, admired and loved, and the man which he had prayed to be.

Ashleigh had modelled himself off William's persona, his courage, his honesty, and his compassion towards others. He knew that this day would eventually arrive, but he had wished he could be there with his elder-father to hold his hand and say good-bye as he slipped from this world and into the next.

What was he to do? He was the Captain of the 2nd/10th ISR Striker Company of the 46th Pioneer Striker Division. He had men that needed him and the fate of the AN Uprising was precariously hanging in the balance. He knew what his Ranger Creed had compelled him to do. It would be the same words his elder-father would echo. No one man is greater than the common cause of all men. Regardless of whether or not William was dying, he would curse Ashleigh's return to be with him when there were greater stakes on the line. The decision had been a tough one to make, but the answer was clear, he would stay where he was and complete his duty. It was the Ranger way.

William had been in similar situations, especially during his time in the War of the Great Despair. Uncertainty loomed over every passing day whether or not loved ones remained alive while he was off fighting in the war. Bombs fell like rain in those days as REAMEN forces expanded across the globe. Evonne had lost her elders, he had lost distant elders and the world would suffer an immeasurable cost to life. But through all, William had stayed the course and eventually founded the Ranger Corps Ashleigh belongs to now. His elder-father had laid the foundations which all Rangers live to and abide by to this day. Ashleigh would not dishonour his creed or bring dishonour to William.

Chapter Sixteen

The Light Armoured Tactical Assault Vehicles all moved out in various convoys throughout the following morning. It was to be a coordinated operation. Many other convoys would also depart that morning, leaving from any number of FOBs that now occupied this theatre of war. All had one purpose, one task, one mission; that was to see an end of this conflict. In doing so, the UFTN would at last be united as a single entity with the rights and freedom for all its citizens. He too had been desperate to see an end to it. He was growing weary of battle, tired of the constant struggle to uphold the principles of the UFTN. He despised seeing his fellow Rangers fall in battle, but most of all, he yearned to be with his family.

He continued to believe in the righteous cause of the UFTN, but he now thought of greener pastures. Josephine had just come into his life and questioned just how it would affect her if he was to fall and not return to her. He had never held those thoughts before, not even about his own children and during the many years he fought in the Terran Wars. Many a time it had looked certain that his fate was sealed, but time and time again, he managed to keep himself alive. Once again he thought of the words his elder-parents would say to him. So why now? What was it about having Evonne back in his life, along with a new daughter, that now affected him so?

He wished he had the answer for it was blurring his judgement and was now hindering his every decision. He couldn't bring his soldiers back alive if his mind was not fully focused on the task at hand. Evonne had shown him some meditation techniques from her Graceline Ways, although her mother had advised against it, he practiced these techniques with a calming effect. Crystal had explained to Evonne that men were unable to grasp the concepts and that these teachings could have the adverse result to what she was hoping for. But Evonne had said that Ashleigh was not like most men, not in her eyes anyway.

Crystal sensed that her daughter may have held some truth in her words. Therefore, if Evonne was going to teach him some of her ways, Crystal would ensure that her daughter got it right. Crystal would spend weeks leading onto months training Evonne with these techniques. Care and due diligence was required with every step, for one wrong move, an incorrect saying or misinterpreted ingredient, could result in disaster. So Ashleigh set himself upon the path of a higher plain of existence while still maintaining his faith to the Catholic Church. He reached out to Mother Terra and Father Sky and sort their guidance and direction.

'Sir? It's time to go .... Sir?'

Ashleigh could not believe the time it was, four hours had passed in what had seemed like minutes to him. But he was at least feeling more at ease with himself and his path before him laid true and focussed. Through his meditation, he had felt a presence. Not like the one he felt when he first met his daughter, Josephine, but more of a calming and serene presence. One that gave off a surety and confidence that what he was doing was correct. He had felt as if his journey was only just beginning and more lay in wait for him. With eyes closed and his thoughts almost becoming one, he could swear that something, or someone was physically guiding him.

This had intrigued him, his whole way of life, his teachings and his knowledge of what he thought about life, were now being challenged by another thought. One thing he knew for sure, he was ready to lead his troops into battle and be victorious come its end. Whatever he had just experienced, it had worked. Climbing into his command LATAV, he gave his orders and they were soon headed out the front gates of the FOB. The journey would be long and treacherous, every turn could be their last. The AN insurgents had learnt from the lessons of yesteryear. They were master bomb makers and knew exactly where to place their IEDs and lay ambush attacks.

The particle clouds hung low this morning and a thick mist rose from the terran ground as they cautiously made their way further inland. Further that is into the deep dark recesses of the Congo jungle. It hadn't rained that morning, not one drop, which was unusual. At this time for the last two months and for every day, the rains of the Darkness had poured down upon them with a vengeance. But not this morning.

The bright blue crack of the electro-magnetic storms could be seen off into the distance. It would surely be coming their way, as sure as this day was bound to get worse before it got better. Was this some kind of sign? And did it have anything to do with that morning's meditation?

At his side was a trusted long-time friend and fellow Ranger, Regis Otillio. Sub-Commander Sergeant Regis Otillio had joined the regiment as a Guardsmen and had been with him for ten years. SCdrSgt Otillio had served under him in the many four man Ranger Teams he had operated and commanded. Since then, they have remained close friends. It was during the Terran Wars that Ashleigh had gone out on his own to bring, the then young and inexperienced, Regis back. Regis had been captured and held prisoner by the RFN Rebels and thought to have been dead. But Ashleigh had believed different and so went to his rescue, with success.

Regis was born in the Eurpasian Island of Italy and was therefore, because of circumstance, an Ugbee citizen of the UFTN. This fact and his special skills have served both of them well over the years and as they are now headed into battle once more, there would be no-one else, save Chris, which he would rather have at his side. As the clouds thickened and the Darkness rains set upon them, Regis would have no trouble at all seeing his way through. But the Darkness rains never came, although the thunder and lightning had been threatening all day. It just seemed to be constantly out of their immediate distance, almost encircling them at one stage, looking at them and taunting him.

The first days travel had been uneventful and quiet and they moved into another FOB for the nights bedding. This particular FOB was smaller than the last, in fact a lot smaller. Air transport of the Federal Sky Force couldn't possibly land any fixed wing craft here, only the rotary wing assets of the Federal Terran Aviation Corps could land their craft.

For Ashleigh and his charges, it had meant that they had to park all the LATAVs on the outer perimeter of the defensive walls of the FOB. This made no difference, the Rangers would always set up their defence guard, plus they had the TACs with them, whose job it was to provide force level security. This may have seemed wrong, but the Rangers would be required in full force when once they reached their objective. The TACs had their duty just as the Rangers had theirs.

'DADDY'S DEAD, HE'S BEEN KILLED!'

Josephine had come running into her mother's bedroom shaking with fear and crying her eyes out. Evonne told her to calm herself and to tell her what had happened. Josephine couldn't contain herself and kept repeating her words over and over again. Evonne reached out and told her daughter to reach out as well. Both of them hung onto the pentacle hanging from Evonne's neck, dangling from its chain. Josephine explained to her mother that she had seen a bright flash of light and had felt the effects of an explosion. She said that she seen her father engulfed in flames and smoke and that is when she awoke.

Evonne had heard of past stories of Graceline women having premonitions before, but has never witnessed them first hand. In fact, it was only the Graceline women who had amassed years of experience who were able to possess this skill, none of which were currently still alive today. She was sure that her mother and auntie had never experienced this either, but instead they might have some knowledge of it. Premonitions could hold various meanings, good or bad; she would have to consult her mother Crystal on this and refer to the ancient book.

'Josephine is developing faster than I expected. I always felt that she held more than the rest of us, but she is still too young and inexperienced with the knowledge of her sight.'

Crystal continued explaining that the premonition could be the future and not necessarily the present. And she hadn't actually seen Ashleigh die; the flames in her premonition could represent rebirth or a new beginning, just as the fabled phoenix. Her attention, regardless of what it meant, required her presence and she would be on the next flight out of Melbourne and on her way to Pretoria.

Josephine had wanted to tell her Maynard mother, but Evonne advised against this. If Ashleigh had been killed, the Corps would be the first to inform them of it. And if he was yet to be killed, she wouldn't be able to do anything about it anyway, his path was set. She would have to let destiny run its course. Besides, she believed that no-one would have believed her anyway even if she did tell them.

The next morning, Ashleigh and his Rangers were once again departing their location. It would be another day spent driving through the jungle and then it would be on foot. And just as the day before had started, this day would also be covered in low laying particle clouds and a thick mist that rose from the terran ground beneath. Once again, the Darkness rains were held at bay, though lightning and thunder could still be heard in distance beyond them. This eerie sensation had started to unsettle the TACs, but not for the Rangers amongst them. The Rangers knew that no matter what, their mission had to succeed. Meanwhile Josephine would search through the Graceline book for answers.

Some of the previous matriarchs of the Graceline had possessed this gifted ability of premonition, but of all the women that had, they had only spoken of it when they were in their mid-thirties. Josephine was just sixteen, and so how did she have this ability? Her elder mother was correct in saying that she had been far too young to fully comprehend the meanings behind her vision. Josephine's fear of losing her father filled her with great sorrow. Her personal emotions felt for this man were outweighing her gifted insight. She would know for certain if her visions were correct when next he would contact them.

Evonne and Josephine had tried to hide this from the rest of the family, but with the sudden arrival of Crystal, Siobhan had started to have her own intuitions. She had noticed a change in Josephine and now started to question what was going on. Being too over whelmed by the situation, this task was left to Crystal to answer. She would further explain the Graceline ways to Siobhan and of exactly what Josephine had saw in her vision.

Siobhan tried her best to understand it, but all her years of the catholic upbringing were blocking her thoughts from expanding her own beliefs into that of others. She listened intently as word upon word filled her mind with wonder and questioning amazement. Although she struggled with the concepts, she accepted it for what it was.

There had been many a strange thing happen to her and her husband over the years and she knew that this world, this life in fact, held more secrets than any of them could conceivably see possible. As Crystal and Evonne had thought, Siobhan also wondered and worried about Josephine and her emerging talents. What else would she see as she grew older and developed more? She possessed the blood lines of both Grace and of her husband, the Maynard's.

This day had so far been without incident and Regis asked his commander if the AN insurgents had all been defeated and had gone home. Why hadn't they been attacked yet, considering they were now deep into the heart of the AN Uprising territory? They were surely being watched. Ashleigh informed his young friend not to become too complacent. They needed to remain vigilant and at the ready.

It was now nearing three in the afternoon and Ashleigh had thought of bringing his convoy to a halt for that evening. They would have a long day ahead of them tomorrow, trekking on foot with equipment and then being expected to engage the enemy in battle. He wanted his Rangers fresh and fit to the task.

This time there was no Forward Operating Base or smaller Patrol Base, they would have to erect their defences themselves. A task they had done many times before. Ashleigh spotted a site that would be suited to their needs and gave the order to move in. As his was the lead vehicle, he instructed Regis to cautiously drive their LATAV into position. Suddenly the rear of the vehicle lurched up and forward with an almighty thunderous explosion. Smoke and debris filled the cabin of their vehicle and confusion reigned as they tried to comprehend what had just happened to them.

At that very moment, a cold shiver was also sent through Josephine's body from the base of her neck and down to her toes. She had felt something not quite right, but because of her elder-mother's guidance and teaching, Josephine slowed her breathing and learned to soak in the sensation.

She would not jump to unsubstantiated conclusions without fact of evidence. Because of this, her feelings and emotions were more controlled and the worry and fear she had experienced earlier dissipated. Her connection with her father was strong and she had said she could feel his heart beating still.

The LATAV had been struck by an IED as Regis had manoeuvred it down a slight embankment. It was the perfect location of choice to plant an IED, but their vehicles had been fitted with Anti-IED Counter-Attack Defensive Measures, so why hadn't the IED been detected? They may never know. Had their specialist equipment failed? Or were the AN insurgents becoming more aware and adaptable of their foe?

The IED had detonated just as their vehicle had driven over it with its rear wheels. The explosion violently lurching the rear of the LATAV skywards in a hail of toxic filled smoke and shrapnel. Debris not only coming from the vehicle itself, but also from the underlying terran soil and rock. The Senior Guardsmen that was perched in the rear hatch and who was manning the gun, was savagely thrown out of, and from the vehicle. He had come to land some twenty meters away from where they were.

'Damn it to Saint Michael, that's twice in three days.'

He didn't usually blaspheme towards his Corps patron saint, but his blood was up and he was mad as hell. He already had one perforated ear drum, he didn't need anything else happening to him if he was to successfully lead and command two Companies of Rangers.

This was now a particularly dangerous scenario. Usually if the injured were close by, combat first aid can be administered. But due to the rear gunner landing so far away from them, it could create more havoc and mayhem, leading to more combat injuries. Insurgents will often watch the area they have trapped with mines in order to learn the procedures of

UFTN forces. Unfortunately and by the sound of it, this Ranger required immediate medical attention, and fast. He and Regis and the rest of his command vehicle crew weren't faring that well either.

The IED had been an incendiary high explosive compound with a high yield effect that had now engulfed the LATAV in blistering flames of fire and black smoke. The personnel protection devices within the cabin, the HALON, would provide he and Regis some respite, but they would only have minutes to escape the burning wreckage. HALON gas would extinguish the flames as it worked on removing all the immediate available oxygen that fire required to live, unfortunately, they also required that very same oxygen to breathe.

They would have to be removed from the burning wreckage if they stood any chance at all of survival. But this wouldn't be an issue and fellow Rangers were now coming to their aid, fighting their way through a hail of enemy gun fire to get to them. As the smoke started to clear around them, Ashleigh regained his awareness, realising what had happened. He had chosen to act on his emotions rather than logic and triggered the emergency release hatch, shooting the top of the cabin skyward.

He knew that the area immediately outside and around the perimeter of the vehicle could still contain IEDs. As too did he realise that if exposed, he could come under a direct fire attack from small arms fire and Rocket Propelled Grenades that the rest of his men were engaged in. None the less, he would take that chance and he released his harness and climbed out of the vehicle.

His emergence from the fiery flames when seen by his troops filled them with inspiration and awe as he walked stoically from them. Some couldn't believe their eyes of what they were seeing. Especially the junior ones amongst them. If this was possible, then they could do anything. They would surely see this day through and be the victors in their struggle to bring peace to the AN Territories.

As he hit the ground and his Chief Master Sergeant had reached him and Regis, shots rang out and whizzed by them, only missing their intended targets by inches. With only the thought of the wounded Ranger on his mind, he ran at pace as other Rangers provided covering fire. 30 and 50 calibre automatic fire could be heard coming from other LATAVs in the direct area to where he was. Then suddenly, it all went black.

He had felt like he had been hit in the chest by a sledge hammer and he now found himself on his back looking up at a blurred incoherent image of a sky that was canopied by the Congolian jungle tree tops above him. As he raised his head, he noticed that he had a small hole in the front on his body armour. Luckily the ballistic plate had stopped the bullet from penetrating and entering his chest. With his composure returning to him, he was soon back on his feet again when he finally reached the injured man.

The rear gunner had been thrown from the hatch with his small section attack machine gun still in hand and had landed on both forearms, smashing both his wrists in the process. The man had also suffered a compound fracture to his left femur. Ashleigh needed to go to work straight away and he ignored the bullets that were now coming thick and fast as they flew past him and his wounded casualty.

By now the Company second-in-command had radioed for an aero-medevac, not only for the casualty Ashleigh was attending to, but also for those that were now starting to fall in action. The situation looked dire and because of his current location, he was in no position to effectively assume command and control of his Rangers. The medevac choppers were also some time off from reaching them. It would take an estimated sixty minutes before the first of them to reach their destination and evacuate the wounded because of the environmental conditions created by the Darkness and the thickness of the surrounding jungle landscape.

By now the Darkness rains that had refused to pour down their menacing effects was now coming down in abundance. Ashleigh placed the hood of his PARTNAR Suit over his head and continued to provide combat first aid. Every now and again, he would stop from what he was doing to return fire. This was more than just an outpost he thought for there were AN insurgents now appearing from all locations to his front and flanks. Flashes of blue electro-magnetic lightning crashed to the terran ground and shaking it under foot.

This was no simple booby trap, this had been an early warning sentry for the main enemy contingent. It had seemed that they had found the beating heart of the lion. They had found the head of the AN Uprising. Now all they needed to do, was remove it. He was still out of position to assume effective command of 2nd/10th and 2nd/14th Striker Ranger Companies, as he was way forward of their position and under continual heavy enemy fire.

They were also on their own as they had been the first Regiment to engage the main body. Other regiments were still heading for their given coordinates and had no idea of their predicament. They would have to be contacted and alerted to this new development.

The Company 2IC knew he needed to protect the exposed men to his flank, but he couldn't risk the chance of striking another IED. These were usually banked or peppered around the main charge in attempt to coerce UFTN forces into a come-on. They would seek to cause further injuries to UFTN Federal troops by these secondary devices. The only thing Ashleigh could do was protect the injured Ranger and ride this one out while they waited for the much needed medevac choppers to come. But first they would have to construct and secure an LZ, or Landing Zone.

The success of their mission and that of the very lives under his charge was becoming increasingly desperate by the second. He watched as the accompanying TACs moved this way and that under the fog of confusion and indecisive orders. Younger men panicked while seasoned battle hardened veterans struggled to maintain control. He watched as his own troops, Rangers, pushed on in vain attempts to bring the battle back under their control and will. Something would have to give shortly if he was to save the wounded Ranger and resume command. The Company 2IC knew also that he would have to make a decision soon if they were to escape this.

By now the both of them were severely pinned down. There was nowhere for these men to move. It would be no use anyway, the man's injuries Ashleigh was attending to needed the medevac and couldn't be moved without causing further injuries. For a moment, he briefly stopped treating the wounded man to take aim and fire upon the insurgents that were creeping forward to his position.

He had told the injured soldier to hang on as he fired his weapon, killing two or three in the process, and quickly followed by another. He could hear and see the 30 and 50 calibre rounds being fired from other LATAVs. But to his dismay, the insurgents did not retreat, they simply pressed further on in advance.

Suddenly he saw the figure of a man kneel up and release an RPG round towards their direction. The only thing he could do was cover the injured man's body with that of his own in a vain attempt to shield them both from the blast and shrapnel. Hoping that his body armour would protect the both of them. He felt the initial sting of what seemed like a hundred fire ants biting into his rump and legs. These were tiny pieces of fragments entering his skin, but he was lucky and after a quick assessment and self-administered aid, considered his injuries as minor.

Hope at last he thought, he had heard the unmistakable sound of a Nighthawk Mk IV coming in from the distance. But it still had nowhere to land. Those words his elder-father had said, now echoed larger than life itself through his thoughts. To lead, you must consider all your men, not just one. These words rang louder in his head with each passing minute, he must do something.

Meanwhile, Regis had managed to pull himself free from the burning Light Armoured Tactical Assault Vehicle and was now trying to reach his commander, he needed Ashleigh back in the game. The Company 2IC also recognised this fact and had ordered two of his LATAVs to creep forward up to their position; TAC troops would be in support behind the protection of the LATAVs on foot. The crew commanders of both vehicles had performed very well, negotiating the treacherous and potentially dangerous route to finally reach them.

After receiving some minor medical patch work to his own wounds, Ashleigh was picked up by Regis and he assumed control of one of the LATAVs. This vehicle was now his flag and they surged back into the battle taking up a central commanding position. Ashleigh knew he was no longer in a team of four; along with the TACs, he had over three hundred Federal UFTN Peace Makers at his disposal against approximately four thousand AN insurgents. Now his metal as a commander would be put to the test.

He was quick to take up a defensive posture at the centre and started coordinating orders and strategic positioning for his next move. This would give him time to plan a counter offensive against overwhelming odds. The environment of the previous two days of reasonable and eerie serenity, now turned against all in its wake with a vengeance and anger. So harsh had it become, that medical rotary wing assets had to turn back to base for threat of going down in the blistering and blinding storm that raged around them.

The only way out of this was to fight their way through the enemy fortified positions in their terran based vehicles. Just as he ordered the second wave of counter attacks, two 105mm high explosive shells burst in front of his position and onto enemy lines. It had been a sight for sore eyes as he viewed a squadron of six All Terrain Heavy Armoured Vehicles take up position along a ridge to his rear.

The ATHAVs released volley after volley of deadly explosive ordinance onto the enemy. This was followed by a surge of ground Federation TAC troops coming to his aid. He and his soldiers had held out for four hours as the day became night and as the Darkness of the Coming had belted down on them from above.

The strangle hold the AN insurgents once commanded over the forces of the UFTN were now being pushed back into submission. This would truly spell the end of the AN uprising, but Ashleigh had thought it to be a longer task. As the battle of the AN Congo, as it would become known, wore down and he was relieved of command by the new ranking officer on the scene, one Brigadier General Marsh, his mind would turn of thoughts of home and that of his family. Also, he still hadn't heard anything about the condition of his friend Chris, plus he also required medical care and recovery himself.

In the coming days that followed, he would return home and join his friend Chris in the Johannesburg Centre Hospital. Their wives and family were happy to know that both men would make a full recovery. It would be another month of minor skirmishes and discussions of peace talks until the AN Uprising was finally put down. But his actions that day and that of his soldiers, had turned the tide of war in their favour. He was tired and he was sore of battle. Once again he would relish the time he had with his family and hoped that this was the last final conflict he and his family would have to endure.

Chapter Seventeen

F aith had saw fit to protect him that day and had provided hope. This campaign and the events in between when discovering he had another daughter had been particularly strenuous on him. Now that his tour of duty was over and his wounds healed, he would look forward to spending some quality time with his family prior to taking up his new position at the Federal Continental Ranger School of Airborne Operations. At this stage of his life, he would question the purpose of his calling as a Ranger. He had given so much over the years just as his family had done. It may be time to reconsider his chosen path.

The end of the Terran Wars had taken a huge toll on humanity and this latest conflict against insurgents involved in the AN Uprising, although minor in comparison, had still cost the lives of many. He thought about all those sons and daughters lost over the years from both sides; had it all been worth it? He would never know, but instead held the belief that in some small way, their losses had made a difference. At least, that is, to the people caught up in these conflicts by the wills and whims of their leaders.

The pressure of command, especially over a large body of troops, had obviously sub-consciously played on his thoughts. His initial actions and judgements during the Battle of the AN Congo had been impeded by the words of his elder-father and the self-appointed guardianship of his friend's, Chris's, Company.

Instead of just getting on with the job at hand and letting his natural instincts and ability guide him, he had almost made a fatal error. Had it been so, then three hundred men and women could have perished that day. He would never let this be the case again. The constant thought of his new daughter and extended family also rested heavily on his shoulders and he wondered how he would react now that he was back home in Pretoria.

Siobhan had already seen him jump in startled fright when fireworks were released due to his experiences in the Terran Wars, now he would also have these images and thoughts to add to them. But he would sheath those thoughts for now and focus on more important matters, his family.

William had been seriously ill, but this time the prognosis indicated that he may not have much longer left to live. It had even been doubtful if he would make it back home to Australia in time enough to see his grand-elder. As he still had two months before being required to take up his new post, he and family left Pretoria bound for Melbourne.

'Dad, I'm home.'

Ashleigh greeted his elder-father with a kiss and a hug, a tear slid down his cheek as he did. Something that Andrew and his elder-mother had kept secret from him, was that William had lost the use of his eyes due to the sickness. It had made no difference to William anyway, he knew his boy was home by the sounds of his movement and voice. There was no fooling old pop.

When the boys were younger and he had been teaching them, they had tried, and failed, to sneak up on him. This did not deter them though and time and time again as they tried, time and time again they failed. Pop was just too smart for the boys. He educated the boys that one's movements could always be told, no matter how sleight of hand or quiet they were. One's own movements were like fingerprints he told them, they were distinctive and personalised, no two were the same.

He didn't know it at the time, but Ashleigh would only have six days remaining with his elder-parent, for on the seventh he quietly passed with all the family by his side. This had been a great man; past and present Rangers of the FCR Corps would be in attendance at his Passing of Life ceremony. As Josephine put it; the body will return to mother terra whereas the spirit will ascend to Father Sky.

Ashleigh could still remember the words his elder-father spoke and the look in his eyes, when he had use of them, the last time he left him. He could see the fear and knowledge in them that William knew his time would soon come. As Ashleigh said good-bye, William spoke the words, 'I don't want you to go'.

He had lost family and friends before. He had also lost soldiers fallen in battle, sometimes in traumatic circumstances. War often leads to nothing else when soldiers are either shot or blown up. The few scrapes he had been in himself had sometimes been on the life ending edge themselves, but he very rarely considered the life of his own above that of his troops. Although his death, if came, would take him away from Siobhan and the children, they would know that it would be because he gave it saving someone else.

The current and most recent events would change him however. He would not be the same man he was when he left that last time for war. And he would certainly by no means be the same man, or boy for that matter, which Siobhan had met all those years ago at school. As she had always done, she would do her best to care for and support her husband during the days that followed each one of his returns. Each experience compounding with the next.

However this time, Evonne would be there to assist. He would continue to love both women emotionally and passionately. At William's Passing of Life ceremony, Ashleigh had been given the honour to say a few a words in retrospect of his elder-parent. He would find the words easy to come by and after summing up the man's life, he finished by saying:

'The measure of one's life is not how long one lived for, but rather by what you choose to do with that life while you have it.

How many of us have expended large amounts of time and energy on superfluous agendas only to end in a nil result.

We must sometimes realise that there are more important things in life than just advancing one's own position.

Time is precious and now my elder-father, dad – my Pop, is gone and that cannot be changed.

But what can be changed is the time we all have on this Terran Earth.

Time to spend it with the people we love and care for.

William gave a lot of himself over the years, both to his family and to those people less fortunate to himself.

This came sometimes at the detriment of his own life and that of his family.

But Andrew and I never resented the man for this, but rather we rejoiced and basked in his caring and nurturing way.

We have, as I know many of you have as well, learnt a great deal from William and are now the better for it.

He was a veteran of the War of the Great Despair; a great leader, a great mentor, and a great father.

Over the past decade, I have probably seen my father a dozen times.

Let me tell you that nothing is too important.

Stop what you're doing, pick up that phone and make that call that we all put off from time to time.

Get in that vehicle or take that flight and go see that someone special.

And make a difference.

And don't be afraid of expressing your love, or for that matter, to say it. I love you dad and I will miss you.'

William had indeed lived his life well and was well respected and admired by a vast majority of UFTN citizens. As was testament by all who gathered at the Passing. Ashleigh's elder-mother would later join her husband one year from now to the day. Her grief over her loss was just two immense and she left this world knowing safe in the knowledge that they had raised two very intelligent, sensible and caring boys. They were 93 and 88 years old respectively and marked a time when those who knew of a life before the coming of the Darkness existed.

It would now be left to us who remained to remember the crimes and mistakes of the past and pass on our educated years of knowledge and wisdom to the young. But it had not been the smooth transition of total unity the Consortium of Trust had imagined since forming the UFTN. Although the AN Uprising and the Trap / Ugbee struggles had taken place, both before and after Federation, these held nothing compared to that of the Terran Wars.

It was inconceivable to think that even with the knowledge of the terrible destruction and cost to human life the War of the Great Despair had caused, that something so terrible like this could take place again. But it had and it was now one of the Peacekeepers major tasks to see that it would never happen again.

For the next two years and as peace reigned supreme throughout the UFTN, Ashleigh and his family along with Evonne and hers would live quiet and content lives in Pretoria without incident. Meanwhile, Crystal and Anne would visit to check up on the daughters of the Graceline from time to time. There was nothing stopping them now that Dirk had been removed from the picture and they could all embrace the Graceline as one.

Josephine, who was now quickly becoming of age, revelled in the new life she was now living in and progressed in her studies at an alarming rate. Not only was she absorbing the Graceline path, but that too of her father's way. So advanced had she become in such a short time that in some ways, she outshone the skills and attributes of her mother. She was no longer the novice, she was now an intermediate Wiccan.

Through knowledge and wisdom, Josephine now understood the premonition she had two years ago. Yes she had seen her father in an image of flames, but it wasn't his death she saw, it was inspiration and hope. Inspiration and hope to his soldiers for them to succeed in their task. Ultimately, it was this vision of defiance towards death that lifted his men in the heat of battle to overcome their odds.

Another Christmas Union would pass and with each passing year, Evonne regained her self-worth. Siobhan had helped her along this path and the two were now as sisters; they were inseparable friends. But Crystal was starting to have her own concerns about the longevity of this quaint arrangement her daughter had. She felt that it was unhealthy and unproductive to all their lives. She also sensed a change in the air each time she visited her daughter.

Evonne, it seemed, was growing more reliant on Ashleigh with each passing second, and more in love. Naturally, Evonne would strongly deny any and all claims made against her by her mother that she held more than just a plutonic attachment to Ashleigh. But still, Crystal held true to the visionary proof that Evonne's feelings towards her once saviour was growing to be more than just friendship.

Crystal informed Evonne that it was not only her daughter's lack of foresight that could see was going on here, but it was that of Siobhan as well who was also blind to this fact. Evonne was warned that she was heading down a dangerous path and although the family situation had worked initially, it was now time that she moved out and really spread her wings. For if she didn't, it could threaten her relationship with her surrogate family irrevocably.

Ever since, and before the time, Evonne had joined the FCR Corps as a young fifteen year old had she been in the presence of men. Her father had cared for her in her childhood years, Ashleigh had watched over her in her mid-teenage years, Dirk had used and abused her during her early adult life, and now she was back again in Ashleigh's care. She had never really had a chance to discover herself.

The twins were even referring to Ashleigh as their father, including Jeremy who had initially had rough beginnings with him. Through all this, Josephine remained silent. Oh she could see it, the situation was perfectly clear, but she said nothing. She was happy the way things were, but she also knew that her mother couldn't continue living with Ashleigh and Siobhan.

Regardless of this knowledge, Josephine would not interfere. Her knowledge as a Graceline had told her to let this run its course, for she now understood the way. She also understood the way of her father whom she had developed an inner bond with. Both were able to read the other's expressions with a high guarantee of knowing the thoughts behind them.

Ashleigh had once told her that he did not believe in coincidence or chance. He had told her that everything happened for a reason. Crystal had also previously expressed these pearls of wisdom to her. Whatever came next would be for purpose and task as her life was now only just beginning to open up. Her full potential had yet been gained, she was eighteen and was full to the brim with confidence and achievement. She also knew a few self-defence moves, thanks to her father. One thing she did lack however, were her premonitions. Only two more would avail themselves to her since the coming of the first. But these had been shadowy at best and their meaning hidden.

'What do you mean you are leaving? You can't go.'

The news that Evonne was suddenly leaving shocked Siobhan, as it seemed to have come out of nowhere. It was amazing to think that only sixteen years ago, Siobhan didn't even want her husband having coffee with Evonne. Now she didn't want her to leave.

'I have to go.' Evonne explained.

'Yes I have gained my life back after being under the control of my lunatic of a husband, Dirk. But I need to spend time on my own, truly on my own.'

Maybe she was right, she did need time to herself. Plus it would be nice just to have Ashleigh all to herself again. He would not try and stop her, in fact he was strongly in favour of her departure and had been the one to convince her to go once Evonne had told him of her thoughts. Going with her would be Josephine and the twins. Jeremy and Damian would spend time with their elder-auntie, Anne; while Crystal, Evonne, and Josephine would all travel to their ancestral homelands in the Eurpasian Islands of North England and Scotland in search of self-discovery and meaning.

There, they would meet up with a distant and very much removed relative, named Mieke Sjöberg. Mieke was a High Priestess in the Order of Hope and could provide them training better than anything Anne or Crystal could provide. It was clear that Josephine's talents demanded it. Her never ending questions about her life were becoming increasingly far too complex and her astounding abilities too advanced for even Crystal and Anne to contend with.

They each knew that Josephine had surpassed them in every way, but was still dangerously immature in her application of such talents and therefore required the guidance of the High Priestess. There hadn't been a High Priestess in the House of Graceline since Diana was alive, Crystal and Anne simply did not possess the knowledge to take Josephine any further.

Meanwhile Ashleigh and Siobhan with their children would return to the UFTN capital in Destiny. It was just as well too, for their home in Pretoria just wouldn't be the same without all of them being in it. They too would relish a fresh start. Regardless if in fact they had not wanted to relocate, they would have no choice as their move had been so ordered by the Council of Elders at the UFTN high command in Destiny itself. The Peace Makers couldn't even stop this. It had been the same for Chris and his family. Once again these brothers of the Ranger Corps would follow in each other's footsteps.

The cold snowy conditions of northern England were almost at freezing point when the three ladies stepped off the air transport. 2084 was the year and it promised to be a good one. The citizens of the UFTN continued in their never ending search of knowledge and wisdom. People lent others a helping hand and those less fortunate than others were given food and shelter. The Under Ground Beings in this part of the world aided their Trap neighbours with offerings of underground accommodation. It was almost as if now long past tensions and conflict between these two races of society never ever existed. But it had, and so savagely too.

In the years that predated the founding of the UFTN and with the Ugbees gaining the ability to see in complete darkness, the Traps which remained on the surface had lived by a strict curfew. No Trap was permitted to venture outside the security of their homes after dark, for they would present easy targets if they did.

Floor boards in homes were covered over by thick metal and iron plating so those underground could not penetrate the building. High intensity spot lights were strategically positioned around the structures of the building and left alight all night. These were powered by makeshift generators which consumed precious fuel that could have otherwise been used to provide heat and to cook with.

In the severest of winters, some Traps often ate cold meals and literally froze themselves to death while providing security and defences to their homes, families and communities. The alternative of being frozen to death was a much preferred option over being taken by an Ugbee, which likewise had been the same for the Ugbees that occupied the same territory. Blame could be laid on both sides for much over exaggerated and enflamed stories of cruelty and barbarity of the other.

It was a fact though, that these people, both Trap and Ugbee, just wanted to be left alone and be given the right to forage for food and shelter without interference from the other. There were, of course, at that time those who had organised themselves into local militias that aggravated the already fragile situation. One was granted permission by the local Trap chieftain to kill in order to protect themselves at night, but succeeding orders would later be given granting Traps the right to shoot and kill any Ugbee that was seen on sight in day light hours.

The Ugbees that ventured out into the daylight posed no threat at all to anyone, as these were often only the desperate and starving that risked blindness to themselves in the light of day going in search for scraps of food. They were the weak amongst the Ugbee population and were slowly dying of malnutrition. While some followed through on this order to shoot on site, most did not and instead argued with their Chieftains on the morality of such orders.

The Ugbees as well would question their warlords over the righteousness of attacking helpless families in the darkness of night. For those that knew of a time before the coming of the Darkness knew that monsters where only made up creatures designed to scare and frighten little children. Thanks to the stories that were told and which now had a life of their own, coupled with the actions of a few Ugbee men and women, monsters in the night did indeed exist.

Gradually, as the lawlessness and ungoverned years continued following the end of the War of the Great Despair, dragged on, more and more people on both sides would defy the orders of their Chieftains and Warlords. They grew tired of all this violence and death, they yearned for a peace. The few that believed in the peace, swayed others and those others in turn convinced more and more. These initiators, pioneers if you will, of peace between Trap and Ugbee was the beginning of many who would pave the way to the eventual founding of the UFTN.

Gladly those days are long gone, but not forgotten. These societies that now live and call home to the northern hemisphere, need each other to survive. You cannot have one without the other. Some have even married into the culture and society of the other, mixing the blood lines. Many would agree that through marriage, their offspring is simply restoring the past. After the first of many nuclear explosions took place and the earth begin to heat, thus melting the polar icecaps and flooding billions into oblivion, many people sought refuge in any places they could find.

To that end, there were many cases of members from the same family ending up on opposing sides. Some stayed topside whereas others such as brothers, sisters, and in some cases, children went below. The end result being that years later, these once united families now fought and killed each other over food and shelter. Family unity was one of the tenets the UFTN adopted as part of their overall mantra. It is believed that out of the original six members of the Council of Elders that formed the Consortium of Trust, two were of Trap origin and one had been Ugbee. Though no-one can be sure; for the six have never been seen.

—∿— ✝ —∿—

When Crystal, Evonne and Josephine finally arrived at the old Cragside Manner of a forgotten yesteryear, they were greeted by a figure in a long leather cloak that covered the unidentified persons head all the way down to their feet. The face of this person was concealed with a full face mask that had a dark film shade covering the eyes.

Was this an Ugbee? The only one Josephine had met up close was her father's friend and comrade, SCdrSgt Regis, and he had been kind and also very funny. As a matter of fact, if she had been a little older, she might have made a move on him as a potential suitor. But this, whoever or whatever it was, seemed to be very menacing and stood at least six foot five or seven inches tall. The cloaked figure towered above all three of them, but none of them feared the being. They could sense that a kind heart and gentle soul laid just beneath this person's coverings and hard exterior persona.

Upon entering the manner, all crevices and gaps that could let sun light in were completely covered. This must have been the home of an Ugbee, Josephine thought. Then her breath would be taken away from her as the mysterious figure began to discard the coverings it had been wearing. The leather cloak was the first to be removed. This revealed eight inch plat formed boots that would be next to be discarded. That obviously answered the question of height.

Their purpose would later be explained for use in the sometimes boggy marsh like conditions around the exterior of the manner and the surrounding forested woods, as well as giving the impression that this was not a person to get caught in trappings with. One push of a button and the platform boots could become as wide and circular as banquet plates and allowing a wider coverage over ground surface area.

The moment that really took Josephine's breath away was when the figure removed the mask. As the mask was removed, Josephine and the others could see a reddish blonde hair be revealed as it unfurled itself and fell across the shoulders of its owner. Next came a set of soft and luscious pouted lips and two oval shaped alluring beautiful green eyes. To Josephine's surprise, the dark figure had turned out to be an attractive young woman not much older than herself.

The twenty year old something girl introduced herself as Aine Sjöberg, daughter of High Priestess Mieke Sjöberg. Her namesake being the Goddess of love, growth and light, and meaning bright as she lights up the dark. Well she certainly did that.

Not only were her eyes naturally green in colour, she also suffered with the same infliction that Josephine's half-brother, Marcus, had suffered with, RFN eyes. Mieke had sent her daughter off into the world under the care and protection of Aine's older brother when she was younger. Her purpose was to gain insight and knowledge into the world around her. To understand life, one must experience all life.

Aine was only thirteen years old when she left on her travels to discover the world outside, constantly under the care and protection of Ashwyn, her older brother by ten years. It would be another six years until Aine return home, but not with her brother. To this day, he's whereabouts are still unknown, even with Mieke's gift of vision. But it had been during those travels that Aine had met Anne and Crystal through kindred thoughts and will. And it was now that Crystal had requested an audience with Aine's mother to further her daughter's Graceline learning.

'My mother, the High Priestess of the Order of Hope, will be with you shortly.'

Aine was angelic in every aspect, the way she formed words to part lips and the sweet tender voice that sounded when did were heavenly. She also moved seamlessly and with thought set to purpose as she gracefully walked across the hallowed large empty reception area of the manner. Aine had been born of Ugbee and Trap descent and because of this, was an anomaly of self being.

Her natural born ability of given sight in complete darkness, counter acted the debilitating effects of the Retina Light Focal Aperture Sensitivity she had contracted because the RFN during the Terran Wars. It had actually reversed the light sensitivity to light enhancement. Aine was as focally capable in complete day light as she was in utter darkness. Although she would maintain her glowing green eyes for the rest of her life and would therefore require shaded goggles to conceal her movements at night.

'Hello and welcome to my home.'

Mieke appeared in a door way behind them and ushered them all into more comfortable surroundings. She was nothing at all as they had pictured. Images of ornate flowing robes and decorations were vacant as here stood a woman that appeared like anyone else. This helped eased their anxieties and they knew by this first meeting that they had made the correct decision in coming here.

For the next six months, Josephine and her mother, under the diligent watch of Crystal, would be lessened in the advanced ways of Wiccan Paganology according to the teachings of Hope. But a new question now serviced by all three of them new to Craigside Manner, who was Hope? The only reference of her was chronicled in the ancient book that had been passed down by each matriarch of the Graceline to the next. But this had only been detailed in a single passage, the passage of the writings related to the Lacrimis Speiv. At the same time, Crystal would also immerse herself in these teachings and would seek to further her own capability through knowledge and wisdom.

Knowledge of Pietas, Sophia and Carman would be availed as well as part meaning of the words Evonne had spoken all those years ago from the Graceline book over the peaceful body of her daughter as she slept. Hope was the key to understanding the meaning of the Lacrimis Speiv.

Its substance used in the correct manner would be very powerful, but as she was once informed before, it could also be very deadly if used by the untrained or uninitiated.

It had been just as well that Evonne already had some knowledge of its wielding potential that prevented any major damage. That coupled with the fact she had not fully understood the ingredients that resulted in the Lacrimis Speiv being of weak strength. Never the less, it had still been taken and Mieke would take steps to ensure no future harm could result by it.

A well-educated and experienced decision had been formed that the Lacrimis Speiv, because of its weak potency, would be of no concern to the twins. The potion when produced by Evonne was assessed to have been insignificant to their wellbeing and would therefore have no effect on them. It was also safe in the knowledge, that because Evonne had only just started to take the liquid a month before they were born and never received any more after they were bought into the world, that Jeremey and Damian's body would evaporate whatever liquid was left remaining, never to leave a trace. But the possibility would always remain that something could go awry one day, only time would be the telling factor.

Josephine on the other hand, had received the liquid during every supper consumed; every day for three years. Often her mother had not made enough for the both of them and therefore, she herself went without. Her first consideration would always be her daughter. She was most affected by this as was evidenced by her abnormally young in age visions of the future and past events.

Unfortunately, she had not matured to completely control or understand these premonitions. Mieke, with growing concern for Josephine, decided that the only option left open to her that would correct this action, was to administer more of the liquid. But this time, it would be of the correct and precise dosage at full strength, and governed.

During the next couple of days, Evonne and Josephine relayed the story of their life to Mieke and Aine. Mieke had been impressed by Josephine's courage and strength through all her hardships and tribulations. She had explained that Josephine had reasonably controlled her emotions and desires with clear thought of mind and presence. This was especially notable as she was still only a child and knew relatively nothing of the ways of Grace or Hope.

Mieke looked at her daughter, Aine, and wondered about the future potential Josephine clearly had within her. To her knowledge, she had been the most senior and experienced High Priestess in the Order of Hope in existence, including that of other orders. And that had only been due to her years of constant study and practice. But here was Josephine, someone who had the possessed ability to over shadow her in every aspect, and it wouldn't take her the years to achieve such a position as it had taken her to do so.

Something told Mieke that Josephine was special. There must have been some reason behind this; some higher purpose. Over the next few months, they would ask and search for the answers to their questions. They would do this together as five women holding the points of the pentacle. Mieke would take Terra, Aine – wind; Crystal had fire, whereas Evonne would take aqua; but Josephine would be reserved to hold spirit for her ways with premonition. They would ensure they had the attendance of the goddesses Pietas, Sophia and Carman as they represented life, death and rebirth; and mind, body and soul. It would be a very enlightened next six months, for all of them.

Chapter Eighteen

T he three years that followed the passing of the AN Uprising were fruitful and prosperous for all. This once blue planet now home to just a third of its once growing population, was now completely one under the united banner of the UFTN. All seemed to be right with the world and that of also Ashleigh and the people in his life. Evonne and Josephine had been released from the evils of a maniac, and he was enjoying time spent with his wife, Siobhan, and their children.

He had completed his duty and been assigned to the UFTN Capital of Destiny, but his yearning to remain in the Corps had slowly dissipated over the last couple of years. Ever since meeting Josephine had he began to question the path his life was set on. And despite of his new assignment, which had come directly from the UFTN high command, he considered treasured life with family too important. He would now place family above all else. Chris, who had also received the same assignment as he, and who had now been promoted to the rank of Lieutenant Colonel, tried to persuade him to change his mind. But this was all in vain, Ashleigh had made his mind up. As with all other things Ashleigh committed himself to, once his thoughts were set, he would not be swayed.

Siobhan, with Chris's help, would plan a going out dinner for Ashleigh from the Federal Continental Ranger Corps of Peace Makers. He had always enjoyed evenings like this and would now look forward to his own, as well as the thought of early retirement. The years of service he had given to the UFTN had taken its toll. It was now time to put all that behind him and move onto the next chapter of his life. The only thing that mattered to him was spending quality time with Siobhan and his family. Evonne and Josephine would also be there to join in the celebrations.

But now he suddenly found himself adrift in a sea of emotions and uncertainty as to the fate of his future. How had it all gone so horribly wrong? He couldn't believe it, that just as he was entering retirement, tragic events would unfold and forsake him and his family. In one fateful cruel set of events, a life decision, a decision to retire from the military, would have lasting and widespread effects. Not only to his own life, but to that of the future history of Terran Earth itself.

Ashleigh, the father of three children who were just coming into themselves as individuals and that of a beautiful caring wife, Siobhan, who were about to enjoy his retirement together, would have their lives altered forever in one devilish cruel twist of fate. Was it destiny at play here, or was it the sins of his past coming back to haunt him as he had once thought many years ago? Was there some divine intervention from a higher power that would see him set upon a different path?

Ashleigh and Siobhan had always believed that events and circumstance weren't just mere coincidence. Everything held reason, and for every reason, there was a purpose. But right now, he couldn't care less for the purpose, and as for the reason? Well, he would search the depths of despair to find out. He would give his very soul if only he could turn back time and prevent that evening from ever occurring. This was the night of Ashleigh's farewell from the Oceania Terran Division and Federal Continental Ranger Corps from within.

Twenty-three years of continuous full time loyal service. Twenty-three years of uprooting his family and relocating to parts all over the globe. The year was 2085 and it was now all coming to a climax, as the events of that evening would unfurl. His farewell would take place in the city he had originally joined to become a Ranger in. The event would be held in Melbourne, his home town. As he left Destiny for the last time as a Ranger, he thought about his life up until that point. How fitting that he had finished his career in such a place named as this, Destiny? Perhaps his destiny had always led him to this point.

He was glad to have been going home and the thought of seeing his family filled him with much joy. Although he had not resided in this city for many years, it would always be home to him. It had been ten years since he and his family once lived there. This was the place he was born, it was where he met and married his high school sweetheart Siobhan, the place EJ and Marcus were born, and the place where he said goodbye to his elder-parents and where he recited his elder-father's eulogy. This place held a lot of meaning for Ashleigh, so it would be natural that one day he would take his family back home to Melbourne. It would be where they could find a little place to call their own to sit out the remaining years of their lives together.

Siobhan along with Elyssa-Jayne and Marcus, had gone to collect Alexander from the airport so they would all be able to share in his farewell from the Peace Makers. Alexander was flying in from the west, from the city of Perth, after finishing top in his class at the UFTN Peace Maker Federal Military College for Officers. He would follow in his father's footsteps and that of his lineage by forging his own stamp on military life.

However, unlike his father who had joined the service as an enlisted man, he instead had chosen to take the path of his great elder-father's choosing. He would become a Peace Maker Federal Officer of the OTD. Alexander's future looked very bright and he had received his first choice of career opportunities within the UFTN Peace Makers. He would become a helicopter pilot in the Federal Terran Aviation Corps.

Ashleigh had wandered down to the front gate of the barracks to wait for and to greet his family when they arrived. He had just gotten off the phone after receiving a call from Siobhan saying that they were only minutes away. He hadn't seen Alexander since he left to join up and was looking forward to see how much his eldest son had grown into a man. The excitement was slowly getting the better of him and he nervously paced the length of the gates that shrouded the front entrance of the barracks. Soon he could see into the distance the silhouetted shape of a vehicle that looked familiar to him and which was driving down the road towards him.

As the image got closer he could see that it was his family. This would be a great night to be held by all, by each and every one of them. He would once again have his entire family together in one place, including his surrogate family. Evonne and Josephine had already arrived bringing the twins Jeremey and Damian, and now Alexander was returning. The moment was nearing perfection.

As the vehicle got closer, the sound of music could be heard from behind him gradually becoming louder and louder. He didn't pay too much heed to the noise at the time, as he was too focussed on his families impending arrival. He also figured that it was just a bunch of young kids out for the night in their vehicle. He was so excited by the thought of having all those that he cared about, all those that were his life's blood, all together again, that he didn't stop to realise the trouble coming his way. They would see this night through and then spend a couple of weeks together to go camping up into the high country. They would head for the north-east of Victoria and into New South Wales.

But as Siobhan got closer, he saw from the periphery of his eyes, that another vehicle was heading directly towards hers. It was the same vehicle that he had heard the music belting out from only seconds earlier, along with that of which could only be described as the sound of voices in drunken laughter. Ashleigh could see Siobhan's face fixed on his, she hadn't noticed the driver of the vehicle that was now coming her way. Then just as Siobhan began to turn into the barracks, she witnessed the look of horrifying anguish on her husband's face. It was then that she realised what was about to happen without any power to stop it.

The path had been set and wheels put to motion. She would be helpless to change the course of events that was now about to be bestowed on them. Ashleigh looked on in horror as he heard the loud screech of tyres, followed by the sound of an almighty crash as one vehicle collided into the other. The driver of the oncoming vehicle was travelling at excessive speeds and in the slippery conditions of that summer's big wet, had lost all control. The driver had driven straight through a red light and had careered directly into the BMW-Royce that Siobhan was driving.

The crash was so loud and violent that all those inside the Officer's Mess having their pre-dinner drinks could hear it and they all rushed out onto the balcony to see what had transpired. What they saw seemed to resemble the remains of a midnight blue BMW-Royce as someone quickly noticed Ashleigh running towards the mangled vehicle. All had immediately recognised the transport of that belonging to Siobhan.

Evonne gasped in distress as she cupped her hands to her mouth in one fluid motion. Josephine meanwhile, had turned away in sheer disbelief, burying her head into her mother's neck and shoulder and grabbing her tightly as she did. A flood of tears quickly engulfed the two of them as they remained standing on the balcony both in shock. Was this the sensation that Anne and Crystal sensed the night when they all spent their first Christmas Union together? The sense that these women were not safe, but what of Alexander and Marcus?

For those that remained somewhat still composed, had now started their way down the stair case and out of the Officer's Mess rushing to lend assistance. There was nothing that any of them could do. The force of the crash created by the velocity of the other vehicle and stupidity of the driver who possessed it, had sheered the once new BMW-Royce completely in half. Siobhan had only purchased the vehicle for her husband's retirement present, but this was of little value or concern to him, it was its contents that he now pined for.

The impact of the crash had sent parts of the BMW-Royce in all directions including some of its occupants. Alexander had been thrown to one side of the vehicle, his now lifeless body coming to rest in the gutter that lined the road and which was only a matter of feet from where Ashleigh was standing. This was no place for his boy to be Ashleigh thought and he ran to his son lifting him up into his arms and carried his body to a grassed area just back from the road. Blood and sinew now stained the fresh white colour of his dinner jacket.

He tried to revive his son's life, but it was no use. Alexander had died instantly from the crash. Ashleigh's past experiences with the death and destruction of others, for the most part, had hardened his senses and emotions over the years. He had taught himself to keep control in order to continue with the task set before him. But now, his whole body shook uncontrollably as he tried to make some sense of this. His brain almost shutting down as he was struck with an emotional tide of overwhelming grief and anger. He had not known what to do next or who he would go to? Chris had since come down behind him, grabbing him by the shoulder.

'Ashleigh!' he said, receiving with no response.

'Captain Maynard!' the words coming now a little more forceful.

Chris now grabbed him by both shoulders and while looking

directly at him, shouted his name, but Ashleigh couldn't hear a word his friend was saying. He could see his friend's lips moving, but that was about all. What Chris had been trying to say, was for him to come and sit down and that he and the others would attend to the scene. Suddenly, he realised who it was that had been speaking to him. In his grief, he finally whispered a few words.

'Chris? Why?'

That's all he could say at the time. Nothing Chris could say would make a difference. He was not going to sit down, he needed to find the rest of his family and hoped they would still be alive. With that, he simply pushed passed his friend and rushed to the next closest member of his family. It would be EJ, still strapped into the rear seat of the car, her head slumped forward and blood gushing down from her head and beautiful hair.

He unbuckled his daughter from the seat and lifted her head grabbing it by each side. His eyes filled with tears, while hers remained closed. As he looked at EJ, he told her he was sorry and gave her a kiss on the lips. EJ was placed next to her brother Alexander, both covered in blankets as their lifeless bodies remained forever still and quiet.

There she was, he had spotted his wife and rushed to be by her side. He had not known it at the time but she still lived, breath still yet parted from her sweet lips and filled her lungs. How could any of them survive such terrible carnage? By now, the SDP and emergency branches of the Terran Division Services were on the scene. Fire & Paramedics, and Rescue & Disaster. They had all gone to work at various positions around the crash site and where the bodies of those had come to rest. The driver of the offending vehicle had died instantly taking all but one of his passengers along with him. There would be no need for vengeance to be sought, for it had already been taken by a higher power than his.

But this higher power had also seen fit to take the innocence of his family as well. He was the one that committed the sin all those years ago by having an illicit affair with another woman. For the result of that sin was now standing on the foot path with her mother, Evonne. Why hadn't it been he that died this day, instead that of his family? Although he was yet to locate Marcus and was unaware that his wife still lived, he feared the worst and gave up all hope.

Alexander and Elyssa-Jayne were positioned on the grassed area beside the road and Siobhan was laying in front of him, he thought them all dead. All those combat missions, battles and engagements in many war zones to various locations around the world and yet it was he that still breathed terran oxygen. Was this a way of keeping him alive so that he would be punished as those he loved around him were taken away?

When he had initially reached Siobhan, an SDP Officer had moved towards him and was about to push him back, but he was instead restrained by Chris. They watched as the paramedics placed a breathing apparatus over Siobhan's mouth and nose when she suddenly tilted her head and opened her eyes looking towards her husband. She must have heard his voice as he whimpered no, no, no, over and over. Siobhan then slowly and agonisingly lifted her arm and with outstretched fingers in a vain attempt, she tried to grab for her husband.

She wanted him by her side, as did he want to be at her side. One of the paramedics then made a gesture towards the SDP Officer who had previously tried to prevent Ashleigh from getting any closer. The paramedic indicated to the SDP Officer to let Ashleigh through and then stood up. He whispered a few words into the officer's ear, just low enough so only he could hear but no-one else.

'She hasn't got much left in her this one; I doubt if she'll even make it to the hospital, you can let him come near.'

And with that, Ashleigh was granted access and rushed to kneel down by his wife's side. As he gently grabbed hold of her hand cupping it with the two of his, he looked deeply into her eyes telling her how much he loved her and how sorry he was for all of this. In her response, Siobhan screwed her face up a little and gave a slight shake of her head from left to right, as she simply said,

'No.'

'I love you so much.' he told her.

'Don't leave, you'll be fine, you'll be fine.'

He struggled on the words as they left heavily from his mouth; he was choked full of emotion. He just kept repeating the words over and over again, don't leave, and, you'll be fine.

Siobhan then asked about the children, although she knew in her heart of hearts that they must be surely dead, there was always hope. Ashleigh couldn't bear the thought of telling his wife that they had all perished. That the beautiful children they had created together were all gone, well at least he had thought. He already carried Alexander and EJ over to the grassed area, but where was Marcus? He had yet to lay eyes on his youngest. Siobhan kept looking at Ashleigh and waiting for a reply. She knew by his lack of words that the unthinkable had happened. He struggled as he closed his eyes and then shook his head.

'Quick! Now! The Defib!'

The paramedics were yelling information and directions at each other as they went to work on Siobhan's body which had suddenly began to go into violent convulsions as blood now filled and spurted from her mouth. But just as quickly as it had started, had it soon stopped. Was she gone? Was that it? Chris grabbed his friend again, pulling him back as the paramedics continued working and trying to revive his wife. Eventually an audible tone could be heard coming from the electrocardiographic heart monitor and Siobhan was breathing again. The paramedics would have to get her to the hospital if there was to be any chance at all.

Now that Siobhan had seemed to stabilise, the paramedics loaded her onto a gurney and placed her into the back of the Paramedic Casualty Transport. Ashleigh gave her a loving look and told her that he would be along soon. The paramedic that was loading the rear of the gurney then explained the answer to a question that had filled Siobhan's thoughts, but was unable to ask herself. The paramedic explained that her husband would not be able to travel with her in the back of the ambulance for safety reasons. What he really meant was, he didn't want an emotional person in the back with them if they had to start the defibrillator again. They needed to be able to concentrate on what they were doing instead of trying to restrain a man out of control. Besides, he still hadn't found Marcus.

As the rear door of the PmCT shut, Siobhan, through her mask mouthed the words, I love you. The vehicle soon pulled away and from behind of where it had just been, Ashleigh peered over to a spot where Evonne and Josephine were. They were standing at a spot also surrounded by SDP Officers and more paramedics. He ran over to see what they were looking at, was it Marcus? As he reached their location, Evonne came running towards him telling him to stop and no, he mustn't go in there.

Evonne, her eyes red from all the tears that she had spent, was pleading with Ashleigh not to look. He looked at Josephine who was now sitting on the edge of the gutter looking after her little brothers; Jeremy under one arm and Damian under the other. He then glanced back over towards the large crowd of SDP Officers and paramedics. He told Evonne that he must, and with that, he gently pushed her out the way and ventured in.

He could not believe his eyes with the sight that filled them. Upon returning from the Terran Wars and the AN Uprising, he had wished to never again see such graphic and horrifying images like those he had seen ever again, but his wishes would have to wait. What he saw was a horrifying image. He looked down and there was his son Marcus, his head almost completely twisted around so that it was now almost facing to the rear, diagonally over his left shoulder. There he saw his son's chest which held a large gaping wound down to his son's stomach. The contents which was partly exposed as if it had been sliced open with a meat cleaver.

Marcus's left arm had been severed from just above the elbow and he was covered in blood from head to toe. This was one of the most violent of deaths that he had seen in his lifetime and it had happened to his boy. Why would such a thing happen to his family? Marcus was only fourteen years old and the youngest of the three children he had created with Siobhan. It was one thing that his family were taken away from him, but did they have to be taken so violently?

There was nothing else he could do except watch as his three children were all placed into black body bags to be taken to the city morgue. He witnessed the whole sequence of events which seemed to play out in slow motion as they happened. He racked his brain to think of anything he could have done to stop the accident from happening. It will be a question which would haunt him for years to come.

After all he had seen in peacetime and war; this would almost prove to be too much for him to cope with. As he collapsed to his knees and wept, now comforted by Evonne and his only living offspring still left alive, he thought about where his life would take him. Would he be able to get passed this one day and move on with his life? Or would he want to join his children in the afterlife? But what of Siobhan? She was still alive and had been taken to the hospital. In his grief and the disbelief that had gripped him upon seeing the remains of his son, Marcus, he had momentarily placed his wife from thought.

This would have been the first time since he had known Siobhan, with which this had happened. He had always thought of her, she was a constant presence in his life every second of the day, every day of the year; regardless of where he was or what he was doing. Evonne lifted Ashleigh's head and told him that she would drive him to the hospital. But Chris would have none of that. They were all far too emotional from these events for either of them to drive anywhere. The last thing anyone needed right now was for there to be another vehicle accident that could be avoided.

Chris would walk them both to his All Purpose AutoMobile, but first they would take a short detour back into the Officer's Mess where the both of them would change out of their bloody clothes. Evonne and Josephine would also quickly change out of theirs. Both Chris and Ashleigh had still been wearing their mess whites which now contained blood stains and other muck. While Evonne was still dressed in a blue sequined long evening gown that had also been stained and scuffed up.

They would not spend too much time on this as they wanted to get to the hospital as fast as they could, but they would at least make an attempt to present themselves well. It also wouldn't do Siobhan any good if Ashleigh came in to see her all bloodied with what she could only think of as being the remnants of one thing, the blood of her children.

They arrived at the hospital just after 8:30pm that night. After being received by the medical staff, they were then ushered into the waiting area. Ashleigh was informed that Siobhan was still in theatre being operated on and he asked how long she been in so far. An orderly informed him that she was rushed straight into the operating room when she arrived and that it just about to come up to two hours. Two hours he thought and there was still no indication that the surgeons would be finished any time soon. But he was thankful for one thing, she had made it to the hospital. She had at least made it this far and therefore there was still hope, for there is no life without it. As Ashleigh continued his thoughts towards Siobhan, he tried to regain his hope and hang on to it. While there is a chance, one must always have hope. Soon after, Josephine would also arrive at the hospital with the twins in tow. Buy now they were becoming very tired and restless.

The plan was to only have Jeremy and Damian with them at Ashleigh's farewell dinner for an hour or so. After that, Josephine would take them home where their elder-mother, Crystal would baby sit. They were only seven years old and had not realised or understood much of what was going on. They certainly did not need to be around all this to witness such events at such a tender age. Evonne had asked Josephine to take the twins home and had advised that she should stay there with them.

Josephine was now nineteen years old herself and after everything she had been through, Evonne had thought it would be kinder if she was to leave. But Josephine would have nothing of the sort. She wanted to be near her biological father, she wanted to support and comfort him as he had once done her. She loved him and it hurt her to see him in this much pain. She had also become very close to her step siblings and to her second mother, Siobhan, for she loved them all immensely. Evonne decided they could stay and a hospital counsellor came to mind the twins.

Chapter Nineteen

The medical staff, surgeons and theatre nurses emerged from the operating theatre nearly seven hours after going in. Siobhan was wheeled out connected to machines and tubes coming out from various parts of her face and body. Her eyes were still closed shut, sealed with medi-strips, but you could see that at least she was alive. Ashleigh rushed over by her side as she was taken to the Intensive Care Unit. The Chief Surgeon who had operated on Siobhan turned to talk to Ashleigh, but all he could do was follow his wife into the ICU.

'Well doctor?'

Evonne, who had asked the question of the Chief Surgeon, requested that he follow her and Ashleigh to ICU where he could explain Siobhan's condition to them. The orderly's and nurses gently lifted and positioned Siobhan onto a waiting bed where she would stay and hopefully recover. Other than the tubes sticking out of her and the knowledge of the fact she had just been in a vehicle accident, she looked at peace, as if she was just sleeping.

Ashleigh had many times over the course of their marriage watched her sleep as she had done him on many an occasion. He would sometimes just look at her until he himself fell asleep, while thinking to himself how lucky he was to have found such a beautiful and loving girl. Now that they were here and she was hooked up to machines in the ICU after just coming out of surgery, he wondered if she would ever wake up. Would she recover?

The surgeon had grabbed Ashleigh's attention as he, Evonne and Josephine all listened intently to what he had to say. It was not promising. Siobhan had suffered a lot of internal injuries and had spent six and a half hours in theatre as they tried to reassemble her insides and keep her brain activity alive. Ashleigh had remained awake the whole time, sitting still and in one place just staring at the doors of the operating theatre to open. He had waited patiently when those doors would open and when Siobhan would come walking out throwing her arms around him. He knew off course that this would not happen, but he could dream and wish.

He had seen many a soldier wounded in action and killed. He had seen the damage that bullets and shrapnel could do to flesh and bone, and he had developed an overwhelming appreciation for the critical incident trauma surgeons who put the pieces back together. He had seen miracles performed by these surgeons in the past and had hoped now for that same miracle. Would he be so lucky?

The surgeon continued explaining Siobhan's injuries detailing that she had suffered several broken bones, including her radius and ulnar in her left arm which must have snapped as she was lurched forward in the vehicle. Other broken bones included a fractured collar bone and several cracked and damaged ribs, one of which had punctured her right lung. Injuries were also sustained to her pelvis and hips and a fear that she may have damage to her spinal column which could render her paralysed.

Only when and if she wakes up will the doctors know if she will be able to walk again. Siobhan had lost quite a lot of blood due to suffering a lacerated spleen and liver causing internal bleeding, but the most serious of injuries sustained had been to her head. A neurosurgeon who had been called into theatre, had been required to drill a series of holes into the left side of Siobhan's skull. This was so that a small piece of her skull could be removed in order to release the fluid that was creating pressure on her brain. As a result of this, Siobhan was placed into a medical induced coma.

It would be unsure if she would ever wake again from it. Ashleigh was now watching as his entire life was slipping away from him before his eyes. The words coming from the doctor seemed to cut into him like a cold steel knife; each statement cutting deeper and deeper as each word was spoken. Ashleigh was speechless, he had wanted to ask questions but he simply couldn't and as if reading his mind, Evonne asked the Chief Surgeon what Siobhan's chances were of making a full recovery. The answer came slow and considered, but also painfully honest.

He explained that right now, that question wasn't even on the table. The question he most had fears for, was that of whether she would make it through the next 24 hours. She only had a very slim chance that all their work in the operating theatre would pay off. It was up to God now for the remainder.

Evonne turned to Josephine and told her that there was nothing else that could be done right now and to therefore take the twins and herself home to clean up and get some rest. She would want to stay by Ashleigh's side, but he wouldn't have it. Ashleigh wanted time alone just between the two of them and God to talk. So he requested that Evonne also leave. She agreed but not before convincing him to have a shower and clean himself up.

By now, Chris had returned with a fresh new set of clothes for Ashleigh to change into. One of the nurses nearby, over hearing this comment, advised that he could take a shower in the patient's room just down the hall. Siobhan would be fine for now, Evonne and Chris would stay by her side until he got back. As they left, both Chris and Evonne gave Ashleigh a big cuddle and told him to have faith, he hadn't lost Siobhan yet, there was still hope. Josephine started to cry again with emotion, she had only just become part of his family and now this. It would be some time for all involved to get over the events of last night, if ever at all.

Ashleigh stared at his wife and knelt down beside her clasping his hands and bowing his head. He had converted to the Roman Catholic Church when he was younger just so he could marry and be with the girl of his dreams, but it was not an empty vow he had made. Once he gave his commitment, once he had made a pledge, he would not only honour it, he would embrace it with open arms.

He held his wife's hand as he prayed to God and Jesus Christ above. He did not blame them for the tragic events that have now forsaken he and his family, he didn't even ask why they happened, for he had moved passed that question now. All he wanted was to have his wife back. He just wanted to have her open her eyes and tell him that everything was going to be alright as she had always done.

When morning's sun rose and the streaming bright light filled the sterile rooms and halls of the hospital reflecting off every white surface, Ashleigh had still not gone to sleep. He had stayed awake the entire night watching over his wife, as if a guardian angel were watching over his charge. He had been through sleep deprivation before during his time in the service, but this was obviously different. The way he was feeling, he would not know if he would ever sleep again, though he was badly in need of it.

Siobhan laid there in silence, only the sound of the machines could be heard in the room and the occasional call that came over the PA system. He watched as the ECG monitoring her heart rate and blood pressure beeped and varied at stages throughout the morning. He listened as the breathing apparatus keeping her alive pumped its valuable life giving oxygen into her lungs. The silence was broken by the arrival of Reilly and Lucienne, her parents and who were now in their sixties. They were accompanied by Siobhan's siblings.

In his grief and shock of the night before, he had forgotten to inform other family members of what had transpired that night.

Knowing his anguish and mental state, Chris had asked if he could do so on his behalf and proceeded to do just that. Siobhan's parents had left Melbourne a number of years ago moving to New South Wales into the Hinterland of the Hunter Valley. This was their retirement and they had decided to enjoy the vineyards and lifestyle surrounding the Hawkesbury River just south of Old Newcastle.

Desmond Kelly, the third eldest of the Kelly siblings, had organised a Multi-Person Capacity Vehicle to pick them up in when they arrived from Sydneyton. Desmond was now the only Kelly still living in Melbourne. Siobhan's twin younger sisters Ciara and Caoilainn would also be travelling with their parents, therefore; the MPCV had been the only logical choice. It would be a few hours later before the whole family was together again, as Deaglan and Sean were currently on their long flight from South Africa.

When they all walked into Siobhan's hospital room, they gasped at the sight of their daughter and sister lying on the bed in an induced coma. The attached machines and tubes emanating from her body had painted an image no parent ever wanted to see. Her father had once upon a time tried to keep Ashleigh and Siobhan apart, but eventually succumbing to his daughter's pleas, would see them joined in union. If those events of the past were different in some way, if the path taken was altered, would she be here in this condition now?

Although he thought it, he never dare speak such words, for he considered his son-in-law a good and righteous man. He loved him very much. This was not the fault of his son-in-law, but rather the tragic event caused by the reckless stupidity of others. And of whom also suffered the same fate. If Siobhan was to succumb to her injuries and pass away, he knew that given the chance and even if knowing of her fate, she would still choose to do it all over again. She had cherished every waking minute she had spent with Ashleigh and would not have it changed for anything or anyone.

Soon after their arrival, the doctor re-entered the room to see how his patient was faring. It would also be a good chance to brief her family now that they had arrived and while they were all there as one. He was sorry to say that there had not been much improvement overnight, but on the up side, she had not declined either. Was that good or bad? It didn't matter, it was simply what it was.

When Sean came into the room, tears grabbed him and he lost control. As a member of the SDP, he had followed his older brother, Deaglan, into the calling. It was a similar calling that Ashleigh had towards the FCR Corps. Living life as a person of the law and upholding peace and order had sometimes been a trying time. In his early years before becoming a Lieutenant Detective in the Victims of Sexual Assault & Homicide Unit, he started life as an SDP Traffic Officer.

During that time, he attended many horrific vehicle accident scenes that had been caused by unconsidered thought of action. Most perpetrators were either drunk on intoxicating liquor, or high on herorain. While many of the victims, as a result of the actions of others, were usually the innocence of other passengers or bystanders. And most of the time, these accidents resulted in fatalities. Families would have their lives torn apart forever more by these acts of violence. He had witnessed the horror of others, now it was he and his family suffering the same ill effects.

Ashleigh was quick to stand and comfort his young friend whom he considered a blood brother. It was the first time he had left that seat since returning from his shower and taking up position by his wife's side. Sean was glad the driver of the other vehicle had died and cursed him in the damnation in the pits of hell for his heinous crime. Ashleigh told him that thoughts such as those were harmful to one's spirit and self-worth. It could also act as a virus and infect those around them, something Sean new very well. No good could come of cursing someone who was already dead and had died themselves in terrible circumstances.

Suddenly, Ashleigh was calling on his teachings as a Ranger and that of Saint Michael. He was also considering the way of life Evonne and Josephine had chosen. He had been a Ranger to protect others that couldn't defend themselves against violent aggression. He had saved Evonne and Josephine from the actions of a madman. Anger would only beget anger, as this would lead to violence. He would not see Sean be swallowed up by feelings of hatred.

As the days turned into weeks, Siobhan remained in a coma, only living by the will of machines. Would that night, that most terrible of terrible nights be the last time that Ashleigh and Siobhan spoke? He remembered those words she had said to him just as the Paramedic Casualty Transport left the accident scene, 'I love you' she had said. He had still remembered the very first time she had spoken those words to him.

—⚜— ✝ —⚜—

Siobhan had decided to make his seventeenth birthday a special one. Having come from such a devout Catholic family and strict upbringing, no-one would ever think she would ever entertain the idea of an intimate evening. An evening that would result in the two of them ending up in a very intimate and personal embrace. But the thoughts of others were not the thoughts of hers, and she would have it different.

Ashleigh had never placed any form of pressure on her for anything more than what was already being received. In fact they had both loved and respected each other too much to place that type of sexual innuendo on each other. Oh they did talk about it, of course they did; they were teenagers after all and they knew that their desire to experience such a sensation would one day come. But only if the time was right.

They both agreed that if it was to happen, they would let it, but they would not rush into it and they would both share in its responsibility.

Ashleigh's seventeenth birthday was soon upon them. It would be held at the lands estate of his elder-parents. An estate that his actual father would have one day managed had it not been for his untimely demise. An estate that was currently being managed by his older brother, Andrew. Anyway, you could always be confident that a good party would be had by all when his elder-parents put on such events.

They had owned quite a few acres just out from the northern suburbs of Melbourne where the city life ended and the country began. On their property, they ran a few head of dairy cattle, just enough to provide the milk they required. There was a chook shed down the back and a ewe or two producing lambs for the feasting and providing wool for clothing.

When he and Siobhan first started dating, she would often catch the Public Service Transport out to where he lived where the two of them would go horse riding together. Prior to then, she had never been on a horse and was a little reserved about initially climbing on. She did, however; get on the horse with Ashleigh there by her side guiding her all the way.

Siobhan new she was in the safest of hands when it came to Ashleigh. It was almost like a sixth sense that they had felt for one another that when they were together, they felt the safest. It didn't mean of course that Ashleigh wouldn't play tricks on her from time to time, as he taught her how to ride. The two of them would have a great time together often riding up to where the dam was located at the rear of the property. They would hitch their horses to a fence railing, strip down to their underwear and jump in for a swim.

But the night of his birthday would be something else. The two of them would sing and dance to the early hours of the morning with most of the adults departing or going to bed as the night wore on. Having such a large property and being a bit of a distance from the city, Siobhan's parents allowed her to stay the night. But only if she slept in a separate bedroom all to herself. This meant that Ashleigh had to give up his room for her and move in with his older brother Andrew.

It was a small price to pay for Ashleigh, who despised the noise of grinding teeth as his brother slept. Some of Ashleigh's friends were also crashing out at his elder-parents' home, taking up sleeping positions on the lounge room floor. It would be two o'clock in the morning before they would all go to sleep. None of them wanted the night to end, but Siobhan finally convinced the other boys to rack out for she still had plans of her own for that evening. Or should it be said morning?

Ashleigh had no idea what was to come. His elder-parents had trusted him completely and were by now, fast asleep. The last of their guests had also climbed into their sleeping bags on the makeshift beds in the lounge room. Now as the two of them stood locked together in an embrace, arms around the other, Siobhan looked into Ashleigh's eyes and without saying a word, gave him a long sensuous and passionate kiss. As their lips parted, they were silhouetted by the gleam of the night sky's moon shining down upon them, as they remained standing on the back veranda, forever looking into each other's eyes.

Suddenly Siobhan lowered her arm down by his side reaching out for his hand. That look on her face was the same look she had given him that first day of school when they had met. It was a cheeky devilish look that indicated mischief. And as she continued to look at Ashleigh this way, she gracefully turned her body, glancing at him over her shoulder and led him away to his bedroom. The very same bedroom that she was supposed to have all to herself. He knew right away her intent and would treat her kindly and with compassion.

As they entered his bedroom, he slowly and quietly locked the door behind them. For the next five or so minutes the two of them just remained staring at each other in the dim night light now peering through the curtains. Then slowly, she slid the strap of her dress off her shoulders and let it fall to the ground. He had seen her half-dressed before but never like this. She then took a pace forward and proceeded to unbutton his shirt and removing it as the two then collapsed onto the bed in a loving embrace.

For the next period of time which seemed an eternity and of which the two wished would last for ever, they both shared their love in the ultimate way. They would not rush, they would take their time as this was both their first. They did not want to waste their moment together and would therefore cherish and savour every second of it. For two young people, this was quite an achievement; they had shown wisdom beyond their years.

For Ashleigh and Siobhan, the moment, the place, the time, and the act, all seemed to be right. Once they had finished, Siobhan rolled over on top of Ashleigh, and looking deeply into his eyes, she told him that she loved him. That was the first time she had said those words, and now all these years later, it would also be the last thing she would say to him.

Following his birthday, the next couple of months were like something else, as twice more the two would embrace and share their love. It would be a hard decision to make, but come the end of the year, Ashleigh would be in the OTD and commencing his training as a Federal Continental Ranger. They had met at the start of the year and now he would leave at the end of it.

—ɷ— ✝ —ɷ—

He glanced up and saw his beautiful wife still lying there in a coma in the hospital bed. He was helpless to do anything for her as he once again prayed to God for her recovery. He hadn't slept much over the last month and a bit, as still, there remained no sign of her improvement.

Siobhan just laid there peacefully and with tubes still attached to help her breathe. Her swelling had gone as well as her cuts and bruises. She was as beautiful to him as ever and he prayed each day that she would wake.

He was officially still a Ranger and so the time spent by his wife's side had now started eating into his leave entitlements. Entitlements that he had planned to use for other things. But none of that mattered now, for he had no need of it anymore. His plan of taking six weeks off to travel up the east coast was now a dream. As he stayed by her side over those long days and weeks, he remembered better times and reminisced about where it all began. He went back to a time and place that changed the course of his future and that of hers as well. It would be the day he left her for the Ranger Corps.

—✠—

He had just given his pledge by swearing the oath of allegiance to the UFTN and boarded the Public Service Transport for the airport. From there, he would soon be on his way to Christchurch NZ. All the while, Siobhan looked on from the parking lot as the PST was about to leave. He remembered the tears of sadness that welled up in her eyes. Up to that point, he had led a fairly active life being skilled and talented in sport as well as other endeavours. He and his brother had spent their teenage years playing Oceania Rules Football.

He was also an A grade student, consistently achieving exceedingly high grades throughout his academic life. His future looked bright and promising and he could have chosen any profession he wanted. But instead he left school and his girlfriend, and joined the FCR Corps at the age of seventeen. Much to the bitter disappointment of his elder-mother, who knew what service life was all about. He began his adult working life as a Tactical Communications Specialist.

This was particularly hard on Siobhan at the time. No-one around them except those in their inner circle could understand it. Why was it that an up and coming successful young teenager, who had been popular through sport and academic achievement, would choose to leave the life he knew for another? Especially as he held the girl most desired for by all.

The ultimate question which burned on everyone's lips was not how he could leave the life he knew, but rather why he would choose to leave her. She would surely be angry with him and would not want a long distance relationship. After all, they were basically still just children. They still had a lot to learn about life, for what did they know of it at such a young age? They had the whole world at their feet.

She too had been successful at school and was about to enter her final years with aspirations of being accepted into the Melbourne branch of the UFTN Knowledge & Wisdom Centre. There she would undertake a four year degree in veterinary science. Her times spent with Ashleigh on his elder-parent's property and being surrounded by livestock and domestic animals had sparked her interest. She loved the outdoors and she loved animals. She would seek to combine both her passions and make a career from it if she could.

She was also very attractive and Ashleigh knew that she quite often received the many looks from the other boys at school. Siobhan's three brothers would ensure no-one else tried anything on her while he was away, but her heart and their relationship rested squarely with them. What would happen? Would she stay true to him or would they grow apart? This too would raise questions of others around them about their relationship. Ashleigh and Siobhan knew better though, for the love they shared ran deep. It was a love forged from the inner recesses of their hearts as both beat in unison.

They each knew that this was something Ashleigh had always wanted to do. The House of Maynard was steeped in vast military tradition stemming all the way back to the time before the coming of the Darkness of the Great Despair. Distant ancestors of his had fought in the Napoleonic Wars and had served under the Duke of Wellington at the battle of Waterloo. His own elder-father had served in the War of the Great Despair while one of the first Maynard's born to these shores of Australia was killed at Passchendaele during the Great War of 1915-18. It would now be his turn to carry on the tradition.

But it was more than just this, he was also a very proud Oceanic citizen and Australian. This country he had called home had a lot to offer. It had sport, music, majestic coast lines and inland landscapes, and it had mostly survived the ravages of the Great Despair. Along with this, it also held a great tradition of mateship and as was written in the old text, was forged by Australian soldiers and carried on ever since. Australians, he had thought, had always answered the call whether it be in a military fashion or in humanitarian aid. This was very much like the Ranger Creed. Never the aggressor, but instead there to reach out the hand of friendship to help those in need.

He was proud of what this country had achieved then and what it had become now. As it now housed the government of the UFTN in the capital of Destiny. During the War of the Great Despair, after the cities of New York, London, and Paris were destroyed, the city of Canberra followed in their fate. It was just fortunate that conventional bombs were dropped on the city rather than nuclear ones. When the Consortium of Trust formed the UFTN, they had decided to rebuild the city of Canberra bigger and better than before. However, they would rename it Destiny, for this now held the destiny of all in its hands.

He would choose to serve the UFTN as his elder-father had done, for its principles were worth preserving. Siobhan knew this was in his heart and would therefore not stop him. But his love for Siobhan would also see him serve his calling towards her. Nothing would ever come between them. At least that is what they had thought at the time. As he sat there standing watch over Siobhan in her hospital room, he knew that times were very different now and the events of the past five years have changed all their lives forever.

Chapter Twenty

To everyone's surprise except theirs, their love did survive and in their fifth year, they were married. For the next twenty-three years they were inseparable, except of course when he had gone to war or had to attend military training manoeuvres. But even then, their love for each other just continued to flourish and grow stronger. There was never any doubt that these two were made for each other. They relied on each other and they supported one another throughout their marriage, with love and affection.

Although, do not think their relationship perfect. They had been just like any other couple, for they too shared in their many ups and downs that a marriage, children and life could throw at them. For a time, the two had argued over many of life's constant little challenges. A few of these arguments had been based around financial issues and how they were going to support their children.

Put it this way, a Ranger did not serve the UFTN for the terra marcs. It would only be sometime later, as he was promoted through the ranks and as she started getting constant business as a veterinary doctor that their monetary issues would start to ease. She had remembered her childhood and the struggles of her parents as they tried to care for six children. Although she loved her parents dearly, she had sort not to imitate their life by doing the same for her own.

She became frustrated with him at times and had blamed his military service on the instability and uncertainty of their family life. Their children's education had been inconsistent as they bounced from one school to the next every two or three years; city to city, country to country. The only time her and their children lived in one place for more than three years had been during the Terran Wars, but that had resulted in living without her husband while he was away fighting. She reconsidered her thoughts that relocating so much would be fine compared to the option of not having him with them at all. She would constantly fear for the safety of his life in a sometimes turbulent and unsure world.

Her own work life had also suffered and for this he had been extremely sorry. She had completed her four year degree and had become a very accomplished and successful Vet. She had a special way with animals and people trusted her. But just as she started to build up a cliental base, he would be relocated, again. Each time, Siobhan would have to strike up a fresh rapport with potential new customers as they moved to the next town or city. If she could not gain effective employment as a Vet, Siobhan was then forced to sit through interview after interview, as she applied for any job that would bring them further income.

But these were only little issues in the grand scheme of things. She had loved him and would always do her best to support him, just as he would do for her. This had been another reason for why he had sort to take retirement after twenty-three years of service. He had seen a lot of things in his life and they as a family had seen a lot of the changing world as he moved through his military career. Places such as, Brazil, Johannesburg, Pretoria, Sydneyton, Queenstown, and of course, Destiny.

Now he was going through another challenging time in his life. His children were gone to what Josephine had called, the afterlife and now it looked as though his wife might never wake up, resulting in her also joining her children in the afterlife. It hadn't been mentioned yet, but he may be asked for his permission by the medical staff to turn off Siobhan's life support.

—∞— ✝ —∞—

Later that night, Ashleigh sat there in the hospital room alone, watching over Siobhan. Images of the past rushed through his mind. He recalled the seven years constantly fighting against a worthless cause adopted by the RFN during the Terran Wars. This had taken a lot out of him at the time and the visions of many a bad thing he had seen and done had never quite managed to escape him. Friends he once knew were gone and millions had died to the Xialm. He recounted the AN Uprising and his last battle in the Congo. He thought of his new daughter and what she must also be going through at this moment, living in her own type of hell. All these events were compounding his emotions and he suddenly felt his body start to physically and mentally shut down. The feelings that befell him quickly became overwhelming leading him to sob uncontrollably as he laid his head across Siobhan's chest.

All these nightmares he had gone through and waking up in cold sweats as he tried to sleep, had all been tendered to by his caring wife. Saint Michael's words echoed in his ears as they gave guidance and wisdom. Rangers always took care of their own, for the Corps was family. But Siobhan and his children were blood and that would bind them together as one, more than any words would ever do. Every emotion he had felt up until this point from the events that had so far shaped his life would pale in comparison to what he was going through right now.

It had now been six weeks since the night of the accident which claimed the lives of his Alexander, Elyssa-Jayne and Marcus; and which had placed Siobhan into hospital. She was now out of intensive care but remained in a coma still hooked up to machines keeping her alive. The doctors had advised him that nothing more could be done for her. The only humane thing left to do was to turn the machines off and let her slip away into the abyss of the afterlife. But he would not consent to this, he couldn't even bear to think of the thought. He just continued to hope and pray that she would wake up.

Siobhan's father tried to convince him that it needed to be done. He hated the thought of his daughter living this way and it broke his heart every time he came in to the hospital and saw his daughter in this condition. This is not the way he wanted to remember her. Prolonging the inevitable would only serve to cause more distress and heartache for all involved. But as Ashleigh was the only legal person that could make that decision, the choice would remain with him.

Andrew had also tried to convince him, as much as it had pained him to do so. They had all thought that if anyone could sway his mind it would be his older brother. They were more than brothers these two, they were the best of friends. Andrew had also reminded Ashleigh that his children were still sitting in the hospital morgue. They needed to be farewelled and a service held regardless of Siobhan's condition.

The two of them had never really come to blows in the past, but Ashleigh was furious with his brother and clenching his hand to make a fist, he lashed out at Andrew knocking him to the floor right then and there in the hospital room. It was only by Evonne's presence that Ashleigh stopped. Andrew would of course not retaliate, he loved Siobhan as well; she had been a great sister-in-law. If Andrew could've swapped places with her, he would have gladly done so, but this simply was not the case.

The reality had to be realised, Ashleigh still had a responsibility to his children and to his catholic faith. They needed to be taken into God's care, but while they remained in the hospital morgue, their passing from this life to the next was obstructed. Andrew expressed his deepest sorrow for Siobhan's condition and as he wiped the blood away from his cut lip given to him by Ashleigh, he left the room. But before he walked through the door and exited, he again asked his younger brother to at least start thinking about it.

Evonne put her arms around Ashleigh and squeezed him tight, Ashleigh returned the sentiment. For a moment, he looked into Evonne's eyes with longing and proceeded to rest his head on her chest as his tears overcame him. He hadn't really cried until this very moment and now he had, his arms and hands clenched tighter around Evonne's waist. He held her for the longest time not wanting to let go.

He was as connected to her as any husband would be connected to their wife and in any other lifetime, the two of them might have been joined in union. But the fact was she wasn't his wife, the woman he most loved, the woman he had always loved now rested on a hospital bed connected to machines that kept her alive. He had appreciated Evonne's compassion and gentle caring hand, but he slowly raised his head from her breast, wiped the tears from his eyes and turned back to Siobhan.

He would enter prayer again and ask for guidance from the Lord above on what he should do. He would ask the Lord and Saint Michael to spare the life of Siobhan and return her to him. He pleaded for the forgiveness of his sins and he would thank the Lord for the cherished time he had spent with his wife.

This was taking a huge toll on Evonne and her life. She had quit her job only to seek further employment that offered flexible and casual working hours. She would do this so she could come to the hospital to support Ashleigh. She never missed a day; there every morning before starting work and there every evening after finishing. Had he realised the sacrifices she was making for him? What were these thoughts she was having? How could she think such things? Ashleigh had been nothing but kind and generous to her over the years, she would push those thoughts from her mind and punish herself for ever having such ideas.

Maybe for a brief moment she had wished that it was just the two of them again. Maybe it was the way Ashleigh had cuddled her, feeling the warmth of his body as her heart beat against the side of his face. Or maybe it was the way he pulled away from her to return to Siobhan's side and start to pray again. Who knows? She had been caught up in the moment and would see to it that she would not have these selfish thoughts again. She would remain by his side for as long as was needed. She knew he needed her support, as did he know he required it.

Every day Evonne came into the hospital to visit Ashleigh and Siobhan, she would make sure he was eating right and at least getting some rest. Every so often, she would bring him a fresh set of clothes to change into. She cared for him a great deal and would generally provide him love and comfort. She had always loved Ashleigh, never really letting go of the affair they had all those years ago. She knew she would never again share his bed or ever be considered his partner, but all that was irrelevant anyway. She was his friend and she loved him. She would continue to care and support him and would see to it that he was looked after.

Siobhan would welcome Evonne's affections towards her husband if it meant he didn't have to be alone. It would take some time for him to move pass this, although never really getting over it, Siobhan would rest more peacefully if she knew Ashleigh had someone to care for him. Siobhan new that Evonne was that person and had once said to her that if anything happened, she wanted Evonne to ensure her husband was cared for and loved.

A few more days passed and Evonne had wanted to broach the subject of the children's Passing of Life ceremony, but didn't know how to bring up the subject. She was not sure if Ashleigh would burst into anger against her like he had done with Andrew. Oh she knew he would not physically strike her, but she could still receive a good tongue lashing for her efforts.

She had wanted to provide options for him. Would he agree to turn the machines off and allow Siobhan to accompany their children into the afterlife, or would he send the children ahead first with her to follow later?

One thing was sure, he couldn't continue living life like this. He had to move on and he had to allow others to move on as well. Her parents and siblings as well as his brother and other extended family were all in continual heartache and sorrow over Siobhan. She and the children needed to be farewelled and they allowed to mourn for their loss. Something had to give and Evonne felt that soon she and Ashleigh would be at an impasse.

Up until this point she had provided no opinion, advice, or judgment; she just remained by his side. It was now time to give her opinion and she grabbed Ashleigh by the hand and with the other gently rested it against the side of his cheek to turn his gaze towards hers. The words that Ashleigh knew he would have to listen to, would be the words that could only come from Evonne, were finally expressed.

'You need to let the medical staff turn off the machines.' she explained to him.

'You need to let her go and you need to see your family passed from this life to the next.'

He didn't yell, he didn't get upset, he simply nodded his head in approval. Evonne than put her arms around him, telling him that Siobhan and the children will never be far from him. They would forever remain in his heart and in his thoughts.

Evonne had been the sense of reason and clarity that he needed. She had provided the words of wisdom through compassion and with care, just as Siobhan had done many times before. He would choose to have one more day with his wife to say goodbye. Presently, his prayers had only consisted of the hope she would recover, he had not once said goodbye to her. He would think of all the joyous and loving times they had spent together. He would remember the ice cold winter nights in Melbourne and as they would snuggle into each other when they had gone to bed to keep each other warm.

He also remembered all the times she had supported and taken care of him each time he had returned from war. Siobhan had been a strong woman both mentally and emotionally. Why was his life surrounded in so much tragedy? He knew that he was not the only one to suffer from loss and that he had to learn to deal with all the events of the past. He just couldn't deal with this one. He would give anything to have his wife back and he just didn't know how he could live without her.

The time was now. Each one of the family, her parents, brothers and sisters, and his brother and family along with Evonne and Josephine including Crystal and Anne, would each enter the room to say their goodbyes to Siobhan. Ashleigh had requested that they would respect his wishes by allowing him to be the only one in the room when the machines were turned off. Not even Evonne would be in the room. As they all finished, a doctor and two nurses walked in, one of them handed him a consent form for him to sign. The doctor then walked around to the side of the bed to turn off the machine as the nurses removed all the tubes from Siobhan's mouth and nose.

Ashleigh would want to see her as she was without all the medical devices hanging from her. All evidence and trace that she had been in a vehicle accident was now non-existent. No bruises, no abrasions, no swelling and no tubes or machines, she was as beautiful to him as the first day they had met. The last of the medical staff now left the room and had closed the door behind them as he did.

He was now the only one left in the room and he watched as his wife struggled to breathe on her own for the first time since the accident. Each breath she took grew shorter and shallower then the last as her heart beat became slightly erratic and less frequent. Ashleigh was now lying down beside her on the bed and cradling her head and body, this day she would die in his arms. He looked and stared at his wife, a single tear of his dropping onto her face, and then her last breath was done and she was gone.

For the next ten minutes he just held her in his arms. Eventually he let go of her and walked outside the room to inform all those waiting that Siobhan had died. He would allow them again to all have another moment with her if they felt it was needed or wanted. The last image they all had was that of tubes and machines, he would see that their last memory of Siobhan would not be of that. Josephine asked her father if she could be alone with her second mother. She had wanted to say goodbye to Siobhan in her way and would prepare Siobhan's body for the passing with words sprung from Hope and Grace.

Lastly, Evonne walked to Ashleigh and told him that no matter what it takes, she will be there by his side if he wanted it. She would continue to help him through this.

Chapter Twenty-One

A t home and with dinner about to be served, he opened up a bottle of whiskey and was about to take a bout when Evonne bought his plate of food over to him. It was the first night he had been home in nearly two months. He hadn't left Siobhan's side in the hospital room at all over that time and now he dreaded the oncoming Passing of Life ceremonies that awaited him. He had slept, ate, showered and changed all in that hospital room and now for the first time in a very long while, he needed a drink.

Typically he hadn't been known as one who would turn to the bottle in times of discomfort and distress, and this worried Evonne as it bought back horrible memories of her husband, Dirk. He knew what he was doing was wrong and he didn't want to get caught up in the cycle of drink, but for right at this very moment, he just wanted something to take the edge off. But when Evonne entered the room and he saw the look of concern upon her worried face, he placed the bottled down, got up from the table and went and laid down on his bed.

She would look after him like she said, though it would pain her so. He knew Evonne would not be happy if he started drinking. She had seen the evil power that alcohol could do to a person's spirit. As too had she seen first-hand the resulting actions from an abusive husband taken by the drink. He didn't want her fearing that he could end up going down that same dangerous path if once it took hold.

Ashleigh had returned to their home in the Dandenong Ranges, roughly 35km from the heart of Melbourne city. This was the home they had just moved into after returning from Destiny to commence his retirement from the services. Household items, including his wife's and children's belongings and clothes, were still all contained in moving boxes. He would not look forward to the unenviable task of going through these boxes to discard their items. However this was a task he knew had to be done, but he just couldn't bring himself to start and so avoided its commencement.

Thoughts raced a million miles an hour through the maze that was now his mind. He wondered which of their items he would simply throw out and which he would give away to charity. What would he keep and how was he going to go about it? Evonne and Josephine would offer their assistance and he graciously accepted, but that could wait for now. He still had to organise the Passing of Life ceremony for his fallen family.

Evonne also had to get back on her feet and gain full time employment again, although money wasn't an issue for her just yet, she thought it would be best not to let it linger too long. As well as Evonne's casual work, Josephine was also lending assistance by working as a waitress in a local city café. As too was Ashleigh, he had no issue in supporting Evonne and her family financially, they were after all his family as well, but he still had to pay for the cost for the ceremony. His brother and his friend Chris with the assistance of his Rangers he once commanded, would all provide their support in the coming days. Siobhan's siblings and her parents would also be there for support. Soon he would bury and say goodbye for the last time to four much loved and cherished members of his family.

Once again, this military career which he had given so much and which his family had also given, was still taking. His family had been there for him over so many years and were now taken from him at the end. If their decisions, his decisions, had of been different, they might all still be alive today. The girl he had met in high school, his children, were now all gone. Alexander – eighteen, Elyssa-Jayne – sixteen, and Marcus Angelus – fourteen years old. And finally, his wife, Siobhan, taken away from him with her life ending at age forty.

All had promising lives. Alexander would follow in the path of the Maynard tradition of military service, whereas EJ had decided to go into the performing arts as a singer and dancer. It was only recently that she had been accepted into the UFTN School of Music, Dance and Drama. The once famous learning centre of Juilliard based in New York City had been resurrected to once again take its place amongst those as one of the most sought after and esteemed learning institutions for the performance arts. Siobhan and he had been so proud of their daughter for her achievement and come the following year would have said goodbye to EJ as she started her six years of dance and song.

Marcus on the other hand was just happy that he was at last gaining the academic results he much aspired to for so long. His eye sight was getting better with each passing year and doctors had agreed that come his twentieth birthday, Marcus would have been completely clear of the disease. It was unsure what path would take hold of Marcus, but at least now his opportunities were expanding. Their lives, their futures, and his blood line was all wiped out in a matter of minutes by the actions of a foolhardy and reckless act.

Now at the age of thirty-nine, he was alone, really alone. Even though Evonne and Josephine were there to comfort him, he felt an isolation take hold. He had never ever felt such despair of hopelessness or worthlessness in his life before. He had been with Siobhan for twenty-four years, twenty of those as husband and wife. Now that she was gone, he simply did not know how to live. There was no purpose to it anymore. Everything that had really ever meant something to him for so many years was now gone.

Josephine could feel that the bond she had forged with her father, one which had seemed to have naturally evolved and grown of its own accord, was starting to slip away. She feared the darkness of her thoughts and looked into her inner mind with premonitions of what was yet to come. But thanks to her teachings by Mieke and Aine, and the Lacrimis Speiv which was now engrained in her and part of her life-force, she knew that visions of the future could be changed.

She now knew that her images were only one possibility of events that could happen if one allowed them to happen. She had seen her images of the future change before and had come to realise that the visions would hold a small percentage of becoming true in an incalculable number of outcomes. Images this strong would only avail themselves as true if they were allowed to do so and these were strong images, very strong indeed. The visions she was having now showed a greater depth of darkness, death and despair, all emanating from one man, her father.

Throughout Josephine's learning and education of the Graceline ways and now with the teachings from the Order of Hope, her premonitions containing her father had always been positive and bright. Her father was always seen in the light of day, confident and sure about his actions. She took these meanings to say that all those in his presence would be safe and protected. These new images she was now having, painted a completely different picture, one in which worried and frightened her.

Since she was little and had been made to endure the injustices at the hands of her stepfather's wrath, had she thought there was more to her own and her mother's life. There had to be more, this couldn't be all there was. She had images of her knight in shining armour coming to them and being with Evonne; was this how it was supposed to be? To make one a reality must make others in that reality suffer? It wasn't fare.

The gods and goddesses of Hope and Grace would surely not allow this to be. But it happened and was made so. Josephine realised that the key to bring the light back into her father's spirit, would be her mother. Somehow through her father's grief, she would have to convince him of this, as well as trying to convince her mother of it also.

Ashleigh continued to linger around the home after the Passing of Life was done and dusted. The house was a mess and boxes moved into position by the removalists still resided in their initial space where they had been placed. Evonne tried in desperate vain attempts to convince him to start going through things, but he resisted and said nothing only to have another drink. The urge to supress his feelings with alcohol were now more strongly evident than his urges to ease Evonne's fears. He was getting nowhere with his life, the longer he stayed within that house, the more he regressed into the depths of self-pity and despair.

—w— ✝ —w—

It was now February in the UFTN calendar year of 2086. He decided that he needed to gain some perspective and clear his thoughts. He would therefore travel to the place where the first Rangers were created during the War of the Great Despair and where they would eventually take on Saint Michael the Archangel as their spiritual guide and protector. He would travel to Canaan, the birth place of modern civilisation, to a place once known as Mesopotamia now known as Iraq. From there he would travel on foot into the heartland of Iran where all the Rangers once stood as one, the once formidable kingdom of Persia.

There he would hope to find the answers for the questions that have plagued him since the accident. He would travel this route alone and once there, he would endure the hardships of the northern hemisphere on foot. No vehicles, no luxuries; he would return back to the basics and experience life the way it should be during one's self rediscovery. This he knew was required to be the correct path of enlightenment, the only path to his redemption and salvation. He would turn to his faith of Catholicism but he would now also strongly embrace the ways of his daughter, the ways of Grace and Hope.

He had blamed a lot of the misfortunes of others upon himself. He took personal responsibility for Evonne's life, he was the cause of Josephine's life, Alexander had been born with TerraOxygenen Syndrome because of him, and likewise, he blamed himself for Marcus being afflicted with RFN eyes. The untimely deaths of Siobhan, Alexander, EJ and Marcus, he had thought, had been as a result of his actions. And he even held the self-blame for his own biological parents being killed although he couldn't have possibly effected their outcome.

He would walk this path and see where it took him and he would hope to find something that would spark up his life again. But how could anything really replace what he had lost. Once in Canaan, there was really only one choice left for him to do. That was to let his life go, recycle his so another can be born. He had lived a full and exciting life; it was now time to let it go and join his family in the afterlife. But there would be no Passing of Life Ceremony held in his honour, he would not want it. He would rather simply disappear without a trace.

Ashleigh had now succumbed to the deepest recesses of his soul. That night he would sleep his last night, or as he thought. As he entered a state of R.E.M. sleep, images flashed before his sub-conscious thoughts. He had only experienced this one time before in his life and that had been during the Battle of the Congo during the final stages of the AN Uprising.

It seemed that now, as once again he was having doubts about his life, these thoughts and images again appeared before him. It was almost as if there was something or someone there, leading or guiding him to put him back on track. Those earlier images he thought to have been human now appeared more clearly. He turned and tossed on the hard ground under the Canaan night sky of the Darkness. Slowly the image of a person got closer until he could make the shape out to be that of one belonging to a female form. The figure got closer and closer until?

It was Josephine, but her face remained expressionless and unmoved in her stares towards him. She seem to not recognise the man that was her father. Was this his daughter he thought or was this figure or entity using his daughter's appearance to be a familiar face from his life in an effort to wield a calming presence over him? When she spoke, the sound projected in a monotone non-emotive pitch and tone. The voice coming slow and winding in a whirring wavering way as the figure stood there in an outer haze of shimmering blue light that surrounded her.

She instructed him that his time in caporal form was not yet up. There was more to be achieved for humankind and Evonne and Josephine still needed him more than ever, especially the twins. The un-angelic voice coming from this figure instructed him to believe in his societies' adopted ways in searching for knowledge and wisdom. But this and the answers to the questions he yearned for would not lie on this lone terran rock, but rather out beyond the stars.

Suddenly the skies opened up and the Darkness rains poured down on him in a thunderous roar. This was unusual at this time of the year and he was caught off guard. As he had been sleeping with no shelter erected, the droplets of rain splashed on his face and he quickly panicked waiting for their devastating effects to take hold. However, he was very surprised to the fact that the liquid did not sting his skin and as he licked his lips, the liquid tasted sweet. He hadn't known it at the time, but the rains that fell on him that night weren't as a result of the

Darkness bought on by the Great Despair, it was actually the pure form of Lacrimis Speiv. But it would only be a small amount, just enough to set him upon path.

Regardless of this fact that the rain seemed harmless, he still erected the shelter provided by his PARTNAR trench coat, opening up the inner flaps of the coat to provide a perfectly formed round dome. Now fully awake, he couldn't quite remember everything he had seen or heard from his vision, only snippets. But it was enough for him to realise that the vision had indeed been real. He had learned to take these visions seriously and would heed their words very carefully and wisely, although he was unsure why they had availed themselves to him, a man. The next day and six months later, he was in an air transport back to Melbourne.

It was not time to give his life away. He always said that a life must be worth living and was not to be squandered without thought. He would not give it away so callously without caution, thought or consideration. All he had ever wanted to do, was to serve the citizens of the UFTN. The goal of which was to provide a utopian society where all could be treated with equality and fairness and one could better themselves through the divine guidance of knowledge and wisdom.

Evonne and Josephine were so excited to see him again and jumped with joy at his arrival. Ashleigh hugged them both and apologised for his behaviour of late, but as Evonne had explained, there was nothing for him to be sorry for. None of this had been as a result of his actions and his grieving was just part of the course. Josephine, now very skilled in her ways, reaffirmed the sentiments of her mother. She looked at him and once again they both felt a connection of knowing the others thoughts. He knew by her look that Josephine had known of the rain that fell on him that night and part of the vision he had experienced. She now saw her own vision of her father back in the light, though it would still be a long road ahead.

Jeremy and Damian were also excited to see him return, Damian especially. But Jeremy remained distant, despite of the ground that had been closed between them during those days when they all lived together. He was never quite sure what to make of Jeremy, but didn't consider the matter that critical. Over time there relationship would have to improve, surely.

Back at the house, he saw that Evonne had emptied all the boxes except those belonging to Siobhan and the children. This was something that only he would have to do. Not wanting to be alone, he asked if Evonne, Josephine and the twins, wouldn't mind staying with him awhile until he got back on his feet. Evonne's heart skipped a beat and she suddenly felt faint as she eagerly and internally secretly jumped with excitement. Outwardly, however; she remained calm and composed and simply told him that if that was what he wanted, she would accommodate.

It was hard for him to be back in that home, but at least it was filled again with the sound of children running around. Alexander, EJ and Marcus would never be replaced, but while he had care and love to give, he would give it. There was no time like the present and that first day back home, he opened the first box of many, starting with his late wife's. He held up an old t-shirt and worn pair of jeans that had been her favourite. Though she would not be caught dead out in public with these on, they were more for getting around the house in and lazing on the sofa.

Emotion is a powerful sensation and by this, a lump started to form in his throat, but he pushed on. Next was a see-through black silk and lace negligée with red trimming and highlights. This she had worn on those special nights when she had wanted to please her husband and tease him a little. Siobhan's devil streak never did change. Though her teasing in such a sexy way was usually preceded by an evening of fine dining accompanied with a few glasses of the most exquisite wine. He recalled just how much fun he had removing the said garment and the look in her eyes she gave him. He never imagined that going through her clothes would be so demanding.

None of her clothes would be offered to Evonne or Josephine, not even plain old sweat shirts and pullovers. It would only remind him of her and he would rather use photographs and the kept visual recordings of her for that purpose. Most of the clothes, except for the undergarments would be donated to the local UFTN Sanctuary and Shelter for the less fortunate.

The only item of hers he would keep, would be the very last item of the very last box he opened, her wedding dress. This he would keep and pass down to Josephine if she so wished it. Knowing of course that Evonne had thrown her wedding dress out because of what it represented. On the other hand, Josephine might simply want to purchase a new one altogether, but at least there would be a choice. Josephine had told him that she would be honoured one day to wear this dress and would keep it safe with pride and loving care. He just told her not to make that day anytime soon. He didn't want to lose her that fast to another man.

Later that night while they were all sleeping, a moaning whimpering sound could be heard coming from within side the house. Evonne got up out of bed from where she was sleeping in the guest room to investigate. She already had some suspicion as to the origin and purpose of the sounds, but she still checked on the boys. They were fine and sound asleep.

'Mother, its father.'

'I know Pheenie, I just don't know what to do.'

Evonne had wanted to comfort the man she loved, but did not want to be seen as throwing herself on him during his time of grief.

'Go to him mother, he will not turn you away. He loves you.'

Josephine knew this was the perfect opportunity to set right the course that had beset them all. She continued to quietly whisper her thoughts to her mother. It had been tragic and unfortunate the series of events that have led them to this point, but they were set none the less and now they needed to be followed. There was no coincidence or chance, everything happened for a reason and every reason held a higher cause. The only way to follow that cause and learn its meaning was to follow its calling. And right now, its calling was telling Evonne to go to him.

Evonne slowly and timidly crept down the corridor towards the half open door of Ashleigh's bedroom. As she peered into the room, she saw that he was laying on his side curled up in the foetal position with his back facing her. He was laying there wide awake and quietly sobbing. His position on the bed was almost at the very right edge of the mattress. If he was any further over, he would have fallen off. The left side of the bed, the side that Siobhan had usually slept on, was made up perfectly and remained untouched. Evonne peered in a little more and had surmised that he had not wanted to disturb his late wife's side of the bed. Maybe he was hoping that Siobhan would one day come back in and join him.

Evonne was hesitant to go any further and she looked back at Josephine with uncertainty.

'Go on.' She whispered at her mother.

But it was too late, in Evonne's haste, she had knocked the door making it move with a creaking sound. Startled by this, she froze in place, but Ashleigh did not stir. Had he heard her? Surely the sound of the door moving would have indicated that someone was at his door. He had heard alright, in fact he had known of her presence for quite some time. She was about to turn away when she saw his hand reach out rearwards over his back. With his hand now outstretched behind him, he continued to look out the bedroom window to his front, his back still at Evonne.

Evonne nervously moved into the room slightly where she saw him make a cupping motion as he opened and closed the fingers of his hand as it dangled behind him. He was indicating to Evonne for her to join him. So she moved into the room a little further, gently and cautiously with each step she took. At first she was unsure if she should lay down next to him on Siobhan's side of the bed. But she took the gamble and moved herself into position behind him and lovingly placed her arm underneath his and around his chest.

She had cuddled right up close to him and he hadn't turned her away. For the next while, the two of them stayed in this position without saying a word. He just continued to quietly sob while she held the man she had loved for so long. Her emotions started to get the better of her as tears started to form in her eyes.

Evonne then spoke his name with concern in her voice. This was enough to make him roll over to face her. Now staring into her eyes, he buried his face into her chest and started to cry. Evonne just held onto him tighter until she raised his head and told him that she would always be there for him. She was going to take care of him just as Siobhan had told her to do all those years ago. Ashleigh wiped away his tears and the two of them kissed. They did not feel guilty that night for their actions. They instead embraced one another and made love passionately and with an intimacy as never before. None of the intensity or fire had left their feelings for the other.

Was it possible to have loved two beautiful women in one life time and at the same time? This question he had asked himself many years ago and the answer? Yes it was. The fact was he never stopped loving Evonne, but his decision had been to marry Siobhan. And that had been the correct decision, there was never any doubting that. However, circumstance and fate had saw fit to bring these two back together by removing others in his life.

Why he thought? Some of that question had been answered during his travels to Canaan. There was a higher purpose, he just didn't know what.

The following morning, he was up and out of bed and making breakfast for all of them. Evonne was still asleep in his bed, the very bed he had invited her into the night before. Upon waking, she held fears that the events of last night were just a spur of the moment reaction. She feared that because of it, their relationship would be forever altered and he might ask her to leave. She had felt relieved when she finally learnt that she wouldn't be and knew that things were going improve for them all. They were at least entitled to some happiness. She had also been right about their relationship forever being altered. But it would not be in the way she had originally thought.

'Good morning.'

When she finally built up enough courage to avail herself in the kitchen where he was, she was greeted with a cheerful smile and loving kiss. There was no regret, no shame, just an epiphany in time that had turned his, and as would turn out, her life around. He would never forget his wife and children, the years he had with them or the tragic and horrific way of their passing. But he had found love again, as too did she. For the loved they shared had never really left them.

Being as committed as he had always been, he proposed matrimony and a month later, Ashleigh and Evonne would be joined together in marriage as one under god. But it would be no ordinary marriage. They would seal their vows under the paganistic ways of Hope and Grace. This he now knew was where his destiny lay. Much would await him in the coming years and he knew that his time on this Terran Earth was not yet up. With that, he would return to his beloved Federal Continental Rangers, resuming the position in the Capital, Destiny; the position he had initially walked away from. Upon his return, he would be promoted to the rank of Major and start working closely with his friend Chris, who was now his Commanding Officer, on the New World Project.

But before then and for now, they would take one day at a time and enjoy their life together, for they were finally one as they had both once wished for. Was it destiny that had bought them to this event? After all the pain and suffering she had gone through, after his fight to preserve the UFTN for complete Terran unity, now a reality, and his great loss of family, had it all been ordained by a higher power? Had their lost hope been found at last? The only thing they knew for certain, was that they were one, and happiness and joy had re-entered both their lives.

'Hey Evee, what's that mark on the back of your neck?'

Terran Earth Lore
Part 1 – War of the Great Despair

The time of the Coming began in the early years of the 21st century from when war was declared on North Korea by the Coalition of Western Continents. The CWC was formed as a result of growing concerns by the west over North Korea's aggressive stance on world politics and its unwillingness to agree to United Nations mandates on arms reductions.

History tells us that North Korea had provoked the western free world by the constant threat of their nuclear testing program. In an attempt to distil the hostile nation, the United States of America and the United Kingdom, along with other western nations, presented a case to the United Nations Security Council for trade and political embargos. Along with these sanctions, the UN also agreed to reduce North Korea's sovereignty over its oceanic territory borders and imposed no-fly zones.

This would only serve to incite North Korea further and the CWC had no choice but to once again position troops along the 38th parallel. It is said that in a retaliatory response, North Korea fired the first salvo that began, what was later to be known as, the War of the Great Despair. This war spanning ten years from 2014 to 2023 would soon see other nations align themselves to the opposing factions of both North Korea and the CWC.

The People's Republic of China was the first to be allied with North Korea, along with many other South East Asian countries they now either controlled and/or governed. This joining became known as the Republic of East Asian Nations, later known as the REAN. It had been sixty eight years since the end of the last major world conflict of World War Two and now the world was once again at war. The old text speaks of diplomacy lost and along with it, all hope. How could this have come to pass?

The war was having devastating effects and it was only through the persuasion and intervention of China's governing body that convinced North Korea not to use its nuclear arsenal. China was a natural ally of North Korea, but it was also an emerging nation, which before the war had begun to open its doors to western influence while remaining nationalistic in its heritage and values. It was a major player on the world economic scene providing large industries of commerce, manufacturing and trade.

The inclusion of the People's Republic of China into the war saw the Stock Market crash and along with it many joint multi-national companies folding. Masses of people now found themselves without work. With no end in sight of this conflict and feeling anger and frustration over emerging events, the people flocked in their thousands to enlist into the western armed forces. Soon other nations that had remained neutral began to realise that if North Korea was to be stopped, it would have to be by force of strength and numbers. Mainland North Korea would have to be invaded and its government bought to its knees.

This epiphany resulted in the neutral countries of Brazil and Argentina being the first of two South American nations see joined with the United States. Others would soon follow, including Columbia who set aside their differences with the US. The political landscape was changing, and fast. Past indifferences were set aside for a common cause. In years to come, this alliance set the foundations of what is now referred to as the Americas.

This mattered not to the REAN, it only equated to more countries they would have to defeat. To them, anything less than victory was unacceptable, they must win and to the REAN it was just a matter of time. The REAN continued their overwhelming dominance and they soon pushed further into the West Asian and Middle Eastern territories. Their plan had been to align themselves with the Middle Eastern countries who had been dissatisfied with the west for quite some time. Once achieved, they would set motion to plan for further invasion into the west. This foothold would see REAN forces stage and launch an offensive into Europe.

The war had progressed four years by the time the REAN had convinced a large number of Middle Eastern countries to join with them. Once again the old text details this time. It speaks of this new allegiance with some discomfort and unrest amongst those caught up in the conflict. To this day, it is uncertain whether or not countries such as Pakistan were a willing partner or whether their hand had been forced. However, faced by the threat of the complete and utter dominance by REAN forces, there may have been no other avenue of choice. This new alliance was labelled the Republic of East Asian and Middle Eastern Nations, simply put, the REAMEN.

This did not sit well with the many leaders of nations bordered or regional to this new enemy threat. Countries that had previously sat idle on the side lines, but supported in principle the CWC's stance, would now be seen joined with western forces. In particular, India who had a long tenuous and somewhat violent past with Pakistan and who had been engaged in an un-easy peace with its neighbour for many years, now saw this peace quickly eroded away. It became the catalyst of aggression with haste. Soon artillery fire commenced over the Kashmir as both sides entered into aggressive hostilities.

Likewise, Iran's admittance into the REAMAN had angered the sovereign state of Iraq who still had a questionable friendship with the US after the forces of Saddam Hussain had been overthrown. Saddam himself had been executed by his own people for crimes against the state of Iraq. Never the less and just as with the relationship between India and Pakistan, Iraq's relationship with Iran had been just as volatile. Is was not long before Iraq and a minority of other middle eastern countries found themselves aligned with the CWC.

Western forces found themselves on the back foot. They were losing the war, and rapidly. Hundreds, if not thousands of men were being lost every day. A decision had to be made. Two thirds of Europe were already members of the CWC, but if they stood any chance at all, the entire continent of Europe would have to stand as one. This included the nation of the Russian Federation, who up until now had tried to remain out of this conflict. But even they could see they could no longer just stand by and do nothing.

The old text describes internal political and military turmoil within the Kremlin at this time, as factions struggled to convince the Russian Federation President to offer their assistance to the west. But the President remained steadfast in his defiance. It is said that he had once stated;

'If the west want the help of the mighty Russian people, then they would have to come begging for it on their hands and knees.'

This was not, however; the beleaguered opinions of all in the Federal Assembly of the Russian parliament. Regardless of whether this had been said or not,   European heads of state approached the Russian Federation for their help. Much to their pleasant surprise, they received it. It wasn't much after this time that the Russian Federation President disappeared and a new head of state appointed. The old text does not describe why or how this came to pass and therefore no-one knows exactly what happened to the former leader, but the alliance was set.

The once soviet people of a communist nation were now aligned with the CWC. They had collectively agreed that the REAMEN posed a threat to all and therefore had to be stopped. The alliance between Europa and Eurasia created one unified peoples colloquially known as Eurpasia in the fifth year of the war.

The southern hemisphere had been left relatively unscathed until now, barring of course the island continent of Australia who naturally answered the call of the west. With most of its military forces now occupied in overseas theatres of war, Australia's closest neighbouring country under growing pressure and threat of invasion from REAMEN forces, saw no other choice but to stamp its authority. The opportunity to invade and therefore gain the control of the country's wealth from its natural resources which held in abundance presented a temptation too strong to ignore.

The war, on all accounts, had been going in the favour of the REAMEN and it didn't look like it would fade anytime soon. In fact, another year of this ferocity and pace would see the REAMEN as the victors. So the decision to join with the REAMAN made tactical and strategic sense. Enemy aircraft soon found their targets on Australian soil. What they didn't expect though, was for the Republic of South Africa to come to Australia's aid. This assistance had provided the breathing space sorely required to abate further invasion. It provided just enough time for Australian and New Zealand forces to return home and repel the opposing enemy forces. Later, Australia and South Africa along with India would form the Oceanic Triangle, later to become known as Oceania.

There now wasn't a single country that in some way, shape or form was left out of this conflict. Whether it had been because of the alliances that had been formed or whether they had been invaded and conquered; every nation on the face of the earth was now involved.

People started planning for life after the war. They knew it would not end well and so stock piles of food and various other supplies were being foraged for in preparation. Populations around the globe panicked as the primeval carnal instincts of the human race reared its head once more. In some less fortunate societies, murder for a single loaf of bread started to become common practice. Black market organisations and war profiteers seemed to spring up overnight. There was money to be made and lots of it.

The unscrupulous people that ran these outfits unfortunately prospered well, as there was little to no law enforcement left to provide civil order. The heads of these criminal organisations stemmed from the lives of relatively normal and inconsequential walks of society, but under these conditions, they became something different altogether. Normal everyday people reverted back to their natural primordial basic instincts of survival of the fittest. They struggled to survive under these conditions driven by the desire to provide for and protect their families.

Those still fortunate enough to have money and wealth were either preyed upon by those without it, or they themselves controlled the black market. It was looking unlikely that peace would ever be achieved. Only death and destruction and the utter extermination of humankind looked evident. The end was coming and all knew it. The old text in the archives terms this dark period in history as;

'Global genocide in its purist form.'

China realising that this war could not be prolonged any further, decided to turn its back on the REAMAN and signed a peace accord with the CWC. This historic occasion is listed in the archives as the single most pivotal moment in time that changed the course of the war. This is quickly followed in the text by an act so unimaginable and heinous that one shudders at the thought, it speaks of the unthinkable. As CWC Special Forces paratroopers were dropped into North Korea and Chinese forces positioned on her borders, the button was pushed for nuclear world annihilation. New York was the first to be obliterated in a blinding flash of light; gone in an instant. London soon followed, as too did many other capital cities.

The point of no return had been reached and salvo upon salvo of missiles with their nuclear warheads were fired by the opposing sides. Though thankfully, the numbers of warheads released were comparatively low. Once again it would be the People's Republic of China that would create history and bring an end to the missiles and to the very war itself.

In a bold move, the Chinese military invaded North Korea on mass, losing many of their own in the process. But their goal had been achieved and in a coordinated attack, the CWC seized on this advantage. Amphibious beach landings supported by CWC naval gunfire and Air power attacked from the east coast. North Korea soon buckled and capitulated under the sheer weight and strength of the CWC and Chinese invading armies. The remainder of REAMAN forces would soon follow suit, either by being overrun and killed, or when after receiving news that North Korea had fallen they simply surrendered on mass to the advancing western forces. The War of the Great Despair was over. The victors had won, but their realisation soon became apparent, at what cost?

Most of the nuclear missiles launched in that last year of the war during this vile aggression took place in the northern hemisphere. Their purpose had been served with their resultant deadly effects devastating the entire planet. Consequently, the earth suffered horrific carnage and irreparable damage that could not be undone. The quantities of these nuclear detonations, some in concentrated barrages, were unmeasurable. Each one would serve to shorten the life of their blue planet, causing it to haemorrhage as it fought back at the humans that caused it harm.

These traumatic effects had damaged, what little there was left of, the earth's outer protection layer from the punishing effects of the solar sun. In turn this created a chain reaction of events. The first resulted in the melting of the polar ice cap regions and the second caused the earth's core to heat to excessive temperatures. Deep ocean volcanos that once laid dormant now erupted as tsunamis wiped out complete coastlines and entire countries along the ring of fire.

Although Australia's land mass had changed due to these rising tides, an oceanic rise of some 170 meters, prevailing winds had shifted resulting in most of the nuclear fallout staying north of the equator. Along with South Africa and parts of the Southern Americas, which also gained these same favourable winds, these land masses remained the last reasonable bastions of liveable land.

Terran Earth Lore
Part 2 – Genetic Mutations

Τ he people that survived in the south became known as the Untouched Citizens South of the Equator, better known as the Ucusee. These people managed to go on living comparable healthy lives. They had suffered very little from the nuclear fallout of the north. Although most technology had been destroyed and governed law and order now a precious and rare commodity, the Ucusee favoured better than their northern counterparts.

Most people north of the equator that had firstly survived the rising tides, now turned to life beneath the earth's surface. There they sought sanctuary and an escape from the harsh and poisonous atmosphere of their new environment. The underground abodes they now called home would have life altering changes to their genetic makeup.

These beings would evolve over the years and become gifted with the natural ability to see in complete darkness. They would develop enhanced hearing to an almost sub-sonic level. This ability aided these beings when navigating through the labyrinth of mines and tunnels underground. As sound waves are bounced off the cavernous walls, these underground bound humans can pin point with near 100% accuracy where the sound originated from. Although, these gifts come at a price.

These Under Ground Beings are now known as Ugbees and the price they pay is retina light sensitivity. In fact, it is so severe that they are very sensitive to any form of light no matter how bright. As a result, most Ugbess are rarely seen in daylight hours. For those that do venture out from their underground dwellings will mostly do so at night. Over the years and as technology becomes more readily available and advanced, more and more Ugbees have been seen in the day light hours. You can recognise an Ugbee by their distinctive pale white skin and their specially enhanced vision goggles which they wear to protect their eyes.

It had been a very different story for those who remained upon the earth's surface. Most would die a horrible and painful death proceeding the years that followed the end of the war, but some would survive. These people would be referred to as the Terran Radiated Affected People or Traps for short. This had meant they had overcome the effects of the radiation poisoning while living on the earth's surface. Traps had learnt to adapt to their environment and over time, their genetic makeup evolved and mutated. Most Traps that live with us today are very adaptable to any environment that they find themselves in. From the harshest winter in sub-arctic temperatures to the extremist summer and most desolate places on earth, they can and will survive.

During the twenty three years of unbridled lawlessness that followed the end of the War of the Great Despair, a struggle for power ensued until all became united under the banner of the UFTN. Ugbees and Traps are now very much a part of the civilised world, many of which serve as Peace Makers with their special skills.

—๛— ✝ —๛—

The old text contained in the vault archives of the UFTN describes that of the 7.4 billion people that once called earth home, only about

3.5 billion people would survive. Now fifty eight years later, Oceania stands alone as one of the last remaining masses of terran land considered as sacred by the peoples of the UFTN. It is referred to the Land of the Untouched, as it seemingly managed to escape the brutality and violence bought on by man.

These days, a growing sense of fear still exists amongst some peoples of the UFTN. A perceived uprising in the AN Territories could bring undone years of peace. While the northern parts of the AN Territories had aligned themselves with the REAMAN during the War of the Great Despair, the central parts of the AN Territories had remained somewhat bipartisan and content amongst themselves. That was until recently.

UFTN intelligence reports have it that the AN Territories are organising under one central command. Terrorist style attacks are popping up all over the world and are becoming more frequent and more deadly. Stirred up by large quantities of disenfranchised radicals, the AN Territories are turning to unrest and violence in the outer provinces. Insurgent training camps seem to be growing by the number. This threatens the very way of life that the UFTN is trying to preserve.

The governing body of the UFTN would see this uprising bought down. Right now, more troops are being sent into the AN Territories every day. Small pockets of renegade Ugbee and Trap groups in the north also threaten their way of life and civilised order. The UFTN may still face an uphill battle ahead. These latest threats would have to be quashed if the UFTN is to be seen as powerful and just by its citizens. It was once said that to wage war is easy; but to maintain peace is an eternal battle.

Glossary

Time Line

1956	The term Wiccan is first used
2014 – 2023	The War of the Great Despair
2024 – 2046	23 years of ungoverned society and lawlessness
2025	The creation of the United Federation of Terran Nations (UFTN)
2068 – 2074	The Terran Wars
2079 – 2082	The African Nation Uprising

Civilian Vehicles

APAM – All Purpose AutoMobile

BMW-Royce – Luxury car

XCV – Cross-Country Vehicle

MPCV – Multi-Person Capacity Vehicle

PST – Public Service Transport

OXT – Overlander Cross-Trail (Motorbike)

HTW – Heavy Transport Wagon

APT – All Purpose Transport

PmCT – Paramedic Casualty Transport

Military Vehicles

Nighthawk Mk IV – Attack Helicopter

ATLAV – All Terrain Light Armoured Vehicle

ATHAV – All Terrain Heavy Armoured Vehicle

LATAV – Light Armoured Tactical Assault Vehicle

UTAV – Urban Tactical Assault Vehicle

FPMV – Federal Peace Maker Vehicle

Equipment

VIDCom – Visual Image Display Communications device

APAWS – Air Projectile Alarm Warning System

PARTNAR – Personal Anti-Rain Toxin & Nerve-Agent
Repellent Suit

VEPEW – Vision Enhancement and Protective Eye Wear Goggles

Weapons

TAM – Terra to Air Missile

Terminology

UFTN – United Federation of Terran Nations

RFN – Republic of Free Nations

Terra Marcs - currency

**The Coming/The Coming of the Darkness/
The Darkness/The Great Despair** – The dark skies of the
nuclear fallout from the War of the Great Despair including the
rising of the oceans and the Ring of Fire.

Ancient text – The writing contained in books of a time before
the War of the Great Despair.

Elders – Those people who existed before the War of the Great
Despair. These people are usually in their mid-sixties to mid-
seventies before being given the title of elder. Some of those have
been thought to gain entry as young as fifty.

Grand elder – Grand parent

Twice son or twice daughter – grand child

Thrice son or thrice daughter – Great grand child

War of the Great Despair – The war between North Korea and
the West. The War of the Great Despair signalled the loss of all Hope.

Christmas Union – Christmas and the celebration of the founding of the UFTN.

White Out – Communications Lock Down of friendly forces when an incident occurs involving the death of a UFTN Peace Maker.

Black Out – Electronic Attack against the UFTN military.

TacComRad – Tactical Communications Radio

Passing of Life ceremony – Funeral

Knucks – A curse word.

Family Genealogy & Etymology
including pronunciations

The Maynard Family

1. William Maynard (1989, Australia) m Jocelyn Maynard (nee Armstrong) (1994, Australia).
   2. (s) Marshall Maynard (2022-51, Australia) m Catherine Maynard (nee Lee) (2020-51, Australia).
      3. (s) Andrew Maynard (2044, Australia) m Constance Maynard (nee Cameron) (2050, Australia).
         4. (s) Marshall Maynard (2077, Australia) twin.
         4. (d) Catherine-Lee Maynard (2077, Australia) twin.
      3. (s) Ashleigh Maynard (2046, Australia) m Siobhan Maynard (nee Kelly) (2045, Australia).
         4. (s) Alexander Maynard (2067, Brazil).
         4. (d) Elyssa-Jayne Maynard (2069, Australia).
         4. (s) Marcus Angelus Maynard (2071, Australia).

The Kelly Family

1. Reilly Kelly (2023, Australia) m Lucienne Kelly (nee Murphy) (2023, Australia).
   2. (d) Siobhan Kelly (2045, Australia) m Ashleigh Maynard (2046, Australia).
   2. (s) Deaglan Kelly (2047, Australia).
   2. (s) Desmond Kelly (2048, Australia).
   2. (s) Ciara Kelly (2051, Australia) twin.
   2. (s) Caoilainn Kelly (2051, Australia) twin.
   2. (d) Sean Kelly (2053, Australia).

The Josephine Grace Line Women

1. Father (unknown) m Mother (unknown). Mother from the Angus Rose Line.

    2. (d) Josephine Annabelle Grace (nee unknown) (1832-1940, England) m Aneirin Grace (1827-58, Wales). Josephine Annabelle Grace first of the Graceline.

        3. (d) Caroline Grace (1859-59, Australia) triplet.

        3. (d) Elizabeth Grace (1859-66, Australia) triplet.

        3. (d) Beatrice Grace (1859-?, Australia) triplet m (unknown).

            4. (d) Sarah (1886-?, Australia) m (unknown).

                5. (d) Isabella (1913-?, Australia) m (unknown).

                    6. (d) Dianna Kay Reynolds (nee unknown) (1940-2021, Australia) m (?) Reynolds.

                        7. (d) Summer-Rayne Clarke (nee Reynolds) (1967-2021, USA) m (?) Clarke.

                            8. (d) Paige-Rose Phillips (nee Clarke) (1994-2034, USA) m (?) Phillips.

                                9. (d) unknown.

                                9. (d) Crystal Taylor (nee Phillips) (2021, Australia) m (?) Taylor.

                                    10. (d) Evonne Van den Berg (nee Taylor) (2048, Australia) m Dirk Van den Berg (2043, Australia).

                                        11. (d) Josephine Van den Berg (2043, Australia).

The Van den Berg Family

1. Dann Van den Berg (2020-2101, Holland) m Emma Van den Berg (nee Heidermann) (2018-96, Holland).

   2. (s) Dirk Van den Berg (2043, Australia) m Evonne Van den Berg (nee Taylor) (2048, Australia).

      3. (d) Josephine Van den Berg (2066, Australia).

      3. (s) Damian Van den Berg (2078, Australia) twin.

      3. (s) Jeremy Van den Berg (2078, Australia) twin .

The Sjöberg Family & Order of Hope

1. Father (unknown) m Mother (unknown) Mother is the High Priestess of the Order of Hope.

   2. (d) Unknown (1830, England).

      3. Hope Line Period unknown.

         4. (d) Mieke Sjöberg (nee unknown) (2029, Norway) m (unknown) Sjöberg .

            5. (s) Ashwyn Sjöberg (2056, Norway).

            5. (d) Aine Sjöberg (2066, England).

The Maynard Family

William Maynard

History: The Maynard Family immigrated to Australia from England during the gold rush days in Victoria to Ballarat circa 1850. Family is Protestant.

Notes: William serves in the War of the Great Despair of 2014-23.

Jocelyn Maynard (nee Armstrong)

History: The Armstrong Family immigrated to Australia from England circa 1945 after WWII and lived in the North-East of Victoria at the migrant camps.

Andrew Maynard

Notes: First twice son of William and Joselyn Maynard. Naturally talented sportsman and tracker. Marksman with weapons and an expert in survival skills. Served in the Oceania Terran Division in the Southern Hemisphere Aviation Corps. Fought in the Terran Wars of 2068-74. Discharges from the military to manage and run the family's cattle property on his grand elder's behalf. Marries Constance Cameron in 2075 and has two children, twins, Marshall and Catherine-Lee, both names after Andrew's real parents.

Ashleigh Maynard

Notes: Second twice son of William and Jocelyn Maynard. Many skills as his older brother plus some. His skills outweigh Andrew's and he joins the Oceania Terran Division Federal Continental Ranger Corps. Serves in the Terran Wars of 2068-74. Marries Siobhan Kelly in 2066. Together they have three children, Alexander, Elyssa-Jane and Marcus Angelus. Marcus is given the second name of Angelus, the Latin form of Angel.

The Kelly Family

Reilly Kelly

History: Family immigrated to Australia from Ireland during the last years of the War of the Great Despair to escape the dangers. Reilly was born in Australia. Family is Catholic.

Notes: Reilly marries Lucienne Murphy and has six children; Siobhan, Deaglan, Desmond, twins Ciara and Caoilainn, and lastly, Sean Kelly. Reilly later tries to stop Ashleigh and Siobhan from being married because of religious beliefs and differences.

Lucienne Kelly (nee Murphy)

History: Family immigrated to Australia from Ireland to escape the War of the Great Despair to escape the danger. Lucienne is born in Australia where years later she met and married Reilly Kelly. Her mother was born in France and hence her Christian name, Lucienne.

Notes: Secretly persuaded Reilly to allow Ashleigh and Siobhan to be married.

> **Name:** Lucienne.
> **Pronunciation:** Loo + see + en.
> **Origin:** French, Latin.
> **Meaning:** Light.

Siobhan Kelly

Notes: Eldest daughter and first child of Reilly and Lucienne Kelly. Married to Ashleigh Maynard.

Name: Siobhan

> **Pronunciation:** shiv + awn (Shevaun, Shavon, Chevonne).
> **Origin:** Irish.
> **Meaning:** Siobhan is an Irish form of Joan meaning 'God is gracious.'

Deaglan Kelly

Notes: Second born to Reilly and Lucienne Kelly.

Name: Deaglan.

Pronunciation: deck + lan.

Origin: Irish.

Meaning: From dag 'good' and lan 'full' suggesting 'full of goodness.' St. Declan was the founder of a monastery at Ardmore in County Waterford and may have preached in Ireland before the arrival of St. Patrick.

Desmond Kelly

Notes: Third born to Reilly and Lucienne Kelly.

Name: Desmond.

Origin: Irish .

Ciara Kelly (Twin)

Notes: Forth born and twin of Caoilainn Kelly.

Name: Ciara.

Pronunciation: kee + ra.

Origin: Irish.

Meaning: The feminine form of Ciaran, from the Irish ciar meaning 'dark' and implies 'dark hair and brown eyes.' St. Ciara was a distinguished seventh-century figure who established a monastery at Kilkeary in County Tipperary.

Caoilainn Kelly (Twin)

Notes: Twin of Ciara Kelly.

Name: Caoilainn.

Pronunciation: kay + linn.

Origin: Irish.

Meaning: caol 'slender' and fionn 'white, fair, pure.' Several saints were Caoilainn and one was described as 'a pious lady who quickly won the esteem and affection of her sister nuns by her exactness to every duty, as also by her sweet temper, gentle, confiding disposition and unaffected piety.'

Sean Kelly

Notes: Last and sixth child of Reilly and Lucienne Kelly.
Name: Sean.
Origin: Irish .

—ᴍ— ✝ —ᴍ—

The Josephine Grace Line Women

Josephine Annabelle Grace

History: Josephine's lineage is derived from the Order of Hope. A long family line of female matriarchs who still believe and practice the ways of Celtic Neo-paganism.

Notes: Born in England and married a Welshman by the name of Aneirin Grace. Struck with poverty and pregnant with triplets, Beatrice, Elizabeth and Caroline, her husband steals a loaf of bread and is killed in the act. Josephine is sent to the penal colony of Australia as a convict. While in bondage, she gives birth to her fatherless daughters and ends up working for a wealthy land owner of a large estate. The triplets were born when she was 27 years of age. Caroline died three months after her birth from Cholera Infantum; Elizabeth died aged seven when the Master of the house she served lashed out in a rage killing her; and Beatrice lived to continue the Graceline, the first of her kind in Australia.

Aneirin Grace

Notes: Aneirin joins the Royal Welch Fusiliers in 1850 as a means to support his sick mother and five siblings. Aneirin's father died in a tavern altercation with the local publican when he was just a young child. In early 1853, Aneirin met and married a young 21 year old named Josephine. Later that year in October, the Royal Welch Fusiliers were sent to fight in the Crimean War. Aneirin returns home to England in 1855 as a crippled war veteran without work and husband to a now pregnant Josephine. In 1858 and in desperation, Aneirin is killed at the age of 31 by police for stealing a loaf of bread.

> **Name:** Aneirin.
> **Pronunciation:** a + nei + rin.
> **Origin:** Welsh.
> **Meaning:** A boy's name is of Welsh origin. Possibly (Irish, Gaelic) 'noble, modest.' Originally Neirin, the A- was added in the 13th century.

Beatrice (unknown) (nee Grace)

Notes: Beatrice is the only surviving child of Josephine and Aneirin Grace. Her husband is unknown. Beatrice gives birth to a daughter, Sarah, when she is 27 years of age.

Sarah (unknown)

Notes: Daughter of Beatrice, husband unknown and gives birth to a daughter, Isabella, when she is 27 years of age.

Isabella (unknown)

Notes: Daughter of Sarah, husband unknown and gives birth to a daughter, Diana Kay, when she is 27 years of age.

Diana Kay Reynolds (nee unknown)

Notes: Married a US Navy Sailor in 1964 and relocated to the United States of America. Started practicing Wicca circa 1960. Cherishes in Mother Nature and a strong vocal supporter of the women's liberation movement of the 1960s. Diana was killed along with her daughter during the War of the Great Despair. Bombs were dropped by the enemy on their home in San Francisco during the battle for California. Diana gives birth to a daughter, Summer-Rayne, when she is 27 years of age.

> **Name:** Diana.
>
> **Origin:** French/Latin.
>
> **Meaning:** The pagan goddess, the most popular of the Wiccan goddesses viewed as a Triple Goddess—maiden, protector, hunter/destroyer. She is Goddess of the Moon; Hunt and/or Vengeance; Woodland and Wild; Female Sovereignty; Magic, and Childbirth.

Summer-Rayne Clarke (nee Reynolds)

Notes: Born a flowerchild during the peace movement in San Francisco, USA, she was taught the Wiccan ways of her mother which in turn she passed onto her daughter. Summer-Rayne returns to San Francisco to look after her mother and is killed by her mother's side in 2021. Summer-Rayne gives birth to a daughter, Paige-Rose, when she is 27 years of age.

> **Name:** Summer-Rayne.
>
> **Origin:** English.
>
> **Meaning:** Peace and love.

Paige-Rose Phillips (nee Clarke)

Notes: Paige-Rose and her first daughter relocate from the USA to Australia during the 6th year of the War of the Great Despair in 2019. There she gives birth to a second daughter, Crystal. Paige-Rose gives birth to her first daughter when she is 23 years old and gives birth to Crystal when she is 27 years of age.

Crystal Taylor (nee Phillips)

Notes: Second daughter to Paige-Rose. Crystal gives birth to a daughter, Evonne, when she is 27 years of age.

Evonne Van den Berg (nee Taylor)

Notes: Evonne joins the Federal Continental Rangers but later discharges from the service when she gives birth to a daughter, Josephine, when is 18 years old. Married to Dirk Van den Berg, they raise their daughter and twin sons, Damian and Jeremy.

Josephine Van den Berg

Notes: Josephine was born on her mother's 18th birthday and her destiny is unknown. She is the last known descendent of the Graceline and may not be able to bear a Graceline matriarch.

The Van den Berg Family

Daan Van den Berg

History: Daan and Emma where two of thousands of European children sent to the southern continents to escape the War of the Great Despair. Daan was just three years old and Emma five years old when they left Holland for Australia in the last year of the war in 2023.

Notes: Daan marries Emma Heidermann and has one son, Dirk Van den Berg.

> **Name:** Daan.
> **Origin:** Dutch.

Meaning: Daniel.

Name: Van den Berg.

Origin: Dutch.

Meaning: From the Mountain.

Dirk Van den Berg

Notes: A successful lawyer working in one of the biggest Law firms in Oceania. Dirk marries Evonne Taylor and together they raise three children; a daughter Josephine and twins Damian and Jeremy.

Name: Dirk.

Origin: Dutch.

Meaning: Ruler of the People.

Damian Van den Berg (Twin)

Jeremy Van den Berg (Twin)

Name: Jeremy.

Origin: Hebrew.

Meaning: God will rise up, God will set free. Form of Jeremiah

The Sjöberg Family

Mieke Sjöberg

History: Mieke's lineage is derived from Celtic Nordic origin. She is one of the last known High Priestesses of the Order of Hope still living. Her husband is unknown, but she gave birth to two children, a son, Ashwyn, and a daughter, Aine.

Name: Mieke.

Pronunciation: Mee + kuh.

Origin: Nordic Female Name. Denmark, Sweden, Norway.

Meaning: German form of Marieke.

Name: Sjöberg.

Pronunciation: show + berg.

Origin: Nordic Surname.

Meaning: 'Sjö' means sea and 'berg' means mountain.

Ashwyn Sjöberg

Notes: First child and son of Mieke. Ashwyn travelled the world with his younger sister after being sent on the journey by their mother. Ashwyn did not return and his whereabouts are still unknown.

Name: Ashwyn.

Origin: Anglo-Saxon.

Meaning: Anglo-Saxon male first name derived from Aescwine, composed of the elements AESC ('Ash, spear, lance, ship') and wine ('friend, protector, Lord'). Important names bearers include:

Aescwine, King of Essex (527-587 AD),

Aescwine, King of Wessex (674-676 AD).

It could mean 'Spear Friend' in English or the Germanic word 'Friend of the Gods.'

Aine Sjöberg

Notes: Second child and daughter of Mieke.

Name: Aine.

Origin: Celtic.

Meaning: Goddess of love, growth, cattle and light. The name of this Celtic Goddess means 'bright' as she lights up the dark. Celebrations to this Goddess were held on Midsummer night.

Other Characters of Destiny

United Federation of Terran Nations

Chris Parker

Notes: Captain in the Federal Continental Ranger Corps. A native of South Africa and long-time friend of Ashleigh Maynard.

Regis Otillio

Notes: Holds the rank of Sub-Commander Sergeant in the Federal Continental Ranger Corps and is a native of the Eurpasain Islands. Regis is an Under Ground Being and a close friend to Ashleigh Maynard.

Patterson

Notes: Major General Patterson is a Divisional Commander in the Federal Continental Ranger Corps assigned to the South-East Group of the Oceania Terran Division.

Republic of Free Nations

Richard Henning

Notes: Richard is the founder of the True People of Trust, an opposing faction to the Consortium of Trust spreading lies and deception. He was also one of the main leaders of the Republic of Free Nations.

>   **Name:** Henning.
>   **Origin:** Dutch.
>   **Meaning:** Home ruler.

Freesensuade

Notes: Doctor Freesensuade is a key member of the True Peoples of

Trust and the Republic of Free Nations. He designed the deadly Xialm contagion.

> **Name:** Freesensuade.
> **Origin:** No origin.
> **Meaning:** Freesensuade is just a made up name.

Emerson Harris

Notes: Emerson is a native Under Ground Being and a friend of Dirk Van den Berg. He is known to be a terrorist and a former member of the Black Ops in the Republic of Free Nations during the Terran Wars. Emerson Harris is an alias, his real name is Emery Horus.

> **Name:** Emery.
> **Origin:** English; German.
> **Meaning:** Brave; powerful.
> **Name:** Horus.
> **Origin:** Egyptian.
> **Meaning:** Egyptian God of war, sky, and falcons.

Wanda Mae Bell

Notes: Wanda Mae is Dirk Van den Berg's girlfriend who lives in Syndeton.

Political &
Socio-Economic
Structure of the UFTN

Structure of Terran Earth

Structure of Terran Earth in order of seniority. The CoT have overall governing control and administration of Terran Earth and of the UFTN. This is delegated to the UFTN Council of Elders which is again subsequently delegated to the TCDs. There are various levels of hierarchy, all of which contain a Council of Elders with different seniority positions and ranks. The TCDs are then formed into Groups which administer and govern their own Districts. The Sub-Structures of Terran Earth are located in all TCDs in various sizes of composition and availability.

1. Consortium of Trust (CoT – Founding Council of Elders).

2. United Federation of Terran Nations (UFTN Council of Elders made up from State Leaders, Judges, Politicians, and High Ranking Officials).

3. Territorial Continental Divisions (TCDs – Continents of the new world).

    a. Oceania – Oceania Terran Division (OTD).

        i.   Oceania South-East Group.

        ii. Oceania North Group.

        iii. Oceania South-West Group.

    b. Eurpasian Islands – Eurpasian Terran Division (ETD).

        i.   Eurpasian Island Group.

    c. The Americas – The Americas Terran Division (AmTD).

        i.   North Americas Group.

        ii. South Americas Group.

    d. Canaan – Canaan Terran Division (CTD).

        i.   Canaan Group.

    e. Asia – Asian Terran Division (AsTD).

        i.   Asia Pacific Group.

        ii. North Asia Artic Group.

f.   The African Nation Territories (The unsettled wild frontiers).

Note: All groups of the United Federation of Terran Nations contain the following Sub-Structures of Terran Earth:

1. Peace Makers.
2. UFTN Knowledge & Wisdom Centre.
3. Terran Division Services.
4. Terran Division Emergency Services.

Sub-structure of Terran Earth

1. Peace Makers.
    a.   Federal Territorial Navy.
        i.   Surface Group.
        ii.   Sub-Surface Group.
        iii. Aviator Group.
        iv.   Federal Terran Marines.
            (1) Amphibious Operations.
            (2) Ground Operations.
            (3) Air Operations.
    b.   Federal Terran Force.
        i.   Terran Artillery.
        ii.   Terran Engineers.
        iii. Terran Armoured Carbineers (TAC).
        iv.   Terran Logistics & Technical Support Corps.
        v.   Federal Terran Aviation Corps.
    c.   Federal Sky Force.
        i.   Fighter Command.
        ii.   Bomber Command.

    d. Federal Special Forces.

        i. Peace Maker Black.

        ii. Federal Continental Ranger Corps (FCR).

          (1) Ranger Brigades.

          (2) Pioneer Brigades.

    e. Federal Galactic Space Force (This element of the UFTN military forces draws upon other elements of the UFTN that undergo specialist training).

2. United Federation of Terran Nations Knowledge & Wisdom Centre

    a. Education.

    b. Science & Technology.

    c. Medicus & Genetics.

    d. Robotics & Animatronics.

    e. Astronomical Sciences.

    f. The Arts.

        i. UFTN School of Music, Dance & Drama.

3. Terran Division Services.

    a. State Division Police (SDP).

        i. Regular Constabulary.

        ii. Tactical Special Operations Division (TSOD).

        iii. Victims of Sexual Assault & Homicide Unit.

    b. UFTN Sanctuary & Shelter for the Less Fortunate.

4. Terran Division Emergency Services.

    a. Central Division Medical.

        i. District Central Hospitals.

    b. Fire & Paramedics.

    c. Rescue & Disaster.

Acknowledgments

Writing and publishing a novel one day has always been a dream of mine. I am glad to say that I have now been given that chance and opportunity to do just that. Along the way, there were many people that provided encouragement and support. One of the very first was Colin Foard, a colleague of mine whom I worked with overseas when I first started this project. I also include many other colleagues at that same time that provided me very positive feedback when I described the story line to them. They always wanted to know more and even asked me when the movie would be released. This indicated to me that I was on the right path.

Back home in Australia and I was ready for the draft manuscripts to be edited. The following people are acknowledged for providing detailed critiques: my mother, Pat Elliot, sister-in-law Joanne Elliot and friend Jacqui Langdon. Their critique provided constructive feedback on what they liked and which they disliked. And although I did not make every change that was recommended, I did re-structure some passages and rearranged chapters. In some cases, I deleted complete sentences. But by doing this, I believe the final product is a much better presented product and story.

My final thanks has to go to my wife, Robyn Elliot, for her support and patience as I spent many a late night editing. Robyn has supported me in every endeavour I have undertaken, and this has been no different during this one. Robyn has provided feedback on every aspect of this story including book design and front cover artwork. And to all those unmentioned, thank-you.

www.ingramcontent.com/pod-product-compliance
Lightning Source LLC
Chambersburg PA
CBHW050206030726
47505CB00005B/1540